T0281979

'You always get a strong sense of place in Staalesen's books and frosty Bergen, a place I've never visited, came alive ... one of the best' Sarah Ward

'Translator Don Bartlett has an excellent understanding of Staalesen's writing. Haunting, dark and totally noir, a great read' *NB Magazine*

'There are only two other writers that I know of have achieved the depth of insight in detective writing that Staalesen has: Chandler and Ross MacDonald' *Mystery Tribune*

'Readers ... will feel drawn to the characters and their intertwined lives' Reviewing the Evidence

'The godfather of Nordic Noir is on top form with an action-packed and dramatic story whose culmination blends the tragedy of two funerals tinged with the tenacious hope of a family reunion that will leave you choked up and wanting more' Crime Fiction Lover

'Gunnar Staalesen is a master of the PI genre, and with *Fallen Angels* he is at the top of his game' Live Many Lives

'A meticulously crafted story which intelligently unfolds with some sections of high suspense where the themes of family, betrayal, revenge and environmental militancy feature prominently' Fiction from Afar

'A masterclass in plotting, pace and characterisation ... The translation by Don Bartlett is as accomplished as ever, sharing the tenor of Staalesen's voice and humour so beautifully' Raven Crime Reads

'A classic murder mystery, while also offering the reader a snapshot of Norway through the eyes of the resilient and stalwart Varg Veum. Don Bartlett's translation is excellent ... Engaging. Atmospheric. Current' Swirl & Thread

'Hints of menace coupled with a chilling climate make this the perfect locational mystery' Bibliophile Book Club

'There's a poetic, lyrical quality to Staalesen's writing, he's not all action and fast-paced plot. His ability to produce much more than a thriller, with the beautifully evocative sense of place and the masterfully created characters, is a joy to read' Random Things through My Letterbox

'With all of Gunnar Staalesen's hallmark storytelling, that real, authentic PI vibe, and a mixture of deception, tension and the occasional flash of high-threat action, as a fan of the series, I am left feeling very satisfied' Jen Med's Book Reviews

'Whether it's the younger Varg Veum or the more seasoned man, I know I am in for a treat when I read a book in this superbly insightful series and the intricately plotted, surprising, elegant *Bitter Flowers* is no exception. Very highly recommended' Hair Past a Freckle

'A complex, layered plot in which human tragedy and mystery combine to play out beautifully in a classic Nordic Noir with a touch of Christie' Live & Deadly

'A brilliant example of Nordic Noir, full of dark secrets and chilling characters' Have Books Will Read

'There are some dark and emotional twists and turns … With an addictive plot, believable and relatable characters, this is a novel I highly recommend' Hooked from Page One

'There is something just so fantastically absorbing about Staalesen's work that I'm always longing to read more … Every time I think I've read the best book I will in a year, Orenda drops a new Gunnar Staalesen that jumps straight to the top of the list' Mumbling About

'Another intriguing and entertaining read' By the Letter Book Reviews

Also in the Varg Veum series
and available from Orenda Books:
Fallen Angels
Bitter Flowers
Mirror Image
We Shall Inherit the Wind
Where Roses Never Die
Wolves in the Dark
Big Sister
Wolves at the Door

ABOUT THE AUTHOR

One of the fathers of Nordic Noir, Gunnar Staalesen was born in Bergen, Norway, in 1947. He made his debut at the age of twenty-two with *Seasons of Innocence* and in 1977 he published the first book in the Varg Veum series. He is the author of over thirty titles, which have been published in twenty-four countries and sold over four million copies. Twelve film adaptations of his Varg Veum crime novels have appeared since 2007, starring the popular Norwegian actor Trond Espen Seim. Staalesen has won three Golden Pistols (including the Prize of Honour to Varg Veum). *Where Roses Never Die* won the 2017 Petrona Award for Nordic Crime Fiction, and *Big Sister* was shortlisted for the award in 2019. He lives with his wife in Bergen.

ABOUT THE TRANSLATOR

Don Bartlett completed an MA in Literary Translation at the University of East Anglia in 2000 and has since worked with a wide variety of Danish and Norwegian authors, including Jo Nesbø, Karl Ove Knausgård and Kjell Ola Dahl. He has previously translated multiple titles in the Varg Veum series for Orenda Books.

Pursued by Death

GUNNAR STAALESEN

Translated by Don Bartlett

ORENDA
BOOKS

Orenda Books
16 Carson Road
West Dulwich
London SE21 8HU
www.orendabooks.co.uk

First published in Norwegian as *Forfulgt av død* by Gyldendal, 2023
First published in English by Orenda Books, 2024
Copyright © Gunnar Staalesen 2023
English translation copyright © Don Bartlett 2024
Photograph of Varg Veum statue supplied courtesy of Augon Johnsen

A catalogue record for this book is available from the British Library.
ISBN 978-1-916788-24-4
eISBN 978-1-916788-25-1

The publication of this translation has been made possible through the financial
support of NORLA, Norwegian Literature Abroad.

Typeset in Arno by typesetter.org.uk
Printed and bound by Clays Ltd, Elcograf S.p.A

For sales and distribution please contact *info@orendabooks.co.uk*

'Wild salmon are either fighting fit or dead, but our farm-bred salmon are like a stressed-out, overweight man who suddenly has to sprint for the bus.'

—Simen Sætre & Kjetil Østli:
The New Fish, Spartacus, 2021 (translation by Don Bartlett).

1

It all started the day the Sogn og Fjordane police took it upon themselves to confiscate my driving licence.

It was a sunny day towards the end of September. After my trusty Toyota Corolla had been forced off the road and wrecked on Sotra island in January, I bought myself another car: same brand, previous year's model, in an equally discreet colour – as grey as the sky above Bergen was for the majority of the year.

I was coming from a job in Nordfjord, where I had done my diplomatic best to resolve a forty-year-old boundary dispute that started on New Year's Eve 1963, when neither of the two neighbours had been entirely unaffected by home-made hooch. As so often, it was the next generation who were banging their heads against the wall, trying to agree on a two-state solution a Middle East peace negotiator would happily accept. Whether I had succeeded or not, time would tell. I had my misgivings, as the heart of the dispute concerned a man with family connections in the area who was relocating from the eastern side of the country, and who had a burning desire to build his cabin on the bit of the property that had a view but encroached on his neighbour's land by somewhere between twenty and eighty centimetres. Now I was on my way back to Bergen with a contract and the promise of an imminent fee in my inside pocket, national-romantic music on the car radio and countryside that was filling its lungs with long, drawn-out breaths around me: out by scenic Sandane village; in through Våtedalen valley; out again as Lake Jølstra unfolded on the left.

I took all the time I needed to digest everything. At regular intervals I glanced at my rear-view mirror. A large, white animal-transport vehicle had been on my tail the whole way from the ferry terminal in Anda, without showing the slightest sign of wanting to overtake me.

As I was approaching Vassenden, I felt I needed a break and a cup of coffee. I indicated by Jølstraholmen, where there was a camping site and a café. I had hardly swung in to park in front of the café when a car with a flashing blue light on the roof drove in so close to me that we could have got engaged. I gazed over and met the eyes of a uniformed policeman, who motioned from the passenger seat that I should buzz down my window.

I saw no reason to refuse, and the first thing he said to me, in *nynorsk*, was: *'Are you on medication or what?'*

I looked at him in amazement. 'What?'

He studied me for a few more seconds. Then he pointed to the car park further ahead. *'Drive over there and park.'*

I did as he said, and the female officer I glimpsed behind the wheel followed suit.

The policeman got out of their car, strode with determined step over to mine and leaned over. *'We've received a number of phone calls about a motorist weaving in and out of traffic and generally driving dangerously.'*

The man spoke a polished version of *nynorsk*, the official Norwegian of the Sogn and fjords county, as opposed to the *bokmål* of Bergen, but I didn't find him difficult to understand. The content of what he said, however, was another matter. 'What are you talking about?'

'It looks as if we'll have to confiscate your driving licence.'

Still I found it hard to grasp what he meant. 'Based on what evidence?'

'A number of phone calls. Let me see your vehicle-registration card and your driving licence, please.'

'There must be some mistake. It cannot be my car.'

He started to bristle. *'Registration card and driving licence please!'*

His female colleague had got out of the car, too. She was standing with what I could see was a breathalyser in her hand.

The policeman examined my cards and assiduously studied my face before returning them, as though he suspected that I was posing as someone else.

'Varg Veum?' he said, and I nodded. *'Strange name.'*

'And yours is?'

'Joralf Smalabeit.'

'And you think my n—?'

He interrupted me. *'We'll have to run a breathalyser test on you.'* He nodded to his colleague. *'Sylvi.'*

I politely asked her what her surname was, opened my mouth obediently and blew as hard as I could into the plastic tube she placed between my lips. For an instant our eyes met. In hers, I discerned no obvious sympathy. She took the tube out, waited for five seconds before checking the screen and almost sounded a little disappointed when she reported back: 'Zero point zero zero.'

Joralf Smalabeit regarded me with a thoughtful expression. Then he turned to Sylvi. *'Has the complainant parked up?'*

She nodded.

'Have a word with him.'

I watched her leave. 'I assume the misunderstanding will be cleared up then.'

'Doubt it. The vehicle reg is correct.'

For a few seconds my head seemed to whirl. It was many years since I had read Franz Kafka's *The Trial*, but all of a sudden it was as though I recognised the situation. *'My* vehicle registration?'

He looked at me with the same serious expression as before. *'Let's have a few personal details then, shall we. I've got your name. Profession?'*

I sighed. 'Private investigator.'

'What did you say?'

'Private investigator.'

His eyes became even more suspicious. *'Not a former colleague, I trust?'*

'Depends on how you define colleague.' I let him reflect on that. 'Not from the force, if that's what you were afraid of.'

'I'm not afraid of anything.'

'Good to hear. Sleep well at night, do you? Dream about solving life's mysteries from the passenger seat of a VW Up?'

'Where have you come from?'

'Nordfjord.'

'In a private capacity or…?'

'No, doing my job.'

'Which in this case means…?'

'I can be anywhere. Have you heard about the Palestinian conflict?'

'Eh?' But he was interrupted by the return of Sylvi.

They moved further away. In the side mirror I could see her reporting back, waving her arms in wide circles and continually pointing in my direction.

Joralf Smalabeit came back to me. *'You stay here. We're going to call the police solicitor.'*

'Which one?' I mumbled.

'And don't try to leg it, or we'll have to arrest you.'

I arched my eyebrows in what I hoped was a suitably ironic way. But when they returned a few moments later, it turned out that the police solicitor, he or she, was not on my side either.

'We've decided to confiscate your driving licence. Do you consent?'

'No, I do not. You can be dead sure about that. Does that help?'

'No. But it does mean we'll have to present the confiscation order to the district court within three weeks.'

'And in the meantime, you'll treat me to a stay at one of the camping cabins here in Jølstraholmen and pay me for the work I've lost?' I didn't say that the latter would cost them considerably less than the stay.

He smirked. *'We'll drive you to the police station in Førde and do a formal interview there. If you can budge over onto the passenger seat, I'll take the wheel.'*

'Your driving licence is valid, is it?'

'You can cut out the jokes. You're wasting your breath. They won't help you one tiny little bit.'

'No, I can sort of see that. That's the fate of us stand-up comics. One day no one will laugh at us anymore. You do know the way, I take it?'

2

I had been to the police station in Førde, the county town, before, in the mid-eighties, in connection with a case involving a young lad known as Johnny Boy. But the station had moved since then. Now it was in a street spelt Fjellvegen; it didn't have anywhere near as nice a view as there was from the Fjellveien in Bergen. On the other hand, they did have a solid mountainside at their back: Hafstadfjellet, Førde's answer to Ålesund's Sukkertoppen mountain.

Here, Joralf Smalabeit handed me over to a young policewoman. And after that, I didn't see either him or Sylvi again. They were probably already racing around the dangerous Vestland roads on the lookout for more big-time criminals with animal-transport vehicles in their wake. It transpired quite quickly during the interview that the huge number of phone calls complaining about my driving emanated from a single person – the man who had been behind the wheel of the aforementioned vehicle. This was more than enough to suggest either that it was him the police should have been breathalysing, or that he had been hallucinating, but they had kindly failed to follow this up.

The young officer who interviewed me was otherwise pleasant company and polite enough. She introduced herself as Solrun Storehaug and asked me to give my account of the day's events. While I talked, she busily took notes. When I had finished, she referred to the conversation with the man in the vehicle behind me. In his judgement I had been holding a mobile phone the whole time without regard for road conditions; he had seen me almost collide with oncoming traffic a few times, almost leave the road and commit a variety of other road-traffic misdemeanours; in other words an experience of our shared drive from Anda to Vassenden that was totally at variance to my own. I passed her my phone and told her that she was welcome to check my chat log. The phone had been as silent as a meditating monk throughout the whole journey. The only people I had listened to had been Edvard Grieg and his composer colleagues on the car radio. She noted this down too, but opted not to check my phone.

'The police lawyer in Florø has agreed that we should confiscate your driving licence,' she said.

'And his justification for that is…?'

She inclined her head and looked at me. 'All the complaints we've received about your driving.'

I could feel indignation rising inside me. 'All the complaints! How many were there?'

'I'm afraid, there's nothing I can do about this. It's the lawyer's decision.'

I made a resigned gesture. 'So what do I do now?'

'We'll impound your car. Your driving licence will be sent to the lawyer. You'll be hearing from us. As you haven't consented to the confiscation, the case will be brought before the court within three weeks at the latest.'

'And how do I get to Bergen?'

'I'll point you in the direction of the bus station.'

'Can I ring my solicitor?'

She pushed my phone back across the table. 'By all means.'

I got Vidar Waagenes on the line. He chuckled when he heard what the call was about. 'This is not the first time I've heard this sort of thing from Sogn og Fjordane,' he said. 'I'm sure it didn't help that you're a Bergensian.'

'Can you help me?' I asked impatiently.

'Not right this minute. It will take a few days at best. Perhaps an appearance in Førde court in three weeks. Drop by when you're back in town.'

'Back in town? I have to catch the bus.'

He chuckled again. 'You're not the first to have undertaken this journey, Varg. Regard it as a challenge.'

'OK,' I said, ringing off.

Solrun Storehaug looked at me with something approaching sympathy in her eyes. Then she told me how to get to the bus station.

The next bus to Bergen left in two and a half hours. I killed an hour and a half eating an excellent lunch at somewhere called Pikant, by the banks of the Jølstra, and sat in the bus-station waiting room for the last hour.

There weren't many passengers getting on the bus from Ålesund to Bergen this afternoon. I counted twelve apart from myself. Some of them were travelling alone; several were school age. An elderly couple sat down at the front; they were going to Vadheim. Two young women in hiking gear had brought along some broad rolls of canvas, which they stowed in the luggage compartment at the bottom of the bus. They brought their small rucksacks inside. I looked up as they passed me down the aisle. They had that featureless appearance good-looking young people have before life leaves its marks on them. One had blonde hair tied into a ponytail; the other girl's hair was dark, in a short, practical style that used to be called, and perhaps still is, a summer haircut.

A man in his fifties wearing a cloth cap and coat bore such a lugubrious facial expression that I put him down as a condolence-card salesman. The similarly aged buxom woman who sat down a couple of seats behind him, chatting away on her phone and giggling, was unlikely to be a potential customer of the salesman. It turned out that she would keep talking through all the mountain bends on Halbrendslia and deep into Langeland before considering the time appropriate for a rest.

By then I was well engrossed in the novel I had bought in the kiosk at the bus station – a crime thriller that took place in

Iceland. An elderly man had been found murdered in a cellar in Reykjavík, and among the evidence the police discovered at the crime scene was a photo of an old grave where a child was buried. The story went back a good number of years in time to a locale in which, in many ways, I felt quite at home. At least it distracted me from my annoyance at having my driving licence confiscated.

On the ferry across Sognefjord, between Lavik and Oppedal, most passengers got off the bus to stretch their legs and go to the toilet, or to buy a cup of coffee, a pancake or a hot dog in the lounge. Eeyore was left on his own. The buxom woman stood on the deck and had started another telephone conversation, this one slightly more impassioned than before. The two young women remained on the deck too, chatting during the crossing; they had returned to their seats before I made my way back from the lounge, the taste of bitter coffee lingering in my mouth and my bad mood on the rise again.

We were leaving Sogn og Fjordane behind us and driving into Hordaland county when the driver pulled into the verge and came to a halt by a bus-stop sign. At the crossroads, down a side road, there was a two-tone, brown and beige VW minibus – a vintage model, the type manufacturers call a camper van. You saw a lot more of them in the seventies and eighties than this side of 2000.

In front of the camper van stood a young man with longish, dark-blond hair. He had a sharp profile with an aquiline nose that made him easy to remember. The two girls alighted from the bus. The dark-haired one ran over to him, gave him a warm hug and stood close to him while the girl with the ponytail collected the two canvas rolls from the luggage compartment. Holding them with some difficulty, she stood beside the road and said something to the other two. They disengaged themselves and came over to her. But by then the bus had already set off for the first of two long tunnels that would take us through Masfjorden and Lindås towards Bergen.

The following week, I saw one of the young people again – in a photo in the newspaper. It was the man with the aquiline nose, beneath the headline: 'YOUNG MAN MISSING.'

3

The weather had been changeable for a while, like my mood, which varied according to the progress of the case against me.

Vidar Waagenes had called the police lawyer in Sogn og Fjordane on Wednesday morning. He brought me up to date on the phone: 'She's going to review the case and email us the reasoning behind the confiscation of your driving licence.'

'And how long will that take, do you think?'

'She promised she'd have a look at some point during the day.'

Nevertheless, it was Thursday afternoon before Waagenes emailed me those reasons. I hit the roof. Once again, the email described how I'd almost had collisions, almost swerved off the road, almost had accidents – as reported in a series of phone calls to the police.

I phoned Waagenes. 'And how many people rang in?'

He still thought this was a chuckling matter. 'Well, it was this animal transporter who was on your tail from Anda to Vassenden.'

'Exactly. Why the hell didn't he honk his horn or flash his lights when he saw all these incidents? I remember his vehicle very well. I kept checking to see if he wanted to pass. But he clearly didn't. He must have been sitting up in his raised seat laughing himself silly at the lunatic in front of him – his hilarity only briefly punctuated by telephone calls to the police.'

'Yes, it's a bit strange.'

'Tell me, does this nutcase have a name?'

He did. 'Atle Helset.'

'Well, would you believe it?'

'Does the name mean something to you?'

'I told you I'd been to Nordfjord to mediate in the case of a boundary dispute that's been going on for years, didn't I?'

'You did.'

'Well, the man who had to give way in the case is called Zacharias Helset. A mature gentleman, who would not drive round, transporting animals. But he'll have younger relatives, I suppose.'

'Interesting, Varg. You may well have a point. In which case perhaps we should consider reporting him for acting under false pretences?'

'But then we'll have to go to Førde. I don't know if I can be bothered. The most pressing thing for me is to get my licence back as quickly as possible.'

'Fine. You decide. We can come back to it. I'll call Florø and inform the police lawyer about the new development. You'll be hearing from me.'

I did, after roughly five minutes. The police lawyer was off sick, but was expected back at work on Monday.

I hit the roof again. 'What! So that means…'

'We'll have to wait until Monday to clear up this mess.'

I took the weekend off, and spent it alone. I didn't need a car to traverse the plain between Mount Fløyen and Mount Ulriken. I managed a run in Isdal valley as well. Both of these put me in a better frame of mind.

I searched for an Atle Helset on the Net, without finding much more than his address in Nordfjordeid. His name was entered as the CEO of A/S Helset Transport, but that was all I discovered. It was impossible to find out what his relationship to the Helset in the boundary dispute was. If necessary, I could make a few telephone calls.

On Monday morning, skimming through the newspaper I had delivered to my door every day, I spotted the headline 'YOUNG MAN MISSING', and that gave me something quite different to think about. The young man with the aquiline nose was easily recognisable in the picture. His name was Jonas Kleiva and he was twenty years old. He had last been seen during a

PURSUED BY DEATH 13

demonstration against a salmon-breeding farm near Solvik in Masfjorden municipality on the previous Tuesday. The newspaper said he had been driving a brown-and-beige VW T3 camper van with a Vestland number plate. He was a student at the University of Bergen, and lived in the city, but he hadn't returned to his bedsit in Sandviken after the trip to Masfjorden. Any information regarding his disappearance was to be passed on to Bergen police station or the closest police authority.

I rang the police and told them I might have some information about the case. The person I spoke to asked if I might be able to pop into the station.

'So long as I can pop out again,' I muttered under my breath.

The man at the other end said: 'Sorry, I didn't catch that.'

'That's fine. I'll be right over.'

Once there, I was taken up to the third floor to see Inspector Signe Moland, who was handling the case. I hadn't met her before. She was in her thirties and had blonde hair cut to a practical length. She was wearing a blue blouse, grey trousers and a light-grey suit jacket.

She received me with a professional smile and invited me into her office, which looked out onto the backyard.

Her surname interested me. 'Are you by any chance related to Atle Moland?'

She nodded. 'Did you know him? He was my paternal grandfather.'

'Then I believe we might actually be related.'

'Oh, yes?' She looked at me with curiosity.

'Your grandfather was my mother's cousin. I must be second cousin to your father, although I don't recall us ever meeting.'

'Harald Moland. He was in the police as well. I'm the fourth generation, in fact. But most of the time he was in PST, the security service.'

'In which case, I hope I went under his radar.'

'Well, I can't remember him ever mentioning you. Veum, wasn't it?'

'Yes. Varg even.'

'Hm.' She smiled politely at that. 'Well, let's put the family to one side for a moment. You rang in to say you had some information about the disappearance of Jonas Kleiva?'

'Yes. That is to say, I had no idea what his name was until I saw it in the press. And I don't exactly have any information, either. What I have is a sighting. I think that's the right term to use.'

'A sighting could be of assistance to us.'

Without touching on any of the unfortunate circumstances in Sogn og Fjordane, I told her that I had caught the bus from Førde to Bergen the previous Tuesday and that I'd seen a man I was sure answered to Jonas Kleiva's description, because of his appearance and the camper van he was standing next to. I told her about the two young women who had met him and described them as best I could.

She listened attentively to what I had to say and made a few notes on the keyboard in front of her, then checked the results on the screen.

'Interesting. Is that all you have?'

'Yes. The bus drove off while they were still standing there talking. My understanding from the newspaper article was that they'd been on their way to a demonstration against fish farming?'

'Yes, near Skuggefjorden. A place called Solvik. There was a board meeting planned at the fish farm they were protesting against. Apparently, it was a spontaneous demonstration – no advance warning. From what we've gathered there were just a handful of protesters, and I assume these three were among them. You said the two women were carrying rolls of canvas. They were almost certainly banners for the demonstration. Young Kleiva has family in Solvik, by the way.'

'Close family?'

'Mother. His parents are divorced. Father lives in Bergen, but from what we know, he has little contact with the son.'

'You've spoken to the mother, of course?'

She nodded condescendingly. 'He'd been to see her after the demonstration. That was the first she'd heard about it. Just a brief visit, she said, along with a girlfriend. Then he was going back to Bergen.'

'A girlfriend? Probably one of the two I saw him with then. Did you get any names?'

She raised her eyebrows with a hint of irony. 'No, we did not. But now that you've given us a hand, we might be able to find out who it could've been.'

'So who reported him missing?'

'That was his landlady in Bergen. He'd arranged to help her with a DIY job in the house the following day, so when he didn't return from Solvik, she started to get concerned. She'd even spoken to Jonas's mother on the phone, but it was actually the landlady who contacted us about him having gone missing. We waited for a few days. The mother told us about this girlfriend, so ... well, we thought it wasn't exactly unlikely that they'd go off somewhere together. But she wouldn't give up, this landlady, so after conferring with the mother and the landlady again we decided to launch a search.'

'And has it produced any results?'

'Not so far.'

'But these girls...'

'Yes, actually your information's been very useful. Especially the fact that there were two of them. We'll try to find out who they are and take it from there.'

The conversation had come to a halt. She leaned forward and shuffled a few documents that were lying in front of her. 'Was there anything else you had on your mind?'

'No, not for the moment.'

She looked at me with arched eyebrows. 'Later perhaps?'

'I hope not. But, you know, in my line of business…'

'Which is…?'

'I sort of thought I had my own section on the information board here. "Beware of the Wolf", it might've said.'

'Really? I'm afraid it doesn't.'

'No horror stories over coffee in the canteen?'

'Now you're piquing my curiosity.'

I gestured with my hands and angled my head. 'Private investigator. No history with the force though, as more and more of my competitors seem to have.'

'OK. Now the mists are clearing. In fact, your name has been mentioned a few times, if only *en passant*.' She shuffled her documents again. 'So, thank you very much, Veum. It was good of you to drop by with the information.'

I nodded and made a move to leave. 'You can call me Varg. Perhaps we'll see each other at a family reunion one day?'

'Has there ever been any? I don't recall hearing of one.'

'Nor me. Perhaps they've crossed us both off the invitation list.'

She smiled wryly in a way that I vaguely seemed to recognise from her grandfather.

On the way out I nodded to Atle Helleve, who was sitting in his office with the door open, embroiled in a telephone conversation. After Hamre left the force, Atle had taken over as section head. He nodded back, without any visible enthusiasm, but then in these circles my appearance didn't seem to excite any kind of welcome. Helleve was usually one of the more congenial officers, so perhaps his conversation wasn't the most uplifting.

I walked back to my office to mope a bit more about the loss of my driving licence, which was currently in quite a different place – either Førde or Florø. It wasn't with me anyway.

4

I received my driving licence through the post after approximately two weeks. The postal service was to blame for the long delay. In the meantime, I'd been in a position to print out a temporary licence from my own computer. This was all down to Vidar Waagenes, who'd done his job quickly and efficiently, persuading the police lawyer in Floro to drop the case, however reluctantly. I did have to go back to Førde to pick up my car though, which meant another bus trip to our northern neighbour.

The Corolla was neatly parked beside the chief of police's office, in the same place Joralf Smalabeit had left it. They hadn't confiscated the key, so I didn't have to exchange any pleasantries with the police. I got behind the wheel, started the engine and headed back to Bergen without extending my stay in Førde any longer than necessary. I was meticulous about keeping to the speed limit all the way to the ferry terminal in Lavik, slowing down where the terrain and bends demanded, of course. When I reached the top of the climb up from Instefjord and came to the crossing where the two girls had got off the bus, I took a decision. I pulled in and checked my map before deciding on a little detour down to Solvik, out of sheer curiosity more than anything else.

Skuggefjorden, the shadow fjord, was well named. The tall mountainsides cast long shadows over the fjord, making the sea, which lay there rippling in the breeze, resemble unevenly laid tarmac, which was normal for this county. From the road I could make out some buildings around a bay screened by a headland in the south of the fjord. The B-road down from the mountain had been narrow enough, and it didn't get any wider as I turned off and twisted and turned down the last few kilometres to Solvik. If you had to characterise the surroundings, 'sparsely

populated' would be the right words. On my descent I espied a
few unoccupied buildings – ghosts of abandoned farms. Only
one of them – where a flock of goats was grazing on what was
left of the grass – was bordered by a fence. I didn't see anyone
on the farm.

It was only when I reached the bottom of the hill that I saw
any signs of life. Solvik became more built up the closer I came
to the old quay, to the extent that the approximately twenty con-
structions could be called built up. There were cars parked in
front of most of them. By the gate to one of the houses was a sign
saying *ROOMS FOR RENT*. Down by the quay there were three
holiday cabins beside a white house with green-stained cladding,
where another sign said: *CAMPING & FISHING LICENCES*.
Above the entrance I read *SOLVIK STORE & CAFÉ* in large
letters. A red sign with a post horn and crown hung beside the
door to announce that it was also a *POST OFFICE*. The signs
suggested I had come to the indisputable centre of Solvik.

I parked and got out of the car. Now I could see that a newish
road went south from the quay to an area further out on the
headland. Large, open salmon pens floated in the fjord, as
though a gang of boys had thrown extra-large frisbees out there.

Along one side of a house I saw a white Ford Transit van with
SOLVIK TRANSPORT written on the top panel. In front of one
of the holiday cabins was a grey 1980 Opel Ascona.

I went up to the white house and peered through the glass
pane in the door, but couldn't see any activity. Stuck to the
window was a typed note: *Mon-Fri 9–18, Sat 9–16, Sun closed*.
When I opened the door, a bell rang above my head. From a
back room I heard a chair scrape as it was pushed backward.

The store had a limited selection of goods. At first sight it appeared to be catering for campers rather than local people. In a
cooler with glass doors I saw mineral water, pop and cans of
Coke. But a cooler in the opposite corner contained milk of all

varieties, pots of cream and yoghurt, cartons of juice and a selection of canned beers, with and without alcohol. On the shelves they had mostly tinned food and dry goods. There was a choice of two types of bread, both wrapped in paper advertising a bakery in Hosteland. To the left of the entrance there was a small freezer with various kinds of ice cream, anything from ice lollies to desserts, and a modest number of frozen items. In front of one window, facing the street, was the part that constituted the café: two small tables and four chairs.

In the doorway behind the cash desk appeared a man I assumed was the owner. He seemed to have adopted a crouched posture, as though ready to defend himself against an assault. I guessed he was in his forties: dark hair, but flecked with grey. He was thinning on top, with a few tufts standing in the air – perhaps he had just come in out of the wind. He had a stocky figure, wore dark-blue jeans, a blue shirt that didn't look quite fresh and an open, well-worn leather waistcoat. On his belt he carried a sheath knife. He eyed me suspiciously, as if a customer at this time of day on the first of October was an unusual phenomenon.

'Hello,' I said. 'My name's Veum. Do you run this place?'

That didn't seem to allay his suspicion. '*I do, yes. Stein Solvik. What do you want?*'

'Actually, I'm only passing through.' I could hear how unconvincing that sounded.

It did to him, too. '*Uhuh? Where to?*' As I didn't answer at once, he continued: '*I s'pose you're going to Sunfjord Salmon, like most people we don't know.*'

'Sunfjord?'

'*Yes, it sounds completely crazy to those of us who live here. I imagine they're trying to appeal to the international market, using a name that sounds familiar, so it's Sunfjord, with just one n. The English sun, then fjord.*'

I nodded towards the fjord. 'Is that the farm on the headland you're referring to?'

'*It is.*'

He looked at me, waiting for a response.

'Wasn't there some kind of demo there a couple of weeks ago?'

'*A demonstration? I suppose you could call it that. There were a few young people who bowled up here and then left. No one was bothered. They didn't get as far as the company premises. No one does without permission.*'

'Not even you?'

'*What would I go there for?*'

'Well…' I looked around the store. 'To deliver food, for example.'

'*Would be nice. They do their big shopping elsewhere, like so many of the folk in this area. This business won't make me rich, I can tell you.*'

'Did you see any of the demonstrators?'

'*Did I see them? They came in their toxic cars and gathered in the car park here.*' He gesticulated to the door. '*A couple of them came in and bought ice lollies, a few bottles of mineral water and some chocolate. That was all. Then they all went to the headland together. Afterwards they went home. I haven't heard anyone say they miss them.*'

'Well, that's the point. Have you heard that one of them is actually missed? Or missing?'

He sent me a sharp look. '*No, I haven't … Missing? Who?*'

'His name's Jonas Kleiva.'

He nodded, deep in thought, and repeated the name. '*Jonas?*'

'Apparently he's from this area, or so I've been told.'

'*Yeah … The Kleivas have been around here for generations. I know very well who Jonas is. His mother lives here.*'

'Yes, that's what I was told.'

'*Her name's Betty.*' A glint of something indeterminate appeared in his eyes, a mixture of cunning and schadenfreude.

'Betty?'

'Yes, her real name's Elisabeth, but everyone calls her Betty. Even she does. She's the one with rooms for rent, if you saw the sign, but I'd better warn you if you were thinking of renting one: they say Betty eats men for breakfast. Widow twice over. The third escaped by getting divorced.'

'Sounds dramatic. It was Jonas's father who survived then, I take it?'

'Yeah, but his successor wasn't so lucky. He died while hiking two years ago. He fell down the side of a mountain and was found by two guys out looking for him.'

'And the first husband?'

His eyes narrowed as he focused on me. 'That was more mysterious, if I can put it like that. They found him dead in bed one morning. Heart attack, it was said at the time, but folk here are saying something else now. She's handy with herbs and the like, Betty is. That's what folk say.'

'But if there was anything suspicious about the death, surely it would've been investigated?'

'Investigated? Don't think so. Didn't strike anyone as fishy, and we would know, coming from an area that has survived for generations by catching fish. And long before the fish farms came here too.'

'Jonas lives in Bergen, I gather.'

'Yes, I suppose he does now. He doesn't come home often, at any rate, and it's news to me that he took part in the demonstration, I have to admit.'

I waited a moment to see if he would continue. When he didn't I said, 'Actually, it was the café sign that drew me in here. What have you got on the menu?'

He looked at me almost open-mouthed. 'We've always got coffee on the go and if you're peckish, I can bung a few rolls in the microwave. I've got cheese and sausages too. Take the weight off your feet in the meantime.' He pointed to the two tables by the window and disappeared into the back room.

I sat down and looked out. A lean, slightly stooped man wearing a black bobble hat, worn padded overalls, dark blue with reflector strips on the sleeves and chest, was coming from the quay. On his back he had a blue rucksack emblazoned with *DNT*, the Norwegian trekking association. When he arrived at the forecourt, he turned to the café and squinted at the window where I was sitting, as though wondering who I was.

The bell above the door rang as he stepped inside. He glanced in my direction and nodded in a measured way – it was someone he didn't know. His face was sinewy and narrow, his eyes a piercing light blue. He had a couple of days' stubble on his chin, streaked with grey, and an upper lip that revealed that he had *snus* underneath. From under his hat protruded some long, greybrown wisps of hair that he had gathered like a little rat's tail on the nape of his neck.

I nodded back without saying anything.

Stein Solvik appeared from the back room. *'Hi, Edvard. Would you like a cup of coffee as well? We have townsfolk here on a visit.'*

'Thank you very much,' the new arrival said. 'And a roll too, if you have one.'

'On its way. I'll throw in a couple more, so…' Solvik nodded in my direction and disappeared into the back room again.

'A Bergensian, I can hear,' I said.

The man nodded, pulled out a chair and sat down at the same table as me. 'Edvard Aga,' he said by way of introduction and looked at me.

'Varg Veum.'

He nodded, without seeming particularly interested.

'I was just curious to see what it was like down by the fjord. I've never been here before.'

'No?' He gestured towards the window. 'I have a cabin here. And for the last few years, I've been a resident.'

'I see. What's the attraction?'

He cast a pensive eye over me. 'The quiet. The silence. The absence of other people.'

'"A place where no one would believe people could live", like the eponymous TV series?'

'That sort of thing.'

Stein Solvik reappeared, this time with a Thermos of freshly brewed coffee, a tray with two cups and a plate of four rolls cut into two. Half of them had cheese on, the others oval pieces of dark, reddish-brown salami. *'Edvard's my best customer. If it wasn't for him I'd have had to close the shop.'*

'Come on now, don't exaggerate,' Aga said with a little smile. *'He lives off the fish he catches in the sea, the potatoes he grows on his land and the bread he bakes himself, but he buys the flour here, and if he needs anything else, he comes to me for it.'*

Aga pulled a face. 'Well, I have to go further and further out into the sea to fish. Those bastards out there…' He motioned to the headland where the salmon pens were. 'They've as good as emptied the bloody fjord.' He turned to face me. 'And it isn't just the wild salmon that have suffered. You should see the cod and the pollock I fish from the sea. They're so emaciated and ill that even my cat won't eat them.'

'And that's because…?'

'I'll tell you: the bastards breeding the fish have spread so much sea lice and poison in the fjord that I wouldn't even bloody swim in it. They should be taken to court. They've killed the whole sodding fjord. Once upon a time it was a jewel.'

He looked up at Stein Solvik, who nodded. *'You are so right, Edvard. A jewel is the right word. That's in the days when tourists used to come here.'* Now he looked at me as well. *'Fishing for salmon. And not just Norwegians. The English and Germans, too.'*

Edvard Aga gazed over at the window. 'Is that your car parked there?'

'The grey Toyota, yes.'

'If you have time to drive along the fjord, I can show you the source of all the misery.'

I hummed and hawed. 'I have to be back in Bergen tonight, but ... How far down?'

'We can drive there in about fifteen to twenty minutes. And it's worth the trip if you're interested in haunted houses.'

I glanced at Stein Solvik. He was watching us with clenched lips and scepticism in his eyes, but didn't say anything.

'Well, if you say so, then OK. But surely we should...' I gestured to the food on the table.

'Yeah, yeah, eat first, ha ha. Isn't that the Sunnfjord motto?'

After we had finished off the rolls, drunk the coffee and chatted about what Aga had done before he moved here – teaching and selling properties – and how I made a living, we thanked the owner, left and got in my car.

Aga pointed. 'Over there to the right, and then it's a straight road the whole way.'

I nodded, started the car, turned round by the next house down towards the quay, passed a few more buildings and then we were out of the compact village of Solvik. The road narrowed and was soon a standard Vestland lane: one carriageway and passing places at regular intervals.

Aga chuckled beside me. 'Private investigator, ha ha. First one I've ever met, I reckon. But to quote Elvis: "If you're looking for trouble, you came to the right place."'

I cast a quick glance at him. 'Oh, yeah?'

'Solvik village is divided into two parts, and those living on either side of the line barely talk to each other.'

'Uhuh?'

I had to keep my eyes on the road, but he continued talking unprompted:

'You saw the sparse selection of goods in Stein Solvik's grocery store. He's tried to stay neutral in the dispute, with the result that many people have boycotted him, regardless of which side of the fight they are on.'

'So what are they arguing about?'

'It's been like the Middle East here over the past few years, and there are no signs of peace coming soon. It became even more dramatic when Klaus Krog died two years ago, while hiking.'

'Stein Solvik mentioned him. He was married to Betty Kleiva, is that right?'

'Not sure if they were married. I think they lived together. And there were ten years between them.'

'OK. But what did his death have to do with the local dispute?'

'You're right to be confused. The whole reason for this witch's brew lies there.' He jabbed a finger at the fjord. 'And what they've done to it. But when someone began to shed some light on the matter, things … ended as they did.'

'By which you mean?'

'The accident in the mountains, if it was one. Many have their doubts.'

'But it was investigated?'

'They call it so many things. A local policeman came here and walked the route they assumed Krog had taken, up to the summer farms in Fossedalen. He came back down and said it was perilously steep. Then he drove back to Duesund, or wherever it was he came from. After a while the police ruled that it was a case of misadventure and no further investigations would be undertaken.'

'And that was accepted by … everyone?'

'Absolutely not. I believe Betty contacted a lawyer, but never got any further, and I suppose the case is stuck there.'

'When did this happen, did you say?'

'Two years ago, in September 2002.'

We were round a headland now. From here we could see the
end of the fjord. A white waterfall plummeted down the mountainside from high above. On a piece of land in the foreground
I glimpsed some dirty, grey buildings and a pier jutting into the
sea.

'There – you can see it,' Aga said. 'Markatangen. That's where
we're going.'

'OK. But this dispute you were mentioning – what's it actually about?'

'To put it simply, as far as that's possible: breeding salmon
and money. Should a salmon farm be in the fjord or on land?
What's best for the fish? What's best for the fjord? What's best
for the environment?'

'I don't know a great deal about this, but I've followed the
discussion. On land, I assume, in answer to all three questions.'

'Precisely. And that's where the conflict lies. Between – if this
were a gangster war – the Marken gang and the Sørnes gang.
And to put it in a nutshell, again, those from Marken were in
favour of the land solution because they had experienced for
themselves how destructive their own fish farm had been for the
fjord. The Sørnes gang, however, who now have big, international capital behind them, back offshore cultivation and have
established Sunfjord Salmon on the Sørneset headland.'

We were approaching our destination of Markatangen. The
road led to a big gate surrounded by tall wire fences on both
sides. But the gate was wide open and there were visible holes
in the fencing, so there was nothing to stop us driving straight
onto the forecourt. I swung up in front of the closest building
and parked.

Aga had been right. It was like arriving in a ghost town. Three
buildings with dark façades faced the car park. Several window
panes were smashed. A sign above the door announced that
MARKEN SALMON FARMS resided here, but the paint was

faded and the primer coat grey. Nothing tempted you to go in to see if there was a ghost sitting in reception.

Aga stopped and looked down. 'Actually, someone's been here recently,' he said, pointing to the tyre marks visible in the gravel. We raised our eyes and followed the tracks. They led straight to the pier.

Aga headed off in that direction. To the right of the pier were the remains of the old salmon pens, like abandoned UFOs in the fjord. 'This is where the salmon were jumping when they started up in the 1980s. Now they're not only dead in the pens but also in the whole bloody fjord. First came the salmon lice. Then they used poison to kill the lice. And we can see the consequences of both now.' With a broad sweep of his arm, he indicated the fjord. 'A dead fjord. Dead as a dodo.'

We had reached the end of the pier. The tyre tracks we had seen didn't stop here; from what I could see they extended into the sea.

We stood staring down into the dark water for a moment.

Then Aga shouted, 'Jesus Christ!' and stared at me in alarm.

I nodded slowly, as if agreeing with him.

Beneath the surface we could make out an almost indefinable, light-coloured, rectangular form.

It was the roof of a vehicle. And if I wasn't much mistaken, it was the same VW camper van I had observed up on the E39 just two weeks before.

5

'What the hell shall we do?' Aga asked.

I sent him an anxious look. 'Just report what we've seen. I'm seriously worried – the van could well have been there for close on two weeks now. We'll just have to cross our fingers and hope there's no one inside.'

Aga leaned over the edge and peered down into the sea. 'Looks to me as if the driver's door is open. What do you think?'

I leaned over as well. 'It's definitely not jammed shut anyway, from what I can see.'

'What number should we ring? 112?'

'I'll do it. I know the officer on this case.'

No sooner said than done. The operator on 112 noted down where we were, who I was and promised to pass on the message to Signe Moland or one of her colleagues. It wasn't long before I had her on the phone.

'Varg? Have I understood correctly? You've found the vehicle Kleiva was driving when he went missing?'

'Yes. But it's in the sea – and most likely has been ever since he disappeared, I'm afraid.'

'OK, can you see if there's anyone inside?'

'Impossible to see from this angle, and jumping into the water to check isn't exactly tempting.'

'No, we'll sort that out. I'll contact the Masfjorden chief of police, but I'm sure a few of us from Bergen will come, too. Will you be there?'

'I'm in no great rush, so if you need me to stick around…'

'We'll have to talk to you anyway. Are you alone?'

'No, there's someone with me. A guy who has a cabin here. We discovered the camper van together.'

'Good. Stay there until we arrive.'

I glanced at Aga. 'Looks like we'll have to stay here a while.'

He nodded by way of response, and I confirmed to Signe
Moland that we would be here, both of us.

After I had rung off, there was something of a strange atmosphere. It was as though the camper van below was drawing us
down, and we both automatically took a few steps back along
the pier. Neither of us said anything for a while. It was a bit like
Edvard Aga and I had both applied for the same job and now we
had met each other in the waiting room before our interviews.

In the end, he gestured towards the fjord. 'Was ... Jonas
Kleiva driving the van?'

'It's registered in his name, at least. He's been missing for
almost two weeks, since they were here for the demonstration.'

He looked at me, downcast, then he nodded vaguely, almost
imperceptibly. 'Hm.'

'Can you tell me a bit more about the local dispute? Did
Jonas Kleiva have anything to do with it?'

He nodded, again in such a way that it was barely perceptible,
and surveyed the countryside around us. 'You know, in commu-
nities like this everyone has something to do with everything. Close
relationships and family lines intersect everywhere.' He pointed
inland at the abandoned buildings on the run-down works site. 'It
was Mons Marken who started the business here, way back in 1976,
the so-called pioneering days. But he died early, in 1978, as far as I
remember. Then his widow – Betty that is – took over responsibility
for the place. She was young then. She got some help from others
in the village, and one of them – Kåre Kleiva – ended up marrying
her. She had Jonas with him, so actually Jonas would be the next in
line to inherit this, when his parents go. But Kåre and Betty divorced, and I have no idea what the ownership situation is now.
Besides...' He made an eloquent gesture towards the abandoned
buildings. 'Not exactly much to inherit now, is there.'

'No. On the way over, though, you said that the people who
ran the business here wanted to have a closed fish farm, on land?'

'Yes. I think that was Kåre's proposal, actually. But then the Sørnes lot got some pretty substantial funding for a traditional farm in the fjord and started planning for it. Kåre, though, struggled to get financial backing for his idea. A closed farm requires a huge amount of investment, and as the profits are much lower than from the gigantic farms in the sea, of course, it is more tempting for big capital to finance something that provides the greatest yield in the shortest time. In that line of business, it's the laws of capitalism that hold sway, and no government has been able to resist them, not in the current situation anyway. In the end, Kåre gave up. Perhaps that's what led to his divorce from Betty. Who knows.'

He pointed to the fjord.

'See Storfossen waterfall there. It doesn't flow directly into the fjord, but via some long, narrow lakes, connected by rapids, that culminate at the mouth of a river into the fjord. I've stood in it fishing for salmon since I first came here, at the end of the seventies.'

'Have you had a cabin here ever since?'

'No, I built it in 1985. For the first few years I rented a room at Betty's.' And, as if it were an afterthought, added: 'And Kåre's.' Then continued: 'But what I wanted to say is that salmon are fascinating creatures. Since the dawn of time, long before humans came here, salmon travelled up to Storfossen. They spawned there, the spawn grew there and became smolt, which, when they were big enough, left their home in the river, swam out through the fjord to the ocean, crossed it and carried on to Greenland and drifted around there before starting on their homeward trip. And by then they had an internal compass that not only guided them back to Norway and Vestland, but right to the end of Skuggefjorden and up into the rapids, where they originally came from … It's so incredible. I'm still just as fascinated – and moved – every time I think about it.'

'And there they're caught by people like you.'

'Some of them. But many stay to spawn and create new generations of salmon who undertake the same journey. Year after year, generation after generation. Have you seen a salmon jumping the rapids? Have you seen young salmon playing in the waves? They're athletes. Strong little bundles of muscle. You have to take your hat off to them from the grassy river bank as they pass. And' – he looked at me sternly – 'there are limits to how many you can catch. There are strict regulations, and river owners are observant. A fishing licence is not exactly something you pick up at a flea market. If you're caught breaking rules, you can be banned for years.' He swallowed and looked almost grief-stricken. 'And you don't want that of course. That would be … a living death.'

I smiled wryly. Yes, indeed, I had met people like him before: such passionate anglers that they trembled when they got a bite, and tears could flow when they had the catch on land. As for myself, I had to confess that I belonged to the small-timers, who could fish for trout on occasion, or cod, saithe and mackerel if the opportunity offered itself, but I didn't feel the same passion as Edvard Aga, not at all.

'Who were the landowners?' I asked, motioning towards Storfossen.

'The Marken family, too.'

'This Mons … was he the sole heir?'

'He inherited it outright, so he managed the estate. He had a younger brother, who moved to the States and stayed there, and a sister, who's dead.'

'In reality then, Jonas is the heir to the defunct works and the land?'

'Yes, they didn't have any more children, Betty and Kåre, and she didn't have any from before.'

We sat in silence for a while. Dusk was beginning to fall. On the other side of the fjord, a round moon had appeared. In three-quarters of an hour we would be in complete darkness. We were on our way into what on more pleasant occasions is called 'the blue hour'. An hour for poetry reading, a warm fire and interested listeners. The only sounds we heard were shrill cries from a seabird that was dissatisfied with what was on offer for supper and had no one else to complain to except the tall, sheer mountainsides. They returned the sound as if they were grumpy ghosts, irritated that they had been disturbed in whatever else they had planned to do on this afternoon at the very beginning of October.

We agreed that we would go and sit in the car while we were waiting. It was half past six when the first police car pulled up. We saw their headlights from several kilometres away and got out, ready to receive them.

6

I thought I had met the large man emerging from the passenger door before. *'Karl Sætenes, chief of police in Masfjorden,'* he said, introducing himself. He nodded to his companion, a much younger and not quite so large man. *'This is Constable Hans Hosteland.'*

Edvard Aga and I duly introduced ourselves.

Sætenes studied me. *'I reckon I've met this fella before.'*

I assented with a nod. 'We met in Gulen, on the island of Brennøy, six years ago.'

His eyes narrowed. *'That's correct. Who could forget that?'*

'Yes…' I couldn't forget, either.

He shifted his gaze to Aga. *'You say you've found a camper van in the sea?'*

'Yes.' Aga pointed to the pier. 'Over there.'

'We've contacted Bergen police as well,' I said.

'So we were informed. But our journey's shorter.'

Without another word, he nodded to his colleague and began to walk towards the edge of the quay. There he stopped, leaned forward and peered down into the water, which was now greyish-black and rippled with small, breaking waves. *'Get your torch out,'* he said to Hosteland. The officer did as ordered, switched on a powerful flashlight and shone the beam into the depths.

The chief nodded. *'Yes, look there.'*

Aga and I had come alongside them.

'I'm pretty sure I know that vehicle,' I said. 'I saw it myself a couple of weeks ago.'

Sætenes turned to me with a sullen expression. *'Oh, yes? But not down here, I imagine.'*

'No, it was up on the E39, at a crossroads.'

'And what made you two come here today?'

'Aga kindly offered to show me the disused salmon-breeding farm.'

'Why?'

I waggled my head. 'Well, why not? We happened to be talking to the owner of the general store in Solvik, and then Aga suggested a trip out here.'

He glanced at Aga. *'Just like that?'*

Aga looked at him slightly despairingly. 'Veum was interested in what folk do for a living around here.'

'And you thought a disused salmon-breeding farm was just the ticket?'

'Well, not quite.'

'You know, of course, that there was a demonstration here at the beginning of last week? Against the salmon farm in Sørnes.'

'We suspect some of the demonstrators came here in the camper van that is now underwater,' I said.

'Thought so.' Sætenes glanced at Hosteland. *'Interested in what folk do for a living around here. Did you hear that?'*

Hosteland nodded, but apparently without much sympathy for what his older colleague was thinking. Instead he pointed across the fjord. *'Here they come from Bergen.'*

'Yes, still a way to go though,' Sætenes smirked, and stood erect, as if to demonstrate his status.

There were two vehicles approaching: one a police car in red, white and blue; the other a red Mercedes *Underwater Search Unit* from Sandviken fire station. From the police car stepped Inspector Signe Moland and a male colleague, Arne Melvær. Both nodded to me, Melvær with the same distance officers from Bergen police station soon adopt towards me; Signe was friendlier already.

Two firemen jumped out of the Mercedes, one in his forties with thick, curly hair and a small moustache, and a younger man whose head was completely shaven, both ready for action.

'Tor Monsen,' the older of the two said.

'Lars Midthun,' the other man said.

Together we walked to the edge of the quay and stared down. Hosteland shone his flashlight on the camper van.

Signe turned to me. 'Is this the one you told me about last time we met?'

'It's strikingly similar, anyway.'

She looked at the older of the two firemen. 'Can you do a quick dive to see if anyone's inside?'

Monsen nodded. 'Lars is doing the first dive.' He turned to his colleague, but Lars Midthun was already on his way to the Mercedes; he opened the rear door and selected the equipment he needed. He quickly changed into a tight-fitting wetsuit, strapped an oxygen tank to his back and returned to the quay.

'I'm going down,' he announced. He climbed down the ladder at the side of the quay, pulled a mask over his head, switched on the head-torch, gave a thumbs-up and dived down to the camper van, which lay no more than one and a half metres under the surface of the water.

From the quay we could clearly follow his movements. He skilfully manoeuvred his way down to the van, grabbed the external door handle and pulled himself down so that he could see inside. With his head-torch he shone the beam through the side window. A line of air bubbles rose from the purge valve in his mask and burst on the surface. We all stood watching him without saying a word. Everyone was focused on what was happening below.

The diver let go of the right-hand side of van, swam around the front and to the door on the left, which appeared to be ajar. He moved backward along the van, bent forward and moved his head in such a way that the beam lit up everything inside the front compartment. Then he pulled himself away, kicked his legs and allowed himself to float slowly up to the surface. He swam to the ladder and grabbed hold. Only when he was back on the quay did he pull off his mask and look at us, with a serious expression on his face.

'There's a woman in the passenger seat. The driver's seat is empty – the safety belt's undone and the door on that side isn't quite shut.'

'Oh,' Signe exclaimed. 'Nothing else in the immediate vicinity?'

'Not that I can see. But there's a current in the fjord here, so…' Midthun shrugged.

'Hm,' Signe said. 'Then we'll have to contact an undertaker. Are there any local ones you use in such cases?' She looked at Sætenes.

'It'll have to be the one in Knarvik.'

'Can you inform him?'

'Do you want them here now?'

'The sooner, the better. Ambulances won't take bodies, and we have to transfer her to Gades Institute as soon as we can for an autopsy.'

He nodded and glanced indicatively at Hosteland, who decoded the message and headed for the police car.

I looked at Signe. 'The girls I told you about,' I said. 'Did you contact them?'

There was an expression of concern on her face. 'Only one of them.'

I focused on Midthun. 'Did you see … the woman? Did she have short hair or a ponytail?'

He appeared to be considering the question. 'No ponytail, no. I'm fairly sure about that.'

I turned back to Signe. 'The woman you contacted, did you meet her personally?'

She cleared her throat. 'Varg … I think you should leave the investigation of this case to us now. Thank you for reporting the camper van. For formality's sake you should drop by my office over the weekend so that we can log the details of why you and Aga came out here.' She glanced at Sætenes. 'I think we can leave the local enquiries to you, and then we can liaise afterwards. Is that alright?'

He nodded sullenly, without making a comment.

'So Aga and I can leave the crime scene?'

She grinned. 'You can.' Then she turned her back on us, faced Arne Melvær and pointed to a spot down the quay to show that what they needed to talk about definitely did not concern us two civilians.

Before we got into the car, we gazed across the fjord.

'Sometimes when I'm out fishing alone,' Aga said, 'late in the evening or early in the morning, I stand like this and look around. Then I often think … people have lived here for thousands of years.' He pointed to the waterfall. 'Remains of stone-age settlements have been found there. And I've tried to imagine them. Perhaps not stone-age folk, but those who settled here later. Before the Black Death – and after. In the twelfth and thirteenth centuries, and then again, from the fifteenth onwards. The human fates that have been acted out in these surroundings. How many secrets do you think this fjord is hiding? How many stories could the mountains on both sides tell us if they were living beings? How many human dramas have they witnessed?'

'And now another – is that what you're thinking?'

'Yes, now another one. I really hope they find him.'

'Jonas, you mean? You think it was him in the driver's seat?'

'Yes. From what you yourself said, surely it must've been.'

'Yes, I suppose so.'

Then we were in the car again. The four police officers were studying a map one of them had spread out while the two fire officers stood apart, chatting quietly. It was ever thus. A body or two always put a damper on proceedings. It rubbed off on us in the car as we drove back to Solvik; we had not the slightest inclination to talk during the whole journey.

Outside Solvik Store & Café a woman was in conversation with Stein Solvik. He was standing in the doorway; she was at the bottom of the steps leading up to it. When I parked by the fence, they both turned their faces in our direction.

'Betty,' Edvard Aga said, and he seemed to hesitate before opening the door on his side and getting out of the car.

7

If the atmosphere back at Markatangen had been muted, here it was tense. Betty Kleiva took a few steps towards us while Stein Solvik stayed where he was. *'Edvard,'* she said. *'What's happened?'*

'Happened? Nothing, I…' He looked at me.

'We saw the vehicles driving past. Two from the police and one from the fire service. What's going on? Tell me!' She fixed her gaze on me.

Betty Kleiva was about one metre sixty tall and squarely built. She had a broad face with strong features, sensual lips, and eyes that didn't deviate for a second. She was bare-headed, with thick, medium-blonde hair cut in a short, practical style suited to a working life in the country. She was wearing dark-blue jeans and a green windcheater with a hood, lined with orange fleece. On her feet she wore blue boots with a white edge around the soles.

I stepped closer. 'Varg Veum.'

'Betty Kleiva.'

'Jonas's mother, I understand.'

Her eyes held mine, but it was as though her pupils grew and filled the iris. *'Yes, I am. Is it him? Have they found him?'*

'No, they haven't. Only his camper van.'

'Camper van? Where?'

I paused. 'In the sea.'

'Out by Markatangen,' Aga said.

She clutched her throat. *'In the sea? That can only mean…'* Her lips trembled and her eyes moistened.

'We don't know that, Betty. Veum and I were there and … The camper was in the sea at the end of the pier.'

'Was anyone inside?'

I cleared my throat in an admonitory manner. 'We can't answer that question,' I said, meeting her stare.

'You can't? Who are you, actually?'

'I'm a private investigator.'

'Private investigator? Have you been looking for Jonas as well?'

'Not really. I passed him and a couple of friends almost two weeks ago, when they were on their way to demonstrate against the fish farm over there.' I nodded towards Sørnes.

'Yes, when he came by that day, that's where he said he was going. But then later, his landlady in Bergen was worried about where he was, and eventually we agreed with the police that they should initiate a search … And now, this evening, when I saw all the vehicles, the police, the fire service and … I thought they'd found him.'

'When he came by that day, was he with someone?'

Her eyes wavered. As though something was buried deep inside her, she hesitated before answering. 'Yes. There was a girl with him. I'd never met her before. I wasn't used to him bringing someone home and I … I suppose I was a little confused.'

'But she did introduce herself, did she?'

'Yes. Mona, I think she said. Nothing else.'

'Are you sure? No surname?'

'No. Not that I can recall anyway.'

'I see. Well, there's still hope he might turn up.' Mona, however, was another story, I said to myself.

She looked at the other two, first Aga, then Solvik, as though one of them might be of some support. But they stayed silent, both of them.

'Well, I'd better be going home. They'll probably contact me if they find anything. Have a nice evening. See you later,' she said, looking at the other two again, then nodding to me and walking away.

We stood watching her for a while.

Stein Solvik came down the steps. 'What does it mean, boys? Did they find his camper van in the sea?'

'I'm afraid so,' Aga said. 'And there was someone in it, too.'

'What do you mean? It wasn't Jonas?'

'No, it was a woman.'

Solvik glanced at me.

I nodded. 'You heard what Betty Kleiva said. He had a girl with him when he dropped by to say hello.'

'One of the demonstrators?'

'Most probably. But I think you should keep this under your hats until it becomes public knowledge.'

'Yes, of course.'

I cast a glance up the mountainside. 'I'd better be going home, too. This might've ended dramatically, but I have to say it's been nice getting to know you two.'

'We'll see each other again, I reckon,' Solvik said, sending me a sly wink.

And I thought: Maybe that isn't so unlikely.

'Have a good trip back. I'm going to chug back to my cabin,' Aga said.

'It's not on the mainland?'

'No, I have to cross the fjord,' he said, nodding towards the water, where the moon shone even stronger now that darkness had fallen. You had to admit there was an air of enchantment about the fjord with the steepling mountains on either side.

There wasn't much more to say. I got into my car, switched on the radio to listen to the news, and drove along dark Vestland roads punctuated only by a few illuminated houses and factories until I approached Knarvik and the lights on Nordhordland bridge appeared in the south-west like a diadem, warning me that I was closing in on more populated areas. My speed was well within the permissible limits. I was still taking no chances on that score.

8

Bergen in October can be anything from all-out autumn storms to unseasonably summery days. This weekend was more like the latter, with the temperature up to sixteen degrees and variable cloud cover on the Saturday; then still mild, but with intermittent rain the following day. According to the weather forecast, the tail-end of a tropical storm would announce its arrival on Monday, with such strong winds that even locals would find their deft handling of umbrellas under threat. I followed the meteorologist's advice and left my umbrella at home, but donned a raincoat and hat and took the quickest short-cut down to my office. There I entrenched myself behind the computer while waiting to be contacted by Signe Moland.

It got to almost three o' clock in the afternoon and I still hadn't heard anything, so I rang the police myself and was put through to her.

'Veum?' she confirmed with no tinge of joy audible in her voice.

'Varg,' I said.

'OK. What do you want? I'm pretty busy here.'

'You intimated on Friday that you wanted me to come in for a formal interview over the weekend.'

'We've had our hands full here talking to relatives – and others – so today's busy enough as it is.'

'Relatives? So, you've identified the young woman?'

'Yes, but as I said—'

'Mona...'

'Could be.'

'And no one else has turned up?'

'In the sea, you mean?'

'Yes.'

'No ... Let me see, now. If you come in tomorrow at one-thirty, we can talk then. Is that convenient?'

'I can manage that, yes, but—'

'Then I'll carry on here. Talk tomorrow, Varg.' The way she said my Christian name reminded me of my history teacher at Katedralskolen a hundred years ago, who loved to lengthen the 'a' in my name as if it were a rubber band she was aiming to hit me between the eyes with.

I made a note that I had an appointment with Moland the following day. But that didn't mean I could relax. I sifted through online news sites about the demonstration by Skuggefjorden in the hope of finding an organisation that claimed responsibility for it. I didn't find many articles. There was a little story in *Bergens Tidende* and two columns in *Nordhordland*, the local newspaper. In neither did they talk about any centrally organised action. I made a call to both the Nature Conservation Association Hordaland and the Green Warriors of Norway, who had their headquarters in Bergen. Neither of them had been involved. At the Green Warriors I was transferred to their founder, Kurt Oddekalv. With obvious conviction, he stated that he supported this action one hundred per cent. Time after time he had himself stated, on record, how salmon breeding polluted the fjords, but he thought this particular demo had arisen spontaneously, led by local, seriously committed young people. When I mentioned Jonas Kleiva, he checked the membership list and was unable to find his name there. *'But that doesn't mean I don't support him!'* he asserted vehemently in nynorsk, and then we finished the conversation.

Now that I was on the Net, I kept searching for articles about fish breeding. Most of them were simply news stories, generally supportive of breeders and full of encomiums about how Norway was going to live on this industry once the last oil had been pumped up from the sea bed. But there were also some critical articles, which, among other things, pointed to the widespread problems with vibriosis, a bacterial disease that had a terrible impact on salmon. Huge amounts of antibiotics were used to combat it, so much so that the salmon became resistant to them. Many breeding pens had been destroyed by violent storms, which led to a mass breakout of the farmed salmon and an uncontrolled spread of diseases to the wild fish in the surrounding waters. And not only the salmon, but also cod, saithe and other varieties were affected.

An even bigger problem emerged when infestations of salmon lice struck in earnest. The salmon louse was a calanoid copepod that bred and proliferated at a frightening tempo, which was exacerbated by the closed farms' habit of keeping far too many salmon together in one place. Some of the articles were illustrated with pictures of lice-stricken salmon. They looked terrible, with open sores and large abscesses, which didn't exactly make them appetising. These specimens were hardly going to front the campaign for Norwegian salmon on the international market.

In the fight against salmon lice, everything was being used, from garlic to hydrogen peroxide. Other remedies were being researched to save the whole seafood industry, which was now in the process of establishing itself along the coast, from Lindesnes to Lofoten and even further north. The names of some of the investors were testament to the big money involved. The energetic and unsuspecting salmon breeders who had started in the 1970s as happy amateurs, more or less, were gradually being replaced by large concerns that were on an upward curve on the major stock markets. Or they would be if it weren't for the damned calanoid copepod...

Seeing the name of the journalist who wrote one of the articles pulled me up short: Torunn Tafjord. Her name awoke some vivid memories, the clearest from a dramatic incident in connection with organised human trafficking north of Haugesund a number of years ago; another when she helped me with a case in Vigra in the autumn of the same year. My memories of saying goodbye to her at the airports in Flesland and Vigra were lodged in the back of my mind like two scenes from *Casablanca*. She worked as a freelancer out of Dublin, and covered large parts of the world. It came as a surprise to me that she had now added fish breeding to her list of causes, but it probably said something about the position this industry now occupied on the international news scene. In a world where we stared catastrophic hunger in the face on a daily basis and where increasing the availability of food was a question of life and death, the burgeoning production of seafood was a vital project that was not to be held back.

I took out my phone and rang the first number I had saved – her home telephone in Dublin. I was informed that this number was no longer in use. I went onto the Yellow Pages website and looked there. I found both an address in Oslo and a mobile number. I dialled and got a nibble on my first cast, which I had never experienced in all the time I had ever tried to catch a salmon.

'Torunn,' she said as she picked up the phone.

'Varg,' I said.

'Wow. Well, this has to be telepathy. I was just thinking I was going to try and get in touch.'

'Really?'

Her Ålesund dialect was as marked as it had been eleven years before. 'Yes, I've been thinking of going to Bergen very soon. I haven't been there since we last met.'

'And that's a few years ago now.'

'Far too many, if you ask me.'

'That's not down to me.'

'No?' she replied with an equivocal little laugh.

'I wonder if the reason for your Bergen trip has something to do with salmon?'

This time she laughed out loud. 'That *is* telepathy. Or else you can read minds. One of the two. Does the name Fredrik Martens mean anything to you?'

'Not immediately. But Martens Bakery is a name we all know in Bergen.'

'Yes, but that's a different family. Fredrik Martens is a very active investor in a variety of industries. Recently he's turned his attention to salmon breeding. And as is so often the case, the headquarters of his company is based in Jersey, one of the islands in the English Channel and a well-known tax haven.'

'Yup, I know all about that.'

'It turns out that his business spends more time and effort making a profit than it does developing foodstuffs that are meant to be good for us all. The problem is, developing healthy foods costs money. What's more, the quantity of fish the company breeds and sells has to be reduced significantly as there are concerns about the animals' welfare, and because the quality of the product doesn't bear much scrutiny. All of which makes me want to have a chat with Fredrik Martens himself, but that's not proving so easy. First, he divides his time between Jersey and Bergen, and second ... well, he says he doesn't talk to the press.'

'And so you thought I should pay him a visit, twist his arm and force him to?'

'Yes, something like that.' She laughed. 'The last time we confronted the businessmen of Bergen, I had you along as a kind of bodyguard, didn't I?'

'I'm still at your service, albeit a few years older. When are you thinking of coming over?'

'I don't know yet. I still have quite a bit of background work to do. I can ring you when I know more. But actually it was you who rang me this time, so why—?'

'Yes, I did. Your name appeared in the byline to an article I was reading – about salmon farming, in fact, and then I thought—'

'So you aren't a mind-reader after all? How disappointing.'

'…Why not go straight to the source?'

'And why the sudden interest in this topic?'

I told her as briefly as I could about what had happened in Solvik and the dispute between Sunfjord Salmon and the local population, or at least some sections of it.

'A camper van with a dead woman inside?'

'Yes.'

'Has she been identified?'

'According to the police, yes. But they haven't gone public with her name yet. And unofficially no one seems to know who it is, either.'

'Sunfjord Salmon is one of Fredrik Martens' companies.'

'You don't say. Then that's another reason for our paths to cross again, don't you think?'

'Actually I do. Can you keep me posted if something new comes up in the case?'

'I'll do what I can. To the extent that there is a case, and that I have any involvement in it.'

'If I know you, you're already deeply involved.'

Was I so easy to read, or was it just that she was sharp-witted? I had no reason to doubt the latter; I hoped I could refute the former.

'Let's put it this way,' I said. 'We'll be in touch.'

'We will. Anyway, it was nice to hear your voice again. I'm looking forward to seeing you.'

'Me too.'

We concluded the conversation with a couple more pleasantries. Then I had another go at her article, but I couldn't concentrate. I was back at the airport in *Casablanca*, with the same words echoing through my brain: *Of all the private investigators' offices in the world…*

I must have missed her more than I had actually realised.

9

The following day I made a few telephone calls to various acquaintances, most of them with experience and knowledge of the economy and business, in an attempt to find out a bit more about Fredrik Martens. There wasn't much. If anyone could live up to the term '*éminence grise*', it was him. It was no exaggeration to say that he didn't talk to journalists. There was not a single interview with him to be found in newspapers, on the Net or in the TV and radio archives. His age was estimated to be in the mid-fifties. One source asserted with great confidence that he was fifty-eight. Another source said he was born in the autumn of 1945, to a German father and with a German surname. He had spent the first years of his life in Germany before his mother brought him back to Bergen in around 1950.

After finishing school, he had gone on to the Norwegian School of Economics. After graduating, he worked in several industries, eventually in shipping and now, in recent years, as an investor in salmon breeding, among other ventures. During the 1970s and 1980s he had bought several properties in Bergen, which he'd had renovated and sold for a huge profit. Unlike many others, he came through the yuppy years unscathed and emerged in the early 1990s as an investor with a good track record. In the list of annual tax returns posted online every October, he was among the highest earners, but generally speaking he had gone under the radar with regard to reporters' articles about the annually published tax-assessment list.

He was a majority shareholder in several companies; they had a variety of names, but the word 'invest' was prominent. The company that was a rising star in the world of salmon farming bore the poetic title of Riverbank Invest. It was through it that he became a majority shareholder in Sunfjord Salmon, which had originally had the far more local name of Sørnes Oppdrett.

Neither Fredrik Martens' address nor his telephone number was publicly available. And from what I could see, it seemed that no one had anything to say about his private life or family circumstances.

Riverbank Invest, however, was listed as having an office in Kokstad. With it came a telephone number and also a secretary, who rebutted all requests from the press to talk to the CEO.

This was how I killed time until I appeared at precisely 13.30 at the police station in Allehelgens gate for my interview with Signe Moland. She received me with a slightly resigned smile and invited me into her office, where she showed me to the chair on the 'guest' side of her desk, if 'guest' was the appropriate word to use in this building.

I tilted my head. 'Anything new?'

'Surely it's me who should be interviewing you?'

'Oh, yes. By all means, fire away.' As she didn't immediately respond, I added: 'I'm just a bit curious. After all, it was Aga and I who found the camper van containing – as it turned out – a dead woman.'

'We'll come back to that.' A pained expression crossed her face. 'Have you ever come across a body that's been in the sea for any length of time, Varg?'

'Well…' I gave the question some thought. 'Only indirectly.'

'Never close up?'

'No.'

'Then I can tell you it's not a pleasant experience. When we got this young woman out of the vehicle and on land, and before we put her in one of the body bags the firemen had brought with them, we performed – as we have to – a superficial examination.'

'And what did you find?'

She sighed. 'At first it looked as though she'd been beaten up.' She pointed to her face. 'Her eyes, lips, her whole face … and down below.' She gestured to her abdomen. 'There was an open

area of skin between her jersey and the waistband of her
trousers, and … it was the same there.' She swallowed. 'The
firemen said that was perfectly normal, and yesterday I spoke to
the pathologist, Tor Flaten. He said the wounds were caused by
a crustacean, which some call a fish louse, and they can appear
in their millions. They're quick to feed on anything they come
across in the sea, such as a body.'

'Related to the salmon louse, perhaps?'

'Definitely. Anyway, we came to the conclusion that she
hadn't been subjected to any obvious physical assault. The initial
examination at Gades Institute suggests the same, although we
might have to consult the more detailed report later. Everything
points to her having drowned, probably because she hadn't been
able to get out of the vehicle.'

'Which the driver *had* been able to do.'

'So it seems.'

'All the indications are that he's the missing man, Jonas
Kleiva.'

'We have to assume so, yes. But until we've found him, in the
sea or elsewhere, we can't be absolutely sure.'

'No, I understand.'

'And now let's come to you, Varg. The formal interview.'

She did what the regulations said she had to: noted down my
name, date of birth, address and telephone number. Then she
handed the floor over to me. I held forth on what I had to say
about the case, from the glimpses I'd had of the person I
assumed was Jonas Kleiva, his camper van and the two young
women who had been on the bus from Førde two weeks ago
now. We had already discussed all this. Then I told her about my
second trip to Førde and the sudden impulse I'd had on the drive
back to go down to Solvik.

'A sudden impulse?'

I grinned. 'Yes, I'd call it that. I suppose I have to confess to an innate sense of curiosity ... And a missing-person case always makes me extra inquisitive. I admit I've experienced this quite a number of times over the course of what I rather tentatively call my career.'

'I see. Well ... carry on.'

I told her about my visit to Stein Solvik's store-cum-café, and how I had met Edvard Aga, who suggested showing me the disused salmon-breeding farm by Markatangen.

'Why?'

'We-ell...' I stalled. 'Jonas Kleiva and these girls had been in Solvik to demonstrate against the fish farm in Sørnes, and Aga was himself very critical of the whole fish-farming industry. He claimed the part of the fjord by Markatangen and Storfossen was now as good as dead. If you were lucky enough to catch a fish, it would be inedible. And ... well, he was keen to show me this. So that was why we drove there.'

'And how did you discover the camper van?'

'We followed the tyre tracks leading to the end of the pier. There were no signs that the van had braked.' I arched my eyebrows.

She nodded. 'We noticed them, too.'

'And when we stared down into the sea, we saw the roof of the van. I recognised it at once.'

'So quickly?'

'I was pretty sure I recognised it, anyway. Don't forget I'd seen the van on my way home from Førde. I'd seen who I thought was Jonas Kleiva and the two girls, so I was probably mentally attuned to this being the same van.'

She studied me pensively. 'And this Aga, did he seem surprised by the find?'

'Absolutely, yes, he did. He reacted in the same way I did – with astonishment.'

'Do you think ...? Did he know Jonas Kleiva?'

'Yes, I assume so, at least as a child. He's had a cabin there since the mid-1980s and before that he'd rented a room at Jonas's parents' house – Betty and Kåre Kleiva.'

She nodded. 'We've contacted them, of course. They're frightened that he's died too, naturally enough.'

'Yes. You said when we met that you'd contacted one of the girls I saw Jonas with.'

'That's correct.'

'And the girl in the van, have you identified her too?'

'Yes, I'm afraid so.'

'Jonas's mother thought she was called Mona.'

'Yes, we heard that, too.'

'Can you reveal her full name?'

'To be frank, I don't know that this has anything to do with you, Varg, and the relatives have asked us to withhold this information. But I suppose we'll have to go public at some point tomorrow anyway, as part of the investigation, so…'

She flipped through the papers on her desk, neatly ordered into piles of varying heights. She lifted one of the documents and her lips moved, then she said: 'Her name's Mona Martens and she was twenty-two years old.'

My throat tightened. 'I see … Related to Fredrik Martens?'

She met my gaze. 'Yes. She's his daughter.'

10

'But … you said that you'd been in contact with the relatives. Does that mean you've spoken to Fredrik Martens himself?'

'Yes, unfortunately. It's not a nice message to have to pass on to a parent.'

'I've heard he's difficult to contact.'

'Well…' She eyed me somewhat condescendingly. 'Perhaps that depends on who's doing the contacting.'

'True.' I had to concede that one. I didn't even have a witty riposte.

'You have tried though, I take it?'

'No, no. I'm not speaking on my own behalf. I talked to a journalist who found that every door she tried was closed. If you search for Fredrik Martens on the Net, you don't find any interviews there and only minimal personal information.'

'Well, people do have a right to a private life.'

'How did you identify her then?'

'That wasn't much of a problem. She had a bank card and a driving licence in a cardholder, so … easy.'

'You also said you'd been in touch with the other girl. Can you give me her name?'

Now she looked a little concerned. 'No, and I'm sure you'll appreciate why not. She's part of the investigation. Why do you want to know?'

'I…' Still no witty riposte. Signe Moland had quite simply reduced me to silence. 'As they got on the bus in Førde I assume at least one of them lives there.'

She smiled. 'So what's the problem? I reckon Førde has a population of about eleven thousand people. I'm sure you can work out the odds.' She rose as a sign that the audience was over. 'And you're a private investigator. You'll manage without our help.'

'It's always good to have a supportive contact in the police.'

'You can find your own way out, can't you.'

'Yes, in fact I did once find my way out all alone.'

'I heard that story. After you told me we were related, I couldn't help asking around about you. There were a fair few stories at the canteen table, I can tell you.'

It was my turn to smile. 'I don't doubt that. I have to say what I usually say on these occasions: if any more dead bodies turn up, then…'

'We definitely won't ring you. Unless you've found one, that is.'

I recognised the family voice at least. We weren't as different as she perhaps might have wished.

I walked back to my office in Strandkaien. There, I went to the desk, opened the third drawer from the top, took out a half-full bottle of Simers Taffel Aquavit, rinsed a kitchen tumbler in the sink, which still reminded me that the room had been a doctor's surgery once, took it back to the desk and placed it beside the bottle. But I didn't pour. I was still unsure whether I might have to drive to Kokstad later in the day, in which case it would be an advantage not to have a drop of alcohol in my blood. Anyway, the mere sight of the bottle and the glass had a calming effect on me.

I had once talked to a doctor about this. He thought it was perhaps the taste of the caraway that produced this effect, as much as the alcohol. And he had reminded me that when aqua vitae, the water of life, was first mentioned in Norway – on 13th April 1531 apparently – in a letter from Eske Bille, lord of a manor in the borough of Bergenhus, to Olav Engelbrektsson, archbishop of Nidaros, it was described as a remedy for all kinds of internal maladies, so long as the correct herbs were used.

I looked around. I'd had the office since 1975, the year Saigon capitulated and the Vietnam War was over. Which was now a very long time ago. Not many people bred fish at that time. Now, on the wall above my desk hung this year's Bergen calendar so that I wouldn't forget either the town I lived in or what year it was. Next year would be my office's thirtieth anniversary. I had lost the adjoining waiting room a year ago during the renovation works.

The view was the same as it had been when I first moved in. Mount Fløyen stood where it had always stood, and there had been no fires in the Hanseatic wooden buildings of Bryggen since the mid-1950s. But the traffic queues that had been there in the 1970s had long been transferred to the Fløyen tunnel, and one day in the future there would perhaps be a light-rail system, if we were to believe those who took decisions on such matters. The Hurtigruten express boat no longer used the Festning quay and sailed from Nøstet instead, but from the Skoltegrunn quay you could still catch the ferry to Newcastle, if you felt the need. Most was as it had always been. Apart from me: I had more annual rings in my trunk and had problems reading everything written in small print, in particular the instructions for computer equipment. In 1975 I had neither a personal computer nor a mobile telephone, two electronic devices that had made my working days both easier and more sedentary than they had been at that time.

I needed to use both devices to track down the second young woman who had got onto the bus in Førde that Tuesday two weeks ago. I didn't have a very clear mental image of her, apart from her blonde hair tied into a ponytail, a perfectly normal, average body type and a practical outfit: trainers, blue jeans and, from what I could remember, a red windcheater.

Initially, I tried a search for Mona Martens. She was listed in the Yellow Pages, with an address in Forstandersmuget, a couple of stone-throws from my own little alleyway. In the Yellow Pages I found two other names with telephone numbers for the same address: Geir Gravdal and Marita Svanøy. When I clicked on

Images, a picture of a centenarian being visited by a mayor some-where in Østland came up. Whether it was the centenarian or the mayor who was called Mona Mertens it didn't say, but the mayor didn't fit the description either, so I could safely ignore him.

So far, I wasn't making any headway.

I tried similar searches for both Geir Gravdal and Marita Svanøy. Something interesting came up for Gravdal. Six months ago, he had an article in *Bergens Tidende*, in which he took a criti-cal position on the growth of fish-breeding farms in Norwegian fjords. I found nothing about Marita Svanøy.

I sat gaping at Geir Gravdal's telephone number. I could try ringing him, of course. But as he lived in the same neighbour-hood as me, I decided that it would be at least as effective to pay him a personal call. It was always easier to put a phone down on someone than to slam a door in their face. Besides, it was clear to me that we had something to discuss.

11

Forstandersmuget is an alleyway named after Bergen's first *forstander*, or minister, for the town's poor, Jacob Wesenberg, who once lived here. One of the houses is claimed to be the oldest preserved private house in Bergen, with a ground floor dating from 1441; a plaque in the entrance hall commemorates the fact. Most of the houses have kept the classic white exterior from the times when painting a house white – the most expensive colour – showed that you were well off – minister or no minister.

Mona Martens' address turned out to be a white, timbered house too, relatively recently painted. The door was green, and no less classic, but the two bells beside it definitely belonged to modern times. There were no nameplates, but I assumed one button was connected to the first floor, the other to the ground floor. You just had to make a choice.

When I pressed the lower button, nothing happened. I waited a little, but there was no reaction inside. When I pressed the top button, there was a reaction after around thirty seconds, in the form of heavy footsteps on the staircase down from the first floor. The door opened and a young man stood in the doorway. He was wearing dark-blue jeans and a well-worn, partially faded T-shirt that had once been black, with *SAVE THE WHALES* on the front.

I guessed he was my man. 'Geir Gravdal?'

He ran a hand over his short, dark-blond hair. 'Yes?'

'My name's Veum. In fact, I'm here regarding a Mona Martens. She does live here, doesn't she?'

'Yes.' He half turned. 'On the ground floor, but … I don't think she's at home.'

'No? Do you know where she is then?'

'What's this about?'

I gestured towards his T-shirt. 'You're committed to similar campaigns, it seems.'

'Yes, and?'

'Perhaps you were with her on the demonstration two weeks ago? In Solvik?'

He appeared taken aback. 'Yes ... and?' he said again, straightened up and pulled back his shoulders. 'Let me repeat what I just said. What is this about?'

'You know of course that one person has gone missing since the demonstration, don't you?'

He hesitated for a second. 'Yes ... Jonas Kleiva.'

'Is he an acquaintance of yours, too?'

'Yes, of course. We belong to the same...'

'Yes?'

'Group.'

'Group?'

'Yes, of eco-warriors, if that means anything to you.'

'Absolutely. Have you any idea what's happened to him?'

'To Jonas?'

'Yes.'

'If I did, I would've told the police.' He stepped back, ready to bring the conversation to a close.

'Don't you think it's striking that neither Jonas Kleiva nor Mona Martens has returned from the action up at Skuggefjorden?' I waited before continuing. 'I suppose you haven't seen Mona Martens since you came home either?'

His eyes wandered to the side, and then back again, more unsure of himself than before. 'No-o. I suppose I haven't.'

'Have you reported her missing to the police?'

'No, I ... Things haven't panned out that way.'

'Things haven't panned out that way? A young man's reported missing. A young woman you share a house with is apparently missing, too. And it doesn't occur to you to report this to the police?'

He began to look pretty grumpy. 'I'm asking you now for the last time: who are you, actually?'

'It's the first time you've asked that, surely? I apologise for not introducing myself properly. My name's Veum and I'm a private investigator.'

'Private ...? So you've been commissioned to find Jonas, have you?'

I sent him an eloquent look, sparing myself a lie.

He seemed to be considering his options. 'The thing is...'

As he didn't carry on, I said: 'Yes?'

Again, his eyes wandered to the side, but this time as if casting around for anyone in the vicinity who might be eavesdropping on what he was saying. Before his eyes came back to me, he said: 'There was a kind of situation up there.'

'Connected with the demonstration?'

'Erm, more afterwards, when we were about to come back home. There was a bit of to-ing and fro-ing, and Mona ended up going back to Bergen with Jonas.'

I tried to read his facial expression; he seemed to be repressing anger.

'In other words,' I replied, 'Mona was going back to Bergen with Jonas, and then some days later Jonas was reported missing while Mona clearly hadn't returned home either. And this didn't make you react, or anyone else who'd been with you in Solvik? Tell me – was there a girl with a blonde ponytail with you? Possibly from Sunnfjord.'

Again, he appeared taken aback. 'What ... Why are you asking about ...? What has that got to do with anything?'

'Let me explain. I'm not investigating this case out of random interest. You see, I caught a bus from Førde to where you turn off to Solvik on that Tuesday. On board were two girls. I saw them meet a young man I'm pretty sure now was Jonas Kleiva. I'm equally sure one of the girls was Mona Martens, but I was wondering who the other one—'

We were interrupted by a young woman turning into the

alleyway from Steinkjellergaten. On catching sight of me and
Geir Gravdal, she slowed down. She eyed me with a wary
curiosity and then Gravdal.

'Oh, hi, Marita,' he said awkwardly.

She had answered my question anyway. Her blonde hair was
still tied in a ponytail and she was just as sportily clad as two
weeks before.

12

Geir Gravdal waved a hand in my direction. 'This is Veum. Apparently he's a private investigator. He's been commissioned to try and find out what's happened to Jonas. And ... he's been asking after Mona.'

The young woman I had to assume was Marita Svanøy looked at me with a peculiar expression on her face, a mixture of anxiety, sorrow and what vaguely seemed like irritation. *'Oh, yes?'*

I ventured a tentative smile. 'By pure chance I found myself on the same bus as Mona and you two weeks ago, and I saw Jonas Kleiva meet you when you got off.'

She studied me. *'On the bus from Førde?'*

'Yes, a bit before there.'

'I don't think...'

'...you noticed me? No, but I definitely saw you.'

'And how did you know ... do you know Jonas?'

'I didn't, but when he was reported missing a few days later, I recognised him.'

She nodded silently.

'Your friend here told me there'd been a situation when you were there, which led to you coming back here separately.'

She spun round to face Geir Gravdal. *'What?'*

He looked even more confused than before. 'Yes, well ... there was.'

I looked around the narrow alley. 'Tell me, what about inviting me in so we can talk inside without disturbing the neighbours?'

I cast my eyes around pointedly. Following my gaze, they saw a few heads retract quickly from the closest windows. It made Marita look even more annoyed.

She glared at Geir and snapped: *'See what you've done.'*

'Me?'

I motioned to the door. 'Shall we…?'

Marita shrugged and walked past me. Geir Gravdal stepped to the side to let her in. I followed her and he made no attempt to stop me.

We were in a rather narrow entrance hall, where a steep staircase led up to the next floor. Marita Svanøy was already halfway up. Gravdal closed the door behind us and said: 'We live on the first floor.'

The narrow hallway revealed the age of the house. It was built at a time when every square centimetre of the plot was used, so there was no room for two people walking abreast. At the top of the stairs was a little landing and two doors. Marita had stopped in front of the one furthest to the left and stood waiting for us.

'Let's do it in yours, Geir.'

'Fine,' he mumbled in a tone suggesting it wasn't, not by a long chalk, but he couldn't be bothered to argue.

I arrived on the landing as well, which meant we had to stand uncomfortably close to each other, bearing in mind the circumstances, in order to allow Gravdal to open the door to his room. I followed him in while Marita chose to stand in the doorway, waiting to see what happened.

We had entered what I understood to be the sitting room. It was pretty tight in here too, but there was enough room for a 1960s sofa and a bookcase that held books, magazines, and what I assumed were various textbooks on whatever subject he was studying. On a green dresser there was a modest portable TV. On the low coffee table in front of the sofa there was a laptop displaying a screensaver, and some stapled sheets of paper, folded over in such a way that the top one could be read. Another prescribed text, I guessed. Above the open door leading to what we could see of the kitchen hung an old street sign saying *Strangehagen*. Above a door on the opposite side hung a print of a wolf, staring between some tall trees. A pretty basic print.

I pointed to the street sign. 'From Nordnes?'

He looked at me sullenly. 'It was left here by the previous owner.'

'Where do you come from then?'

'Fyllingsdalen.'

Marita Svanøy coughed impatiently from the doorway.

Gravdal glared at her. 'Shut the door for Christ's sake. You know how draughty it is in here.'

'And where had you imagined we would sit? All three of us on the sofa?'

'I didn't have a plan, but … you can sit there.' He pointed to a large bean bag in reddish-brown imitation leather on the other side of the coffee table. 'He can sit on the sofa and I'll stand here.' He leaned against the doorframe to the kitchen and sent me a provocative look.

I nodded and did as instructed. There were some clothes, a pair of trainers and some books on the floor but I stepped over these obstructions and plumped down on a sofa I would have had difficulty getting up from if I had been ten years older and my legs less strong. Marita closed the door hard and sank down into the bean bag with an expression on her face that made it obvious she would rather be anywhere than here.

I glanced around. 'You each have your own room on this floor, I see.'

Geir nodded silently.

'And Mona … does she have the whole of the ground floor?'

'She's got more money than us.' After a short pause he added: 'She owns the whole house. We rent rooms from her.'

'Yes, she comes from a family with money.'

Marita sighed aloud. *'Are we going to get started?'*

Geir regarded her sullenly.

I said: 'Yes, let's, by all means. I'm interested in the situation that blew up in Solvik, which you mentioned, Gravdal.'

Marita was still clearly irritated and had her eyes fixed on Geir, too.

'Well, I...' He flapped his arms. 'There was just a bit of discussion about who should drive who home.'

'Oh, yes?'

'The upshot was that Mona stayed behind with Jonas.'

'Stayed behind?'

'Yes, or rather, would leave later. His mother lived there. We assumed he was popping in to see her.'

'Uhuh?' As neither of them said any more, I continued: 'So I suppose that means you drove up to Solvik in separate cars, Jonas and you.' Still no comment. 'As eco-warriors I'd have thought you would use public transport.'

'Eh?' He gawped at me in disbelief. 'You can try to get to Solvik by bus, if you like. The best you can say about it is that there's a choice. There's one in the morning and one in the evening, apart from the school bus, and that comes from Hosteland.'

It was my turn to wait for him to carry on.

'Besides, we both had appointments in Bergen, which made it more practical for each of us to use our own transport.'

I turned to Marita. 'So you didn't have to go back to Førde after the demonstration?'

'To Førde? I live here. But Mona and I had been in Førde over the weekend, to measure up some of the banners we were taking to Solvik. I come from there, and my father still lives in the town. And he has the space and the paint for that sort of job. More than we have. Afterwards, though, I was coming back here.'

'You study, too?'

She nodded silently.

'So you'd have preferred to come back with Geir?'

'No, one of the others offered. One of the girls.'

'The reason for the demo was that a board meeting was going to be held in Solvik, wasn't it?'

'Yes, that's what we'd heard.'

'How many of you were there?'

She shrugged, but didn't answer.

I turned to Geir. 'How many would you say?'

He was still looking disgruntled. 'There were enough of us to make our mark.'

'Have you any names?'

He suddenly raised his voice. 'Who the hell employs you? The security services? The salmon breeders? You won't get any names out of me.'

Whom I represented – which was in fact no one – I kept to myself. Instead, I tried a different angle. 'So Mona stayed behind with Jonas – were they in a relationship?'

'Relationship?'

'Yes, is relationship too difficult a concept for you? Were they dating?'

He shrugged and tossed his head in a way that suggested not that he didn't know, but that he wasn't going to answer that question either.

I looked at Marita. 'I saw them hugging each other when you got off the Førde bus, while you were left to struggle with the banners.'

She clenched her lips, but couldn't hide her reddening cheeks.

A phone rang from the little rucksack she had placed on the floor when she sat down on the bean bag. She took it out and glanced quickly at the display before answering.

'Yes, this is Marita.' A voice spoke at the other end; it was difficult to hear what was said, but it was a woman's voice. 'Yes. No. What!' Her eyes widened and moved at once over to me. 'I see.

In the camper van? No, I...' Immediately tears began streaming from her eyes. She let out a sob. Her voice was thick and strangulated. *'No. Yes, I'll do that. Yes. Yes. Thank you,'* she said, her voice tailing off.

For a moment she sat staring down at the phone in her hand. Then she fixed her eyes on me again. In a choked voice, she said: *'Did you know? Have you been sitting here and taking us for fools the whole time?'*

'What is it, Marita?' Geir exclaimed. 'What have you been told?'

'It was that policewoman ... It was about Mona. She's been found dead.' With the phone in her hand, she pointed at me. *'He knew all the time.'*

'Dead?'

'In Jonas's camper. In the sea.'

'In the sea where?'

She sobbed. *'There! In Skuggefjorden.'*

Now he turned to me too. His eyes narrowed. 'Did you know? You came here pretending she ... And you knew all the time.'

There was nothing I could say in my defence. They were right. I knew they were.

Marita jumped up from the bean bag. *'Get that bastard out of here. I'm going to my room. I can't bear this!'* She grabbed her rucksack, went to the door, pulled it open with a jerk and disappeared into the half-light on the landing.

Geir Gravdal took a couple of steps after her, and called despairingly: 'Marita...'

We heard the sound of a door slamming. Then he turned to me. 'You heard what she said. Now piss off before I throw you out!'

I pressed down on my heels and levered myself up from the low sofa, slightly off balance. 'I had no intention of tricking you. I just hadn't got that far.'

'You hadn't got that far, eh? I'll…' He didn't continue. 'What about Jonas? Have they found him, too?'

I gently shook my head. 'Not as far as I know. But I'm not privy to inside information.'

'This is the worst thing that could have happened. I never imagined this.' He was almost speaking to himself.

'Is there anything else you'd like to say now? About the "situation" as you called it?'

He snarled: 'Anything else to say? I've already said as much as I'm going to say to an asshole like you. Are you still here? Didn't I just tell you to piss off?'

I nodded and went to the door. 'Of course. I got the hint.'

I took it with me all the way down the stairs. Before leaving the house, I glanced at the nameplate screwed to the door to the ground-floor apartment. *Mona Martens*, it said, as pithy and to the point as a gravestone.

13

From Forstandersmuget it wasn't long before I was back at home. Once inside, I took a critical look around, and came to the conclusion that my place was a lot tidier and more presentable than Geir Gravdal's. Were anyone to visit, that is – not that I had any reason to believe they would. I was at a stage in my life where I felt like I had been abandoned on a cartoon desert island, with not so much as a witty caption or a shark fin in sight.

In the fridge I had the remains of yesterday's lunch – fish in tomato sauce – which I could reheat. I boiled a portion of rice, found some light-green lettuce leaves to bring some colour to the meal and pampered myself by accompanying it with a Hansa Bayer beer.

I wasn't sure there was anything else I could do in connection with what had or hadn't happened in Solvik. I would have liked to talk to some of the others who had been at the demonstration, but as neither Marita nor Geir would supply any names, I was unlikely to make any progress with them, for the time being, at least. Fredrik Martens was someone else I would have liked to speak to, but it definitely wasn't the right day for a private investigator to approach him for information.

I could, of course, have contacted Kåre Kleiva, Jonas's father, who lived in Bergen. I found his address on the Net. He lived in Paradis, in what had once been the town's best district; now that Garden of Eden was plagued with snakes in the form of ever-increasing queues of traffic. But it was pretty unlikely that he would speak to me, either. And what would I ask him? I should probably just heed Signe Moland's words and let the police investigate the case themselves, without any irksome interference from my side.

So I had a quiet evening at home. Ben Webster was on the CD player and the bottle of beer was joined by two glasses of

fiery Simers Taffel aquavit while I sat reading the day's newspapers and finally a book. When I went to bed at half past eleven
there was nothing to suggest that anything but a good night's
sleep awaited me. That is how wrong you can be; and perhaps in
my line of work that is particularly true.

At a quarter to two the phone I had placed on my bedroom
dresser started ringing angrily, just so far away that I had to get
out of bed to answer it. Who on earth would ring at this time of
night? Instantly a thought struck me, a sudden fear that something had happened to Jakob, my grandson in Oslo, not yet two
years old…

But no, I was reassured on that point.

It was a woman's voice that spoke to me, in nynorsk, and in
a subdued tone, as though not wishing to be overheard. *'Varg
Veum?'*

'Yes,' I said, suitably gruffly, even at this hour.

'I need help.'

'Who—?'

'I'm so scared.'

'What—?'

'I'm scared out of my wits.'

'Who am I talking to?'

There was a silence. For a moment I wondered if she had
rung off, but then she said: *'You're speaking to Betty Kleiva.'* Her
voice cracked. *'We met in Solvik before the weekend.'*

'Yes, I remember, of course,' I said, suddenly more awake.
'What are you so scared of?'

'You said you were a private investigator.'

'Yes, I am.'

'I need your help.'

'But if someone's threatening you, you'll have to ring the local
chief of police.'

'The chief of police?' she snorted. *'He's a halfwit.'*

'Well … it's still his job to help people who feel threatened.'

'Mm, it's not urgent right now.'

'No?'

'I shouldn't drink red wine so late, and definitely not on my own.'

'No, that—'

'What kind of jobs do you take on? Anything you won't do?'

'Mmm, I do have my limits. And if this is about Jonas, the police are on his case.'

'I was thinking of something else.' She sounded calmer now. It probably helped being able to talk to someone. *'I don't suppose you know anything about me.'* She was quite wrong there, but I didn't contradict her. *'So let me tell you. My first husband died a long time ago. In 1978. My second husband left me after we'd been married for almost twenty years. Two years ago, I lost my third man in what they said was an accident. And now … my son.'*

'Well, we don't know yet—'

She interrupted me again. *'I don't want to sound melodramatic, but I could say that I'm being pursued by death.'*

'Well … But—'

'It's my partner's death two years ago that I'd like you to investigate.'

'Two years can be a long time in a context like this, and especially for a private investigator. The case was investigated, wasn't it?'

'As far as it went. And then it was shelved. An accident, as I said.'

'Well…'

'I've got money. I'll pay you whatever it costs.'

'What do you think I can find out that the police didn't? And after two years?'

Something changed in her. Again, it was as though she was frightened of being overheard, and she noticeably lowered her voice. *'Someone knows something, Veum. Something they've never talked about.'* Once again, her voice cracked. *'And now Jonas has gone missing, too.'*

'Yes, he has, and I definitely can't do anything about that. It's a police matter.'

'I understand that, but … Can't you come to Solvik and hear what I have to say? I can give you more details and then you can decide for yourself. I'll pay you for your time, whatever the outcome.'

'The man who died in the, erm, accident – what was his name?'

'We were just living together when he died, but we would've got married eventually.' She paused for a moment, then said: *'His name was Klaus Krog.'*

'Was he from Solvik, too?'

'No, he moved here from Østland. He was an angler.'

'He could hardly live off that I suppose…'

'No. I can tell you more when we meet. Can you come tomorrow?'

So soon? I hesitated, but to be honest I didn't have any other work, so … 'It'll be in the afternoon then.'

'Wonderful. I have a room to let, so you can stay here for free for as long as you need to.'

She also had red wine, and unless my memory was playing tricks on me, Stein Solvik had said she ate men for breakfast. *They say,* he had added, so as not to risk being sued. Perhaps this was a more dangerous job than it had initially sounded.

'Well,' I said after a pause for reflection. 'Let me drive up and then we can take it from there.'

'Now you've made me happy. Thank you very, very much.'

'I think I'll return to my beauty sleep then.'

'You need it, do you?' she said, and I could see her pouring another glass of red wine to celebrate her catch.

Well, maybe I didn't. After that it took me quite some time to go back to sleep.

14

The first thing I did the following day was see if I could find out anything about Klaus Krog. There wasn't much online. He was born in Skien in 1968 and graduated from the University of Oslo with a degree in geography in 1995. From 1995 to 2000 he had worked as a journalist for a magazine called *Jakt & Fiske* – Hunting & Fishing. I didn't find any more background information beyond that. When I searched for images, what looked like a passport photograph came up, clearly used in connection with articles for the magazine, and a picture of a young man smiling and holding up a salmon, which, according to the caption, weighed fourteen kilos and had been caught with a fly rod in the Skien river in June 1992. There was no connection between him and Solvik in Masfjorden that I could establish.

The next thing I did was to call Torunn Tafjord.

'That was quick, Varg,' she said, audibly smiling. 'Did you think it was *that* good to talk to me again?'

'It was, but I'm also ringing for a specific reason.' I told her the dead woman in the camper van had now been identified as Mona Martens, the daughter of Fredrik Martens.

'What? Then he'll be even less motivated to receive a visit from a journalist right now.'

'I fear so, yes.'

'In that case, I think I'll wait a bit before taking a trip to Bergen.'

I told her I had a job in Solvik and would be going there that day, and I would keep her posted if I found out any more about Fredrik Martens' investments in the area.

'Fine. Shall we leave it that we'll stay in touch?'

We did.

There wasn't much else to do but pack a couple of shirts and some extra underwear, socks and a toilet bag in the most practical travel bag I had, get in the car and set a course north again.

I arrived in Solvik at about half past one and parked in front of the yellow house with the sign saying *ROOMS TO RENT*.

Betty Kleiva was standing on the steps in front of the house before I was out of my car. She was a little more casually dressed than the last time I had met her, with a loosely hanging grey-and-white cardigan, open at the front, a tight, dark-blue T-shirt that emphasised the contours of her figure and stone-washed jeans that were tight around her thighs. On her feet she wore light-coloured trainers. She sent me a serious look, and only a fleeting smile, as I took out my bag and closed the boot.

We shook hands, and she cast a glance around to see if anyone had noticed my arrival. Personally, I couldn't see any signs of life in the village.

'Thank you for coming so quickly. Come in and I'll brew up some coffee.'

We entered a small hallway. To the left was a staircase up to the first floor. To the right there was a long row of hooks for outdoor clothes and on the floor a shoe stand. I put down my bag, hung up my jacket and flipped off my shoes before following her into the rest of the house. We came into a large kitchen with a table by the window so that you could sit there keeping an eye on everyone who passed by on their way to the store-cum-café and quay.

'Take a seat, Varg,' she said, gesturing to one of the chairs at the table. She filled the kettle, plugged it in, placed a filter in the dripper, placed it on top of a Thermos jug, scooped coffee in and stood waiting for the water to boil. She glanced obliquely in my direction. *'I hope you drink coffee.'*

'Like a parish priest. It'll taste good, after the trip.'

She nodded and reprised her fleeting smile, so quickly it was barely perceptible.

'Have you heard any more from the police? Regarding the camper van we found?'

A few dark clouds scudded past. 'No,' she said, with sudden fear in her eyes. 'Nothing. But they promised they would tell me as soon as they had anything.'

'Then they will.'

The water was boiling now. She took a cup and proceeded to pour cupfuls of water into the Thermos; she counted out ten – enough coffee, even for a priest. While the coffee was brewing, she took two more cups, with a flower pattern on, and put them on two saucers on the table. 'Are you hungry?' she asked. 'I can quickly rustle something up.'

'Well…'

The smile lasted a bit longer this time. She went back to the worktop, opened the bread bin, took out a loaf and cut a few slices. Then she went to the fridge, took out some butter, brown cheese, mild white cheese, some plastic containers containing various types of charcuterie, another with smoked salmon, a couple of jars of jam and marmalade and finally a tube of caviar. 'The guests who stay overnight always get breakfast. If they want it, that is. Some have lunch too.'

'But you don't have so many guests at this time of year?'

'Not even in the summer, now that the fish in the fjord have all but gone.'

In next to no time, she had set the table, placed a dish of sliced meats in the middle and all the other options around it. I smiled and thanked her before reaching out for some food. She sat down across from me, folded her hands, bent her head and quickly said grace.

I retracted my hand.

She looked at me and said: 'It's become a habit with me now, a tradition. But … dig in.' She watched with satisfaction as I helped myself to brown cheese and ham, then she served herself.

'You'll have to tell me exactly what it is you want me to investigate,' I said, and she nodded.

Then a bitter expression that hadn't been there before settled on her face. *'The wretched story of my love life.'*

They were her words, not mine. I gently splayed my hands.

I let her talk. For the next fifteen to twenty minutes I got her life story, in broad strokes.

She came from a farm further up the valley. *'If, when you drove by, you noticed some goats on a farm before you reached the village, they're ours. Or strictly speaking, my parents'.'* At eighteen she had married Mons Marken, who had been ten years older than her. *'There wasn't a huge selection of men,'* she said, without a smile. *'But Mons was a great guy. And I wasn't the only girl to send lingering looks after him. But it was me he chose. We tried to make it work, despite the ten years between us. And he was an enterprising man. His parents had a farm further down the fjord, where Mons started the fish farm, where they found ... Jonas's van.'*

It had been Mons who had bought the house we were in now when they married in 1975. Three years later he died, only a little over thirty years old. *'It was a shock,'* she said. *'Totally inexplicable. I've never got over it. Even now, after all these years, I get frightened just thinking about it.'*

'What happened?'

One morning, she had found him dead in bed. She had got up without noticing anything. She had gone to the bathroom to wash and dress, and when she had finished, she was surprised that he still hadn't got up. *'He always used to put on the coffee and I prepared breakfast while he was shaving.'* When she went into the bedroom, he was in bed, lifeless. She had shaken him, leaned over and shouted his name, feverishly felt for his pulse, on his wrist, at the side of his neck, but without detecting any life. Then she had run to the telephone and called for help. Her mother and father had arrived before the duty doctor, who had to come from Hosteland, but there was never any hope of resuscitating him. The doctor confirmed his death the moment he arrived.

She couldn't recall much about the rest of that day, or the ensuing days. *'I was in a daze; I didn't know what day it was. We'd only just started our lives, Mons and I. We had so many plans: him with his fish farm, me with our lives together. And then all of a sudden it was over!'* She looked at me, visibly upset. After a pause, she added: *'I was much too young to be a widow.'*

'Did they ever find out what the cause of death was?'

'Yes, they had to do an autopsy. Heart failure, they concluded. Probably a congenital defect that had never been noticed. We didn't get any kind of warning. His heart stopped, just like that.' She clicked her fingers.

There was another pause. She stared at the window, at the empty road outside. *'I know folk in the area were talking about it. I could feel their suspicious eyes on me. As though it was me who'd done something. As though I'd ... poisoned him ... or whatever it was they thought!'*

It looked as if she needed to pull herself together before she could carry on. Gently, I said: 'But you remarried?'

She sighed and stretched her lips into something that was not quite a smile, more a grimace. *'Yes. Kåre. Another man from around here, but a bit closer in age to me. Two years older. There were so few pupils in our school, we were in the same class in the first years. We got married in 1981. He's Jonas's father.'*

'So I've gathered. But you got divorced.'

'Yes, that's how that one went. Kåre was completely absorbed in his work on the salmon farm. It was him who was fighting to breed them on land. What was called a closed farm. But it was too difficult, especially after the Sørnes lot started their own farm further out in the fjord. They got financial support from outside and we didn't. It affected Kåre so badly that he wanted to move away from the area. But I ... I still had my parents here, and for me Solvik was my whole life, so ... Yes, Kåre and I got divorced although we never really fell out.'

'And now, with Jonas having gone missing, have you contacted him?'

'Kåre, do you mean?' A shiver ran through her upper body. 'I told the police they should talk to him, but he and Jonas weren't in contact. Jonas never forgave him for leaving us. That was in 1999 and Jonas was at a vulnerable age, fifteen. He was going to attend school in Austrheim in the autumn and move into lodgings there. Then, even when he moved to Bergen to study, a few years later, he never got in touch with his father, as far as I know anyway.'

'Right.'

'He wasn't at home much here, either. As good as never in the summer. Even after the first year in Austrheim he and a pal went interrailing all over Europe. And that was how it went on. Working at the weekends and doing evenings in a warehouse or at a till in the local Co-op in Mastrevik Torg and saving up enough money for the summer. If I was lucky, he came home for a weekend or two in August, before school started again. That was how much time he sacrificed for his mother.'

'But he dropped by when he came for the demonstration two weeks ago?'

'Yes, but that wasn't for long. I think he came mostly to show off the girl he had with him.'

'I've been told her name was Mona Martens.'

Her mouth tightened. 'Yes, I was told her name was Mona.'

'So you had no idea he had a girlfriend in Bergen?'

'No. He never talked about that kind of thing. To tell the truth, I was beginning to wonder if he was a bit … you know…'

'Oh, yes? Had you any reason to suspect that?'

'No, no. It's just the way a mother thinks, isn't it? I got married when I was eighteen, and he's twenty this year and has never had a girlfriend, as far as I know. He just had a friend he went interrailing with every single summer.'

'So this was the first time he'd brought a girlfriend home?'

'Yes, it was.'

'But as for you – you were living with someone new, which is actually why you invited me here, isn't it?'

She became serious again. 'Yes. Klaus.'

'Tell me about him.'

She nodded and made a start.

Klaus Krog, a hobby angler, had come to Solvik in the summer of 2000 and had rented one of her rooms. He had paid for a licence to fish in what was called, with some hyperbole, Storelven, the 'big river', a name it had probably acquired from its source, Storfossen, the 'big waterfall'. It had been love, if not at first sight, then soon afterwards, she admitted with slightly flushed cheeks.

'For the first time, I'd found a man younger than me. He was thirty-two. I was, well, forty-three. I'm not ashamed of my age.'

Klaus Krog never went back home. Eventually he moved from the rented room, which was in a separate low annexe at the back of the house, and across the yard into the main house.

'What about his job?'

'He'd been a journalist for a magazine called Jakt & Fiske, *but he resigned because he planned to write a book about fish farming and the problems it caused, not least when the farms were open pens in the sea and not on land.'*

'I see. How far had he got with the book?'

'He was still working on it, collecting material. Not everyone was willing to talk to him when he knocked on their door. Einar Sørnes sent him packing, I was told.'

'Einar Sørnes…'

'Yes, he's the pater familias *out there in Sørnes. The prime mover and the landowner. He was the same age as Mons Marken, but he's still going strong. A big, burly man he is too – which is good to know should you have to pay him a visit.'*

'So Klaus never finished the book?'

'No, it was a work in progress. I've still got the whole manuscript. It's in Jonas's old room, which he gradually turned into a study.'

'What did Jonas say about that?'

'Well, what could he say? After all, he'd moved out and had no plans to return.'

'But he accepted that you had a new man?'

This time she shrugged demonstratively. 'We didn't talk about it. They only met a few times – three or four maybe. It wasn't exactly a meeting of minds.' She gave a wry smile. 'I think that Jonas felt he was too young for me.' Again she stared at the window. 'And they probably thought so too, most of the folk out there. But I will say, when Klaus died, Jonas came here, just to comfort me, and he had great respect for the work Klaus had done. He's the only person who's read the manuscript he left behind.'

'So what happened? When Klaus died, I mean.'

'What or how – I simply don't know. He often went hiking in the mountains, usually alone, once in a while with someone, if he felt he needed to pick their brains. The day he disappeared ... I don't quite know what plans he had that day, but ... it was beautiful weather when he left, though the wind picked up and it became pretty strong. When he wasn't back down by five, half past five, I began to get twitchy. I spoke to some of the guys around here, the volunteer firemen. A couple of them said they'd walk up the ski run and look for him.'

'Did you know where he'd planned to walk?'

'Yes, we'd talked about it the day before. Up to Stølene, as we say. The summer pastures. In Fosse valley, where lots of the farms had grazing in the olden days.' She swallowed. 'That was where they found him. He was lying at the bottom of a steep slope. His head had hit a rock, they reckoned.' She raised a hand to her forehead. 'He had a deep wound here and it had bled a lot.' Her voice cracked. 'He wasn't showing any signs of life.'

The two men had been unsure quite how to proceed. One of

them knew some first aid and felt for a pulse and listened for breathing, but there was nothing. Nevertheless, they called for medical help and phoned the police, as well as Betty, of course.

'So once again, I went through the experience of an unexpected death ... a husband, a live-in partner – same difference. It was no less a shock than the one I'd had when Mons died. And now we don't know what's happened to Jonas. I told you on the phone, Varg – I'll use your first name, if that's OK: death has pursued me, time and time again!' She looked at me with despair in her eyes. 'And perhaps it hasn't finished yet.'

I felt a chill go through me, as if a ghost had flitted across a grave. 'And what did the police say, two years ago?'

She waved her arms. 'Well, what did they say? Some young stripling of an officer came here and carried out an investigation, as they liked to call it. The autopsy was inconclusive. The injuries could have been the result of a fall or someone could've hit him over the head with a rock.'

'That's kind of how it sounds.'

'But the conclusion of the investigation was that it was an accident. I spoke to a lawyer. He said he could take on the case, but he didn't recommend me pursuing the matter. Not unless I had tangible proof that something criminal had taken place.' She sent me an eloquent look.

'And this is what you'd like me to try to investigate now?' She nodded, and I added: 'Two years later.'

Her eyes moistened again. 'Yes, I know it's a long time. But I've been numb with grief. And it's only now that I'm beginning to get some perspective on the situation – not least with what's happened to Jonas.'

'You think there's a link?'

'It isn't only me who's being pursued by death. It's as if the whole Marken family is suffering from the same affliction. Sudden death, no warning. As though someone up there' – she directed her gaze to the ceiling – *'has decided that this is the family's fate. It's just how it has to be.'*

After this there was another pause. I reached out for the Thermos and shook it to see if she wanted any more. She nodded, and I poured, first for her and then for me.

After I had taken a sip, she said: *'You know, those of us who grew up in places like this, we went to chapel from when we were small. So we didn't grow up with Asbjørnsen and Moe's fairy tales. We grew up with Bible stories. Now this has happened to Jonas – or Jonah as the English call him – I can't get the story about Jonas ending up in the whale's belly out of my head. I pray to God he lets my Jonas go free, as he did in the Bible, so that he can come back to me – if only for one last time.'*

'Did you call him Jonas because of the Bible story?'

'No, we didn't even think about it. But maybe it's a sign from God, something we weren't aware of back then, but we're experiencing now.'

I took another mouthful of coffee so that I didn't have to say anything in response. She seemed to have enough sombre thoughts on her mind.

15

Stein Solvik nodded to me without any visible sign of surprise when I entered his shop at three o'clock that afternoon. Edvard Aga, over by the window, also nodded back. However, the woman in her fifties paying for what she had bought eyed me with interest, and I could see her lips tremble after asking the only natural question: *And who's this man then?*

She didn't receive any answer. She left the shop with her purchases in her net bag and such a thoughtful expression on her face that I felt sure it wouldn't be many minutes after arriving home that she was on the telephone to her nearest neighbour to discuss various explanations. After all, so much was happening at the moment. First, a wild-cat demonstration, then a disappearance and finally a body in the sea by the disused fish farm at Markatangen.

I nodded to Solvik. 'Got any coffee in the Thermos?'

'Freshly brewed, Veum. Anything to eat with it?'

'No, thanks.'

'You've eaten where you've just been, have you?'

'Well…' Rumours had preceded me, I could hear.

He smiled meaningfully. *'Sit yourself down with Edvard. You know each other already. Then I'll bring over the coffee.'*

I thanked him and strolled over to Edvard. 'Nice to see you again.'

He nodded. 'It was dramatic, wasn't it. Do you know if she's been identified? The girl in the camper, I mean.'

'Yes, I think the police said they would make a public announcement today.' I sat down on the free chair at his table and pulled out my phone – the latest model, with internet access. 'Have you checked the Net?'

'Not today.'

I clicked onto the *Bergens Tidende* webpage and had to scroll down before I came to the headline 'Dead Woman Identified'. I quickly skimmed the article and passed my phone over to Aga. All it said was that the police had informed the public that the woman found dead in Masfjorden after what was termed a 'car accident' was Mona Martens and she was twenty-two years old. Another person was presumed deceased in the same accident, it also said, without any direct link to the earlier police bulletin regarding Jonas Kleiva.

Aga returned my phone. 'Mona Martens?'

'Daughter of Fredrik Martens, who is one of the principal owners of Sunfjord Salmon.'

'But didn't you say she was demonstrating against the fish farm?'

'Yes, I did.'

'So, she demonstrated against her own father in a way, didn't she?'

'That's what we have to conclude, yes.'

Stein Solvik joined us. He placed a cup on the table in front of me. Then he poured coffee from the Thermos. He glanced at Aga. 'Refill?'

'Please,' Aga said, pushing his cup towards him.

'So what's brought you back to Solvik?' Stein asked, standing with his own cup of coffee in his hand. 'I thought the police were searching for Jonas.'

'I hope they still are,' I said.

Both men stared, waiting for me to carry on.

'Well, I still need to talk to some local people. But…' I shifted my gaze from one to the other to make it clear I was talking to both of them. 'I hope you'll keep your mouths shut about what I'm going to ask you.'

Solvik gave a wry smile. 'If I gossiped about everything I heard behind the counter here, I don't think I'd have very many customers left. I can hold my tongue, if that's what you want.'

'And, basically, I only talk to Stein, so you can trust me too,' Aga said.

'Then I will.' I sipped some coffee. 'So … Betty Kleiva has instructed me to take a closer look at what happened when her partner, Klaus Krog, died in 2002.'

Both men nodded.

'Your use of "died", suggests you have a particular line of thought?' Aga said.

'"Was murdered" is too dramatic,' I said. 'At this stage in the enquiries, however, I have to leave all options open.'

Solvik nodded towards the door. *'The woman who was going out when you came in, Veum, is Klara Kyvik. Her husband, Nils, was one of the two guys who found Krog on the path down from the summer pastures. They went up there because Betty said that was where he'd planned to hike that day.'*

'Do you have any details? They didn't meet anyone on the way there, did they?'

Solvik shook his head slowly. *'I haven't heard anything to that effect. You'd better talk to Nils.'*

'Who was the guy Nils was with when they found him?'

'Their neighbour's son. Both he and Nils are voluntary firemen for the area. Harald Eide. Good, strong lad. He's an electrician. Works in the North Sea, on Gullfaks A oil platform.'

'Do you know if he's at home now?'

'I couldn't say.'

'Does Betty believe there was some skulduggery involved?' Aga asked.

'"Believe" is another strong word. At any rate, she suspects something. And Jonas's disappearance has strengthened her suspicion. You told me yourself about the ongoing conflict between – what was it you called them? – the Sørnes gang and the Marka gang.'

'Well, I was speaking metaphorically. It's never been so

serious that it's actually ended in deaths. But the way it looks at the moment, the Sørnes gang appears to be coming out on top.'

'Betty told me that Klaus Krog had been writing and collecting material for a book about fish farming. Did he talk to either of you about it?'

'That's news to me,' Aga said. 'To tell the truth, I only said hello to him in passing a couple of times, either here at Stein's or in the village. He was with Betty, as I remember. But then I mostly keep myself to myself.'

'Yes, I had that impression last time we spoke.' I turned to Solvik. 'And you?'

'*Lots of people in the village see me as a kind of oracle, I think. Even if I can count on my fingers how many locals come here during the day. But Betty belongs to the faithful few. She had old Krog staying with her soon after he pitched up in the area. He was a chatty sort, and a hobby angler himself. So they probably talked a lot about fish breeding, wild salmon and trout.*'

'You two would've had a good deal to talk about as well then?' I said to Aga.

'Yes, I'm sure we would. But, as I said, it never happened.'

'*But I don't remember him talking about a book,*' Solvik said.

'He would've been given short shrift by Einar Sørnes.'

'*Old Einar, yes. And he's probably not the only one.*' Solvik smiled wanly. '*They've always seen themselves as the big cheeses around here, that lot on the headland. And even more now they've earned millions selling their fish.*'

'Millions?'

'*That's what they say. Both Einar and his only son, Knut, were right at the top of the online tax lists last year, after the sale.*'

'Does that mean the family's no longer involved in the project?'

'*Not at all. They still hold good positions, both of them. Knut is the CEO and his father the operations manager.*'

'That means of course that they live in the district, both of them?'

'Absolutely. Einar lives in the old farmhouse out there, and Knut has built himself a grandiose residence on the adjacent plot, where it was pasture and wasteland before.'

'Family?'

'Einar has his wife, Louise. She runs the primary school here. But there aren't many pupils now. Eight or nine, I think, all the year groups in the same class.' After a short pause, he added: 'Why are you asking about all this?'

'It's a habit I have. I like to get the best possible overview of the terrain I'm going to be working on.'

'Are you planning to walk up to the summer pastures yourself?' Aga asked.

'I haven't got that far in my thinking. But I'd be interested to see where Krog died, of course.'

'In which case I can show you the way, if you can't get Nils Kyvik to help you.'

'I doubt he will,' Solvik said. 'He's not exactly the most amenable, Nils isn't.'

Aga looked out of the window. 'It's too late now. There's a good chance it'll be dark before we're back down. But I can meet you tomorrow morning if you're staying over.'

'I've got a room at Betty's.'

'Mhm,' commented Solvik with a tiny smile.

I nodded to Aga. 'Great. I'll go and see Nils Kyvik now, but let's exchange phone numbers. If you don't hear from me, we can meet here at ten. Does that suit you?'

'I'm a morning person, so that's fine.'

I asked Solvik to explain to me where Klara and Nils Kyvik lived, and Aga walked with me to point out the house.

'It'll be interesting to hear what you find out, Veum.'

'Well, it's two years now since he died, so I'm not very optimistic. Shall we use first names?'

'Fine by me. When I was growing up in the streets at home, I was called Eddie.'

'I was never called anything but Varg.'

'Great.'

16

Klara Kyvik opened the door barely fifteen seconds after I had rung the bell on the green house, two houses down what had to be called Solvik's main street, though doing so risked gilding the lily. But once upon a time Øvregaten, literally the 'higher street', had been the only street in Bergen, so you should never say never.

'Yes?' she said, with an expression that reminded me of a puppy eyeing its big meal of the day. Klara Kyvik was auburn-haired, apple-cheeked and otherwise of standard Norwegian stock, as far as I could see, and wore a blue-and-white cardigan and brown Terylene trousers.

'Hello. My name's Varg Veum. Is your husband in?'

'Nils? Yes, he is. What's this about?'

'I'm a private investigator. I have a couple of questions I'd like to ask him.'

Her mouth hung agape. *'A private investigator? I hope there's nothing wrong.'*

'No, no. I just need to ask him something. May I come in?'

'Wait here and I'll go and get him.' She half closed the door and disappeared into the house.

I looked around me. Down by the quay there was a large, old building where, in earlier times, goods transported here by boat had probably been unloaded. As I'd noted before, Solvik itself didn't consist of much more than a few scattered houses and buildings. Most people had probably lived on farms further down the valley and along both sides of the fjord. A sign above the door of a white single-storey building announced that it was *SOLVIK SCHOOL*, but there were no pupils to be seen outside. Beside the school building stood a classic white chapel with a cross carved into the stone above the door. Two houses further down there was a large, red garage with its broad doors closed.

Above its door was a sign saying *FIRE STATION*. By now I assumed I had seen the most important buildings in Solvik.

I heard someone in the hall in front of me. Nils Kyvik came out with Klara tagging along behind him, no less curious than before. Kyvik was a barrel-chested man with strong arms and powerful thighs – a stump puller in human form and hardly the type to be knocked off his feet by a single blow. His hair was shorn close to his skull and showed the odd streak of grey. *'The wife says you have a question for me.'*

'Yes, it's about when you and a friend found Klaus Krog dead two years ago.'

Klara put a hand to her mouth in outright shock, but Kyvik didn't seem at all affected. *'Uhuh?'*

'Have you got time to talk now?'

'We can do that here on the steps. I haven't got much to say.'

'Well … can you briefly tell me how you two managed to find him?'

His face was unchanged, but his eyes became a little more distant. *'Betty came to our door and said that her partner hadn't returned from a hike. I said I was happy to go and look for him if I could take someone with me. So she spoke to Harald next door and he came with me. Unfortunately, we didn't have to go far before we found him. The guy was lying at the bottom of the path up to the summer pastures. He must've slipped on one of the rocks further up and fallen. It's pretty steep there. He'd hit his head on a jagged rock lying nearby. We could see blood on it, and he had a big, open wound on his forehead. It didn't look good. Harald knows some first aid, so he rushed forward and checked him over, but he didn't seem to be alive. In fact, he was as dead as a doornail, to put it bluntly.'*

'A jagged rock lying nearby?'

'Yes, there was a big rock on the side of the path. It's probably still there now, but the blood will have been washed off after such a long time.'

'There was no suggestion of, erm, any other interpretation?'

'Any other interpretation? What could there be? That someone had murdered the guy?'

'Mm…'

'The police were called, and an officer arrived at the same time as the ambulance, so you'd have to ask them. There have never been any questions about what happened, not here – until now.' He eyed me suspiciously.

'There's so much going on,' Klara said in almost a whisper from behind his shoulder.

He half turned, with an annoyed expression on his face. *'So much going on? Such as?'*

'Well,' she said meekly. *'That camper van they found with the girl in. She's been identified now. It's that Fredrik Martens' daughter, they say. The one they reckoned Knut had been out with.'*

I pricked up my ears. 'Knut Sørnes?'

Nils raised his voice. *'Tittle-tattle. Go and get on with the cooking, Klara.'*

She lingered for a while and then left. But before she did, she sent me a quick nod. Whether it was a polite goodbye or an answer to the question I had asked was hard to tell.

Nils Kyvik had watched me intently as he reproved Klara. Now he stood silently waiting to see if I had any more questions to ask. I did.

'I'm planning to walk up to where the accident took place to-morrow morning. Could you come with me and show me exactly where you found him?'

'Afraid not. I'm busy.' As I didn't respond to that, he carried on: *'I haven't been there since that day, and if it was up to me, I'd never go there again, either.'*

'Did it have such an impact on you?'

Now it was his turn not to respond.

'So you don't fish for salmon in the Storelv then?' I asked.

'*First up, I don't have a licence to fish there, and I'm not going to pay through the nose for it, either. Second up, there are no fish left in the fjord, thanks to the hanky-panky the Marken lot have been getting up to with their first fish farm. The fjord's that thick with bloody sea lice you can walk across it without getting your feet wet!*'

'But they closed that farm down ages ago.'

'*It's no better out on the Sørneset headland, I can tell you.*'

Accordingly, I placed Nils Kyvik on neutral ground in the great debate Edvard Aga had told me about. Although I'd have said he was more on the demonstrators' side.

'Well, I'll have to find someone else to show me the way then.'

'*Try Harald Eide when he comes home. Right now he's on the rig, as far as I know.*'

'In the meantime, I've got someone else who's promised to show me the way.'

'*So why ask me then?*' With a snort he indicated that the conversation was over. He retreated and started to close the door.

'Thank you for the chat – and *bon appetit*.'

He nodded without a word and closed the door.

There wasn't much else for me to do now apart from stroll back to Betty Kleiva's. I guessed a meal would soon be ready to serve up there, too.

17

Betty accompanied me across the yard and unlocked the room I had been allocated in the annexe. It was tidy and attractive. At a pinch, there was space in the bed for two, should that become relevant. In one corner there was a basin and a mirror, and at the end of the flagstone passageway between the two rental rooms there was a toilet with a walk-in shower. Through the window I could see across the yard to the main house. The blue-and-white checked curtains were light and airy, and there was a blind to keep the daylight out, or prying eyes, if you wanted.

'*Happy?*' she asked, looking at me with her big, blue eyes.

'Absolutely.'

'*Supper will be ready in half an hour or so.*'

'Thank you.'

From the window I watched her as she crossed the yard to the house. At the back of my mind, I heard the echo of what Stein Solvik had said the first time I was in his shop: *Betty eats men for breakfast, they say.* But not for supper, I hoped.

There was no reason at all to complain about the meal. She had prepared a fish soup that was so substantial it could undoubtedly have passed as a bouillabaisse. To go with it she served a Bordeaux wine, as though to reinforce the impression that we were somewhere in France. But outside the windows it was pitch-black, a West Norwegian autumn darkness, in which half an hour could elapse between passing traffic.

I told her who I had spoken to in the village, from Stein Solvik and Edvard Aga to the Kyvik couple. When I said that Aga had promised to go with me to what we were still calling the scene of the accident, she nodded and said that was nice of him. '*He knows his way around, he does.*'

'Yes, he's big on catching fish, too.'

'*If there are any.*' There it was again, what I had begun to think of as a standard refrain in this area.

After the meal, she poured us both another glass of wine and invited me into the sitting room, where we sat on opposite sides of a coffee table, her on a broad sofa, me safely ensconced on the chair facing her.

During the course of the evening, she told me more about how life unfolded in Solvik for someone who grew up there. From her earliest childhood she was used to being around animals. When she married Mons Marken, they took over much of the running of the Marken farm, to help his parents, who were beginning to feel the years.

I asked her if she had done any kind of training after her basic schooling.

'*I started. After school I spent a year at Stend Agricultural College in Fana. I lived in a bedsit in Kvernabekkvegen and so on, but when I came home that summer, I turned seventeen, got together with Mons and just stayed here.*'

'And you married?'

'*Yes, but that wasn't until a year later. When I was eighteen.*'

'And you were still around animals?'

'*Yes, a few cows and some sheep. I was in charge of them. Mons was already working on the fish farm. Later, though, after Mons had passed away and the fish farm fell to me, Kåre took responsibility for it, and eventually, after we stopped keeping animals, I did a fair bit of the office work for the fish farm. I completed a bookkeeping course and took responsibility for that side of things.*'

'And it was Kåre who wanted to move the fish farm onto land?'

'*Yes. We didn't have proper control when Mons was running things. There was a particularly bad autumn storm in 1977. It was catastrophic – several of the pens were ripped to pieces by the gales. The salmon lice and hydrogen peroxide spread across the fjord. There was a stench of rotten eggs hanging over the whole area. It made you* want to throw up. So when Kåre took over, a few years later, we both agreed we would move the business onto land.'

'But you never got that far?'

'No, everything came to a halt, primarily because of a lack of funds. And then the Sørneset project started up in competition with us. And things became even more difficult. Investors were putting money into salmon breeding in the fjord because it was the simplest and fastest return on their money. So that put an end to all our plans. And then our marriage ended too.'

She breathed a heavy sigh, reached out almost blindly for the wine and poured herself another glass, right up to the brim.

'I'll tell you one thing, Varg. We had a really nice choir round here once. Louise Sørnes, the headteacher in the village, she started it. The whole village showed up. Singers came from lots of families, and on all the big occasions – Independence Day, end of the school year, Christmas – the choir made an appearance. Something bound us together, no matter how different we were. But then they began with their plans for a new fish farm on the Sørneset headland while Kåre was working to set up his closed farm on land. It split the district in two, and all of a sudden it was impossible even to have choir practice without an all-out row erupting between whoever turned up. In the end, everyone went their separate ways, and since then there hasn't been much singing in the village, I can tell you.'

'Right … Changing the subject, is Jonas against all forms of fish farm?'

'Ermm, not all forms, no. We've talked about it a few times. He isn't against land-based farms. From that point of view, he would've been the right successor to Kåre. What he was protesting against was the pollution from the open cages in the sea. And the lack of precautionary measures.'

'And just by chance there was one such company operating near his home village, so he came to demonstrate against it. That didn't exactly create goodwill here, I'd imagine.'

'No, you can bet your life on that.'

'This Mona Martens. She's a mystery. You see, she was the daughter of one of the Sørneset investors. Fredrik Martens.'

Betty raised her glass and took a long draught. *'Really?'* she said, trying to focus her eyes and failing.

'Klara Kyvik hinted there'd been something going on between her and Knut Sørnes.'

'Mona Martens and Knut Sørnes?' Betty visibly pulled herself together and mounted a crooked smile. *'Mm, if Klara says so, it'll be the pure unadulterated truth. She knows everything about everyone here, including me.'*

My mind was busy with thoughts now. It was easy to see a possible love triangle here: Mona Martens, Knut Sørnes and Jonas Kleiva. But I decided not to go any deeper into this with Betty. She was ill at ease enough as it was.

We sat in the semi-darkness, each with our glass of red wine. A spirit of melancholy had settled over both of us, as it often does when you have drunk too much.

She stroked her hair back from her brow, straightened her neck and tried once more to fix her eyes on mine, with the same floating sensation as before. *'Have you ever experienced true love, Varg?'*

Now it was my turn to reach for my glass and take a fortifying draught. 'Well … I was married for some years and had a child with my wife. But she left me. Later I found a steady girlfriend at the national registration office.'

'At the n-n-national registration office?' She looked dumbfounded.

'We would've probably got engaged. Then she died.'

'Died? What from?'

'Erm, it was in connection with a case I was working on.'

'W-was it your fault then?'

'In a way I suppose it was.'

She slumped across the table and leaned over her glass as though it was a crystal ball in which she could read the future. Almost to herself she said: *'I have.'*

'You have what?'

'Experienced true love. He came late, but he got here in the end, as whoever it was said.'

'Alexander Kielland's Skipper Worse.'

'Eh?'

'It's not important. You were talking about…'

'Klaus. One marriage was cut short. Another hit the rocks. And then he came. This young man entered my life and … He took me by storm. I've never known anything like it, neither before nor since.'

She straightened up and now she found my eyes. *'He was the great love of my life, Varg. A huge, warm presence. And what've I been left with? Memories, that's all I have. Memories and a half-finished manuscript about fish-breeding. Klaus…'*

She stopped there and we swam in and out of each other's blurred gaze, as lost as Jonah in the whale's belly.

Not long afterwards I retired to my room. She accompanied me to the kitchen door that led to the yard. I had the key to the annexe in my pocket.

'I hope you have a good night's sleep here in Solvik,' she said. *'I'm on the first floor.'* Then she added: *'If you need anything.'* As I didn't respond, she concluded the evening with: *'Breakfast at eight o'clock.'*

'That's good. I've arranged to meet Aga at ten.'

She laid a hand on my shoulder, leaned against me and gave me a big, wet kiss at the bottom of my neck. But that was where it stopped. I freed myself and, before crossing the yard, made sure the door was closed securely behind me.

Inside my room, I set the alarm on my phone for half past seven and lay down to read a thriller I had brought with me. I was still on Icelandic crime for the moment. This was a woman detective, the story had elements of the supernatural and it was almost half past twelve before I managed to put the book down.

No one came waltzing across the yard, either. For breakfast she served bacon and eggs and let me eat in peace in the kitchen while she busied herself with other domestic matters.

18

I told Betty I was going out then headed on my way. In the car I found the pair of sailing boots I knew were in there and put them on. They were the closest thing I had to hiking footwear. Edvard Aga was already waiting for me outside the general store when I pulled into the kerb to pick him up.

It had rained a little in the night, but there were glimpses of blue sky above the mountains around us. There was an odds-on chance it was going to be one of the more unusual days in this part of Vestland, where for many years villages had vied to achieve the highest rainfall recorded in the country – Brekke was in pole position with Matre and Solvik hard on its heels.

We followed the same narrow road along the fjord as we had the previous time. I concentrated on driving while we chatted.

'Is it possible to make a living as a private eye then?' Aga asked.

'I've managed it for close on thirty years. But I haven't made a fortune, and when the time comes my pension will barely be acceptable. And you? A man in his prime from what I can see – but it's a working week in October, and you're in your cabin?'

'Mm, in my cabin but not on holiday. I settled here officially many years ago.'

'And how do you make a living?'

'I don't have many major outgoings. I suppose you can call me a kind of pensioner.'

'A local Scrooge McDuck?'

'Well, not exactly. I'm a carpenter by trade. For many years I taught carpentry at a college. In my free time, a pal and I bought old apartment blocks, renovated them, divvied them up and either rented or sold them. As the years went on, I got sick of it. I had less and less free time. True enough, I didn't have a family, but I would've liked to have the freedom to travel up here and other places. To go fishing. So, when prices were high, I sold my share of all the properties and had enough money to invest in interest-bearing accounts and move up here to live – if not on just the interest, then by making such small withdrawals that there's sufficient for when I'm a real pensioner, assuming I keep to the same lifestyle. The only fly in the ointment is, of course, what we discussed last time: the state of the fjord. But it isn't far to Gulen or up to Sogn og Fjordane, and there are enough fish there, in rivers, lakes and the sea. For as long as stocks last.'

'So you don't miss town life?'

'Not in the least. When you can be surrounded by nature like this…' He swept his arm round to embrace the fjord, Storfossen and the mountains. 'What would there be to miss?'

We had reached the summit and looked down on the disused fish farm in Markatangen. The police cordon around the driveway to the pier was still there, fluttering in the wind.

Aga pointed ahead. 'We have to go a little way in that direction. As far as the road takes us.'

The road tapered and there were no more passing points. If you met anyone here, you would either have to reverse the whole way back or swerve off the road. Finally we reached the end, where the road had been widened to allow cars to turn. It was also possible to drive onto a stony area next to it and park. On a post there were two home-made signs, carved from wood. One pointed to the right, to STØLSVATNET, the lake, and the other to STORFOSSEN, the waterfall. When we got out of the car, we could feel its spray, like a gentle shower on our faces.

My walking companion stood with a rapturous expression on his face. He raised it to the spray, closed his eyes, thinking, from what I could judge, about previous experiences in the rapids down from the waterfall and the big fish he must have caught.

I coughed to bring him back into our world. He opened his

eyes and looked at me. 'Right. This way,' he said, pointing – quite unnecessarily – to the lake path, which would take us to the mountain farms.

At first, we walked through dense forest, with branches brushing against our faces if we didn't push them away. 'Years ago, they used to keep these trees trimmed back, but now that the summer pastures are no longer used, they've just let them go.'

Then we started to ascend. After five minutes we reached a steep mountain slope, the path winding up over it and out of sight.

I looked around. 'Nils Kyvik said they found Klaus Krog at the bottom of a steep slope. The evidence seemed to suggest that he'd hit his head on a rock. Actually, that could've been around here.'

Aga nodded.

'A jagged rock,' I added.

We began to make our way carefully up the path while checking both sides. It was so steep that I felt we were walking bent double so as not to tumble backward.

It was as Kyvik had said. All the blood had been washed away long ago. We saw plenty of rocks that could have fitted the description, small ones and big ones, but not so big that you couldn't lift them and use them as a weapon. It was beginning to look as if I would have to contact the local police station to read the detailed report they must have filed away. I wondered if they had carried out an autopsy at the time, and if not, what their reasoning had been.

I stopped and looked up. 'It's really steep here. If you slipped further up, it would be a long fall and you might get badly injured if you couldn't grab hold of something. How on earth did they get their animals up and down here?'

'Oh, sheep are used to mountains. Not to mention goats. They can find paths where humans can barely move forward.'

'It was harder with cows, I suppose.'

'Yes, that must've been tricky.'

'And when Klaus Krog was here, it was probably slippery. It never really dries out here, does it. What was more, it was evening and beginning to get dark. There could be lots of explanations for how it happened.'

'Absolutely.' Aga shifted his gaze upward again. 'It's still quite a way to the farms, so … Or are you happy just to look around the scene of the accident?'

'No, no. Now we're out walking, let's walk. All the way up.'

We continued the ascent. Gradually the slope began to flatten out, and finally we came to what was clearly Stølsvatnet lake. It was oval in shape and lay in a dip, the type the ice age had left behind.

As we studied it, Aga pointed to the other side. 'Over there you can see the Marka mountain farm.'

I squinted in that direction, and sure enough, at the end of the dip, close to the next rise in the terrain, there was a small stone house, as grey as the rock behind it. 'How far away is that?'

'Twenty to thirty minutes. All depending how fast we walk. Over there you have the Sørnes mountain farm.' Now he was pointing to something that fitted that description on the eastern side of the lake.

'So, both the Marka gang and the Sørnes gang have got farms and pasture land up here?'

'Yes.' He pointed down to the beach to the west of where we were standing. Only the foundations of a house on a third farm were left. 'And that's the Solvik farm. But no one's taken care of it for many years. Stein has more than enough to do with his general store, and any family he has stopped keeping animals long ago.'

'I see. With at least three farms, I presume there was every opportunity for rows between neighbours up here, too?'

'Yes, sadly the dispute over the fish farms down below spread up here as well. Before all that, you could buy fishing licences for this lake. But when they started arguing about fish farms, that was the end of any agreement over fishing rights in the lake.'

I gazed across the peaceful surface of the water. 'In other words, there are fish here, too?'

'Do you know a fish called a char?'

'I do indeed.'

'It's an Arctic fish. It's been in Norway since the ice ages. When the ice retreated, a variety of strains of char were left in mountain lakes such as this. They spawn here, and they've kept their breeds alive for all the millennia that have passed since the ice ages.'

'Impressive. So they don't swim out into the sea, like salmon?'

'No, they don't spawn in rivers, either. They stay in the lakes. And it's a delicious fish, Varg.' He was actually licking his lips. 'I've caught a lot of char here, in better times.'

'But now no one fishes here, Eddie?'

'Not with a fishing licence anyway. The owners can come up here and fish, of course, but that doesn't happen often. And if a mountain walker who didn't know any better happened to pass, the odd fish or two might be caught and cooked over a fire. But otherwise, no.' He shrugged, clearly annoyed by the loss of fishing rights.

At the top, the vegetation had become denser again: mountain birch, juniper and heather. However, following the path around the lake was not a problem. It was easier to walk here, and when we approached the Marka farm, not much more than the twenty minutes he had estimated had passed.

To the north-west of us, we heard the roar of Storfossen. Over there, great torrents of water came down from the heights behind the farm, then formed a main stream that continued to the waterfall, but one of its side rivulets ran down into the lake and created life and movement on the surface. A large, black-and-white grebe flew low over us, as if checking to see who these rare guests to the mountain landscape were. After satisfying its curiosity, it croaked a hollow *kuk-kuk-kuk* sound and flew with aristocratic mien back to the middle of the rivulet coursing down into the lake, where it settled in the willow thicket growing around the edge.

Having arrived at the farm, we had a breather. Aga threw down the rucksack he had been carrying. There was a stone bench along what I thought was the west wall of the house, and Aga made a beeline for it.

The house had been built in grey stone with openings for windows facing the lake. There was a solid wooden door and the roof was covered with turf, and at the front of the ridge a chimney had been cemented in place. There were no signs of life.

'Is it OK to go inside?'

'Yes. It's a refuge for long-distance hikers, so it should be unlocked.'

I walked over, Aga behind me, grabbed the door handle, pressed it down and pushed. It was as though the whole structure sighed in nynorsk: *Who is this, coming here and disturbing us? Will we ever have any peace and quiet?*

The house was simply furnished. Through a small porch, with a lot of tools hanging on the left-hand wall, we came into the only room, containing two low bunk beds. In front of the window was a small, scarred table, a bench and two stumps of wood that had been cut in such a way that they could function as stools, even if they were not especially comfortable. In the corner to the left there was a wood burner with a metal pipe leading to the chimney we had seen outside. To the right was a narrow table that might have been used as a kitchen worktop. On it were some dirty plates and a black coffee flask. In a bucket under the table there were some empty cans. When we opened a cabinet above the table we saw a small selection of cups, mugs, plates and a couple of pans as black as the flask. Against the wall under the cabinet was a small gas cooker, the most modern item in the house.

Aga bent down, pulled out the bucket and picked up two or three cans. He poked a finger inside one of them, then another.

'Someone's been here quite recently,' he mumbled.

I walked over to the stove, felt it and nodded. 'Still warm.'

Our eyes met, and I could see we were thinking the same thing. We pictured the camper van we found in the sea outside Markatangen, the driver's door ajar and his seat empty.

Outside the house we scanned the horizon.

I glanced at Aga. 'Are you thinking what I'm thinking?'

He nodded slowly. 'Someone's watching us.'

I looked up the steep mountainside behind the house. 'Where does the path take us if we continue up here?'

'Hm. Quite far west into Stølsheimen, I reckon. Bjørn West territory.'

Some of the last battles of the Second World War had taken place in these mountains, between German soldiers and the Bjørn West resistance forces, the first taste of what could have become the Battle of Fortress Norway, if the Germans hadn't capitulated in May 1945.

'Pretty rugged terrain,' Aga added.

There were some narrow passes between the rocks on the way up, and it was impossible to see if someone was lurking there. If we had been in a western, this would have been Apache country with all kinds of hiding places. Around us, at the bottom, and the whole way around the lake, while the landscape was more open, it was overgrown with juniper and willow thicket. There were enough places to lie low here too, for someone who didn't want to be seen.

'Well,' I said. 'We can tell the police, of course. If they're interested, they'll have to send up a dog patrol. For us there's not much more we can do, other than go back down.'

We took the same route we had come. When we arrived at the last steep slope down to where Klaus Krog had been found, we experienced for ourselves how hard it was to keep your footing during the descent. If you tripped, slid, or lost balance in any other way, there was no vegetation to grab hold of and you would have quickly found yourself twenty to thirty metres below. So, it wasn't difficult to imagine how the local police officer had written this off as an accident in 2002.

In the car on the way back we didn't meet any other vehicles until we were in Solvik.

After parking, I said: 'I wouldn't mind driving in the opposite direction, too, to Sørnes. See if I can look around Sunfjord Salmon. Are you up for that?'

Aga looked sceptical. 'Erm, I'm afraid that'll be a wasted trip, Varg. I think I'll go back to my cabin and spend my time doing something more sensible.'

'Fine by me. Thank you for taking the time to join me on the walk up to the Marka farm, anyway.'

He opened the door. 'I'm not sure that I can help you with much more, though. We'll have to see how this all develops.'

'By which you mean…?'

He shrugged. 'Erm, we are still talking about a missing person, aren't we?'

'Yes, I suppose we are.'

Our eyes met, and once again we had the same name on the tips of our tongues. Then he opened the door wide and stepped out. He leaned down and poked his head back inside the car. 'Good luck in Sørnes,' he said with a wry smile. 'Beware of the dog, as they say.'

'Dog?'

'Wait and see,' he answered, then straightened up, cast a glance in the direction of Stein's store-cum-café and decided on a visit before heading for the quay where his boat was moored. I drove on to the crossroads, where a sign pointed to *SUNFJORD SALMON* and another to *SØRNES, 3 KILOMETRES*.

19

The *SUNFJORD SALMON* sign had a logo: a leaping salmon set again the background of a red sunset. That seemed inviting, but the invitation wasn't quite matched by the barbed-wire-topped fence and massive iron gate, where you needed an electronic card and a code to get in. A surveillance camera kept an eye on who came and went. A small sign near a microphone beside the gate announced in Norwegian and English that, if guests kindly pressed a button, they would be able to speak with someone.

I followed their advice and pressed the button in as kindly a fashion as I could.

The microphone spoke nynorsk. *'Hello. Who is it?'*

'The name's Veum. Varg Veum.'

'What's your business here?'

'I'd like to discuss that in private. Is the CEO present?'

'That's me.' There was a little pause until the voice returned: *'I asked you what your business was.'*

'It's a little difficult to explain like this. If you have time for a little chat, then…'

There was a slightly longer pause this time. I looked up at the camera and waited, trying to look as trustworthy as possible.

'OK then.' The gate buzzed and as if guided by a hand from above, it opened and let me in. I hadn't advanced many metres before I heard it clang shut behind me.

There were two buildings on the large site: a low, single-storey structure to the left and a more compact, workshop-like construction away to the right. In the middle a long road led to the quay and to the piers between the six circular cages, which lay like the perfect throw of a dice in the fjord. Even from this distance you could see that the place was humming with life. On one of the piers, I could make out two men in orange overalls. One was moving a pole back and forth in one of the cages while the second was keeping a sharp eye on what was happening inside. Then the pole shot into the air with a fish wriggling in a net. The first man swung back over the pier, the other grabbed the net, pulled it close and carefully studied the contents.

A door in the middle of the low building opened. In the doorway appeared a tall, fair-haired man in his late twenties. To the left of him, level with his thigh, stood a black Dobermann growling in my direction. Now I understood why Aga had warned me to beware of the dog. But I could see the owner had it on a robust chain, and I walked towards them – calmly, so as not to provoke the dog's instinctive scepticism of strangers.

'Knut Sørnes?'

'That's me.'

Close up, Knut Sørnes had regular features, blue eyes, a square jaw and a powerful body. He was wearing a tight T-shirt emblazoned with the company logo, blue jeans and dark-brown cowboy boots. His hair was cut short around his ears and neck, but on top he had naturally wavy hair.

I stopped in front of them. It was hard to say who was more sceptical: me or the dog. At least the owner wasn't growling.

He shot me a surly look. 'Who are you and what do you want?' As brief and straight to the point as an Icelandic family saga.

'Varg Veum. Private investigator. It'll take a bit longer to explain what I want.'

He looked around. On the pier the net was back in the water and the salmon was free.

'You'd better come in then. Caesar!' The latter was directed at the dog, which looked up at its owner and seemed to nod assent, then they both turned and walked back into the building.

I followed them. Knut Sørnes led me along a short corridor to the only open door and went inside without another word. I saw a sparsely furnished office, a large computer screen and attendant accessories dominating the room. A swivel chair sat behind the solid desk, which was positioned by a window facing the salmon pens. We were right out on the headland now. From here you could see the fjord broadening to the south-west and into the sea.

'Down, Caesar!'

Alongside one wall there was a blanket and a bowl of water for the dog. Caesar strolled calmly over and lay down as his master had ordered. But he turned his head on his muscled neck and stared at me as warily as before, ready to leap into action at the slightest indication from his owner.

Knut Sørnes motioned to the only other chair in the room – a shell-shaped model and relatively comfortable if you were at ease feeling like an oyster before it was gathered and consumed.

He fixed me with a hard stare and said: *'I'm asking you for the last time. What do you want?'*

'Does the name Klaus Krog mean anything to you?'

He appeared to have to give this some thought. *'Klaus Krog? Wasn't that the guy who died in an accident near Storfossen a couple of years back?'*

'That's right. He was an ex-journalist, at that time a freelance writer with a critical view of the fish-breeding industry.'

'He wasn't alone in that.'

'No, as recently as a couple of weeks ago there was a demonstration here, from what I understand.'

'There were a few kids messing around here, yes. But what—'

'Some of them were local, weren't they?' I interrupted.

'You know as well as I do they were, I imagine. But I still don't understand—'

'One of them has gone missing. Another is dead.'

'She ... Mona wasn't from here.'

'No, you're right about that. But you knew her, didn't you?'

He pushed his chair back and stood up, so abruptly that Caesar sprang up as well, fixed his eyes on me and barked loudly.

Knut Sørnes raised a hand for the dog to be quiet. But he kept his eyes on me. *'Who I know and who I don't know is none of your business. What was your name again?'*

'Veum. Varg Veum.'

'Anything else you have to say for yourself? You're a…'

'Private investigator, and I've been commissioned to investigate the circumstances of Klaus Krog's accidental death, as you just described it.'

'My understanding is that it was an accident. That's all I've heard.'

'Really?'

'Really. Criticism's all well and good, even if it's poorly backed up, but you don't seriously think that anyone would resort to physically assaulting people with an opposing view? After all, we live in a democratic society, don't we? Freedom of speech is considered important.'

'So your company received the demonstration two weeks ago with unalloyed joy?'

He sent me a withering look. *'We didn't take it very seriously, anyway, and after a while they gave up. You know, not that many actually showed up here on the headland. And there wasn't a journo in sight, either. Total fiasco, if you ask me.'*

'Did you go out to welcome them?'

'Welcome them? I stayed in my office. I had much more useful things to do than listen to them.'

'So you didn't know that Mona Martens was with them, then?'

'Not until I read about it on the Net, no. And I didn't know she'd died at Markatangen.' A sudden dejected expression clouded his face. This wasn't something he wanted to dwell on.

'I've heard you and she were an item. Is that right?'

He glared at me. *'Used to be. She has someone else now.'*

'Jonas Kleiva?'

'What? Jonas Kleiva? You're way off beam there, Veum. It…'

He paused. In the corridor behind us a door slammed. Heavy footsteps resounded on the floor as they came towards us. Caesar stared at the door, but stayed as calm as his owner in anticipation of the imminent arrival.

A large man, well into his fifties, filled the doorway. He was wearing an outfit that reminded me of the two guys I had seen on the piers: a jacket and trousers made of some hard-wearing material. The ceiling light reflected on his bald head. The hair he did have was shaved so close to his ears that it looked more like a shadow. The lack of any reaction from Caesar confirmed my impression that this visitor was no one less than Einar Sørnes.

The look he gave me was of the same variety as the one his son had shot me. *'Who are you?'*

'Varg Veum. Private investigator.'

'He says he's investigating Krog's death,' Knut added from the sidelines.

'Investigating? Krog? And why's he come here?'

They looked at each other, and I took the liberty of joining in the discussion. 'Klaus Krog had written several critical articles about the fish-breeding industry, as you'll know, and he was on the trail of something here.'

'On the trail?' Einar snarled. *'Of what?'*

'Well, maybe he didn't get far enough to find out.'

'And so what? I hope you aren't insinuating that we had anything to do with the accident, because, if you are, the next place we two would meet would be in the courtroom.'

'Misfortunes never come singly, as they say. I'm sure you're aware of the accident that occurred in Markatangen two weeks ago, the same day as the demonstration against your business. Two of the demonstrators died.'

'Two?' Einar glanced at his son. *'Has there been a development?'*

'Only one person has died, as far as I know.'

'Let's put it like this then,' I said. 'One person's dead and one's missing. The odds of him, Jonas Kleiva, also being out here in the fjord somewhere are quite high, I would think.'

'*I see,*' Einar said. '*And how does that concern us?*'

'Well, it was the daughter of your principal owner who died. Surely that concerns you. How do you two think Fredrik Martens has reacted?'

Knut Sørnes looked at his father, who pressed his lips together, a clear signal that the answer was: *No comment.*

'Perhaps he'll pull out of the whole business?'

Einar Sørnes eyed me fiercely. '*And why would he do that?*'

'For personal reasons perhaps?'

As neither of them seemed to have any further comment to make, I continued: 'There's another thing you might be concerned about: it was here that they were last seen, both of them. If we include Klaus Krog, that's two deaths and one missing person who have criticised the kind of salmon breeding you do. Some people might call that a trifle fishy.'

'*If they're as thick in the head as you, yes.*' Einar Sørnes directed his gaze at his son. '*Can we agree that we've wasted enough time on this wacko?*' He straightened up and towered even higher over the office furniture than before. '*I suggest we show him the door. The sooner, the better.*'

Caesar seemed to react on cue, because he suddenly started growling, with eyes that glowered like those of the other two. I pretended I didn't hear the dog and said to whoever it might apply: 'OK. No reason to be violent – not today, anyway.'

'*Today?!*' Einar yelled and Caesar barked.

'I'm leaving of my own free will.'

Sørnes Senior was in charge now. '*I'll see him to the front door,*' he said to Knut and stepped to the side so that I could pass. When I stood up, Caesar tensed his legs ready to attack if he received the command. He didn't. I emerged unscathed and headed for the main gate before Einar could say anything else.

'Let me tell you loud and clear, Veum. You are not welcome here. If we see you here again, we'll let Caesar loose on you.'

'With what justification?'

'Trespassing on our property.'

'Yeah, you've kicked people out before, I've heard. Klaus Krog, for example.'

'So? Krog came over here and made the most outrageous claims. He wasn't worth listening to. But kick him out? I asked him to leave, that was what I did. No more than that. If anyone says anything different, they're lying.'

'Your word against theirs.'

Again, he swelled himself up to such a size that I had to concede defeat. There was a lot of him. Towering over me, he blotted out the sun. 'Get the hell out of here! Is that understood?'

'Understood and noted,' I said, walking to my car parked outside the fence. The gate shut behind me with the same firm clang as when I arrived. I pressed the key fob. Einar Sørnes stood his ground and watched me right until I had got in my car, started the engine and left the car park. As I passed him, I waved goodbye. He didn't wave back.

20

As I walked up the path from the gate to her front door, Betty Kleiva was almost dancing with excitement.

'How did it go? Did you find anything?'

'There wasn't so much to find after two years, but we went right up to the Marka farm, so I got a proper impression of the terrain there. The slope where he was found is very steep. So an accident isn't out of the question at all. But I'd like to have a chat with the police about the case. Afterwards I'll go back to Bergen and see if I can dig anything up there.'

Her eyes widened. 'But … but…' She grabbed my upper arm and looked left and right. 'Come inside.'

She stopped just inside the door, so close to the entrance that I bumped into her when I crossed the threshold. For a moment we stood in a kind of embrace, before we each stepped away. But we were still standing closer to each other than felt completely natural, given the situation.

'I told you how scared I was! And now you're already going home.'

'I can't exactly move in here, and bodyguard duties are beyond what I normally offer. But you've commissioned me to see what I can dig up about the circumstances of Klaus Krog's death, and we still don't know what might've happened to Jonas. He could be alive for all we know.'

'Alive?' She examined my face suspiciously.

'Anything's possible until the contrary has been proven. He may have his reasons for lying low.'

'What reasons could there be?'

'He was – or is – a young man. The little I've gleaned tells me he could be a part of two love triangles, possibly three.'

'Love triangles? Who with?'

'Well, there are his fellow demonstrators from Bergen, but you

told me you don't know them … There are at least two constel-
lations there. I even observed one of them from the bus the first
time I saw them. And then there's the more local version, which
I mentioned to you yesterday. Apparently, there was something
between Mona Martens and Knut Sørnes, which Knut confirmed
to me today. Actually, he claims it was over and she had someone
else now. When I asked if it could be Jonas, he just snorted. So,
who could it be then? The only thing we can be sure of is that she
was sitting in Jonas's camper van when she died.'

Her eyes darkened. *'Yes, and they came here too – both of them.'*

'Exactly. Jonas came to show her off. But whatever the facts
of this are, I'm afraid we probably still have to be prepared for
the worst.'

She blinked and her eyes were filled with tears. *'Yes…'* She
came closer again, as if to be comforted. I couldn't really do anything else but put my arms around her and hold her tight. Her
body was wracked with barely repressed sobs and I gently
stroked her back.

Then she freed herself and pulled away. She angled a look up
at me, her chin wet with tears, her eyes moist. *'I'm so sorry,'* she
mumbled. *'I didn't mean to … be clingy.'*

'Not at all. There's every reason to be upset.' I nodded
towards the sitting room. 'Let's sit down where it's nice and
quiet. But first I have to call the local police and make an appointment.'

She nodded and forced a resigned, little smile. *'Let me rustle
up a bite to eat and some coffee. Go into the sitting room while I do
that, Varg.'*

I did as she said. The sitting room was where she had served
the bouillabaisse and the red wine the previous evening. It was
a dark room, screened from the brightest sunlight by the canopy
of large trees outside. The furniture was somewhat old-
fashioned, like heirlooms from previous generations. The TV in

the corner was big and not exactly the latest model, either. In the bookcase there was a black Bible, a leather-bound local community register, which on closer inspection was from 1959, and a small selection of various types of books, mostly fiction, but also five or six books about fishing and outdoor living, which I presumed had been Klaus Krog's.

I searched my mobile for the number of the local police station and rang.

'Police.'

'Varg Veum here. Who am I speaking to?'

'Ah, so it's you. You're speaking to Karl Sætenes. I hope you're not ringing me about the car accident. The Bergen police are investigating that case.'

'I know. This concerns another case. I've been asked to look into the circumstances surrounding another death up here. Klaus Krog, who died in what was defined as an accident two years ago.'

'"Was defined as"?'

'The case was investigated by an officer from your police station.'

'Yes, I remember. It was Hans Hosteland.'

'I'd like to have a little chat with him.'

'"A little chat",' Sætenes growled. *'It'll have to be tomorrow then. He's busy on another case at the moment.'*

'That's OK. When can I come?'

'It's Friday tomorrow. Theoretically, we're closed. But I can ask Hosteland to be here at around ten. Do you know where the station is?'

'No.'

He explained, and we rang off.

Betty appeared in the doorway and said that the food was ready.

'Looks as if I'll have to stop over tonight as well,' I said.

'*You can stay here for as long as you like, as far as I'm concerned, just make sure it's a trustworthy outcome this time.*'

'Well, I'll do my best.'

She had set the kitchen table with an assortment of sliced meats, cheeses and bread. I sat down and she poured the coffee.

'*What did the police say?*'

'I have a meeting with the officer who did the investigation tomorrow at ten.'

'*He was just a young lad.*'

'Hans Hosteland. In fact, I've met him. He was with the chief of police the evening we found the camper van in the sea.'

'*Oh? Dig in, Varg.*' She indicated the food on the table, and I did as instructed. She paced uneasily back and forth, though, as if she had a lot to do, but couldn't find the energy.

We made small talk, and she said she was going to get some meat from the freezer for a red-deer stew. I wasn't likely to starve today, either.

After the meal I decided to go for a walk, if for nothing else than to orientate myself better with regard to Solvik itself. I passed the local store and walked down to the harbour. The quay where the coastal steamer used to moor was deserted, and looked like a monument to the shipping of yore. It was built with solid rock and covered with gravel and concrete. In the bay, in the opposite direction from Sørneset, there was a harbour sheltered behind a mole. I counted thirteen or fourteen boats moored there, some smaller ones for sailing in local waters, most big enough to head to sea, if necessary. Or to Bergen for that matter.

It was conspicuously quiet. I didn't see another person until I was walking back up to the main street. A tall woman was locking the door to the schoolhouse. She had dark-blonde hair gathered tightly into a bun on top of her head and was wearing an elegantly tailored brown coat, made from practical, water-resistant material. On seeing me, she stood and waited as if I were a father late for an appointment on parents' evening. As I approached she crossed the schoolyard and stood on the kerb to meet me.

Her face was oval, the gaze in her blue eyes sharp, and there was a classic severity about her mouth, recognisable to several generations of pupils, that placed her firmly behind a teacher's desk.

'You're the headmistress, aren't you?' I said as I came to a halt in front of her.

She nodded quickly and held out a hand. *'Headteacher. Louise Sørnes is the name.'*

We shook hands. 'And how big is the school?'

She sniffed, as if to signal what a stupid question that was. *'Myself and a part-time assistant.'*

'And pupil numbers?'

'Eight.'

'But the school is still open?'

She looked around to make sure she wasn't overheard, and said: *'It won't be for much longer. I'm afraid they'll have more use for a care home for pensioners in this village.'*

'Perhaps I should introduce myself?'

'No need. I know very well who you are and what you're doing. You're staying at Betty's, I understand.' Her face stiffened even further. *'Be careful of her. She eats men like you for supper, I've heard.'*

'For breakfast, I was told.' But I was talking to thin air. She was already on her way to a smart little Toyota Yaris parked by the fence surrounding the schoolyard. At least they didn't have any parking problems in Solvik.

I carried on past the school northward, to Markatangen. I passed the chapel, the fire station and a few more houses. With the village behind me I could walk the same way as Aga and I had driven earlier in the day, if it was a keep-fit walk I was after.

I turned and looked back over Solvik. The house where Nils and Klara Kyvik lived was opposite the school. I probably wasn't mistaken when I assumed it was Klara who had told Louise Sørnes who I was and why I was here. When Louise arrived home, she would probably hear my name mentioned by her husband too, as the day's news from Sunfjord Salmon.

Walking back to Betty's, I decided to pop into Stein Solvik's store. There was no one inside. Like a reprise, the owner appeared from the back room, and he didn't seem surprised to see who had entered his shop this time. *'Ah, Veum. You're still here?'*

'Yes, I've got an audience with the chief of police, but not until tomorrow, so…'

'Is Betty taking good care of you?'

'I haven't ended up on the menu so far, anyway, as more than a few have suggested I would.'

'Alright. The last meal of the day hasn't been consumed yet though, has it? Betty's been full of life ever since she was a teenager. We went to school together, so I know what I'm talking about. And she was no more than eighteen when she and Mons got married, even though he was ten years older than her. Before that she and Einar Sørnes went out, I think, but Mons overtook him on the inside lane, so to speak, which didn't exactly make their relationship any better.'

'Oh, yes? No one's talked about that.'

'You know, the choice is a bit limited here in the country, so … Mons was a nicer guy than Einar in every way. Just such a shame that he died so young. Was it the poet Nordahl Grieg who wrote: "The best of us die; The rest of us are left behind"?'

'Einar Sørnes did marry though, didn't he?'

'Yes, to Louise, but she's not from our parts. She came over the mountains from Brekke, as a teacher first. Fine woman she is, but I don't think she and Betty have ever really hit it off.'

'Betty was just boasting that Louise started a choir in the district.'

'*Yeah, yeah.*' He smirked. '*But that choir has ended up as some-thing akin to the Israel-Palestine conflict, if you ask me.*'

'So I heard.'

It struck me that here was another love triangle in Solvik, with Einar, Louise and Betty as the participants, a drama some of their successors seemed to have inherited. Knut, Jonas and Mona, and perhaps even more.

He didn't offer me a cup of coffee this time, so I thanked him for the chat and ambled the barely hundred metres back to Betty's house.

It was another evening with a meal and red wine at Betty Kleiva's. But she was less talkative this time, and even I turned down a top-up after the first two glasses. 'I'm seeing the police early tomorrow morning, aren't I, and I wouldn't like to be breathalysed on the way there.'

'*Right,*' she said, pouring herself another. She sat slumped forward and seemed to be eyeing me dolefully from her side of the table. '*I've been thinking about what you said earlier today. I think you may be right that Jonas is alive. I have this feeling inside me. I just can't understand how he can be dead.*'

'You're referring to Jonas?'

'*Yes. Men don't understand it, but there's an invisible bond between a mother and the children she's given birth to. His wasn't an easy birth, you know. It was a Caesarean.*' She held her waist. '*I can show you the scar, if you'd like.*'

'No, thank you.'

'*Just a figure of speech,*' she smiled. After a short pause she added: '*Until I see his body with my own eyes, I refuse to believe it. That he's gone for ever, I mean. My boy.*'

'Lots of people are like that. They have to see things for them-selves. Seeing is believing, as they say.'

By the time I decided to retire to my room, at a reasonable hour, she had drunk another couple of glasses. She got up to accompany me to the door, and it cannot be gainsaid that she was a trifle unsteady on her feet. Reaching the door, she held on to my arm and moved as close to me as she had earlier in the day. *'Thank you for coming, Varg. And thank you for sitting with me and listening to all my nonsense again.'*

She gave me a hug and a big, wet kiss on my cheek, but she didn't complain when I left and she didn't cross the yard that night either. Personally, I slept fitfully, but she served me the same substantial breakfast the following morning as before.

I packed my bag and reminded her that I would be driving to Bergen after I had been to the police station. 'But I'll keep you posted if there are any new developments in the case,' I said in conclusion, more formally than I had intended.

She smiled wearily. In the corridor she gave me a fleeting hug, but didn't follow me out onto the steps when I left. I assumed, however, that the rest of the village had made a note of that, plus the time of day and any other interesting details.

21

Masfjorden police station was situated on the ground floor of an eggnog-coloured building, just off the main road between Hosteland and Risnes. It could have been a 1960s private apartment but for the *POLITI* sign clarifying its function.

Through a gateway in the fence I drove into the car park in front of the building and parked. The scenery here was more open than in Solvik. The sky was higher and the forest denser. A couple of trees were so close to the building that they might potentially be a hazard when the autumn storms set in. I crossed the car park and tried the door beneath the *POLITI* sign. It was open. Hans Hosteland was sitting in the main room, safely ensconced behind the counter. But the hatch at the end of it was open, as if to indicate that Friday morning was his free time, and he had no plans to stay longer than he had to.

He was slim, in his early thirties, with an oblong head, sleek, civil-servant-coloured hair, rather large ears made prominent by his short haircut and a worried expression on his face. He was wearing civvies – a checked shirt and grey trousers – and had a light-blue sports jacket hung over the back of his chair. When I bowled up, he rose to his feet and motioned me behind the counter.

'Veum?'

'Correct. We've met before.'

'Yes, it ... I've found the file on the case you asked Sætenes about. It was me who went there and handled it.'

'Investigated it, you mean?'

He smiled dutifully. 'I don't think there was much investigating to do.'

'No?'

'It was pretty cut and dried. I'll show you.'

I followed him to a rectangular table, where he had spread

out a number of photographs and some type-written sheets – by the look of it, the report he had filed.

The pictures of the scene that met the officer told their own story. The deceased, Klaus Krog, was lying on his back, his face severely injured and his mouth agape.

'They'd moved him before I arrived, hoping to revive him with CPR, but in vain. They quickly established that nothing would help. It was the ambulance service that called us and I was sent there.'

'He's not what you would call a pretty picture.'

'No, he isn't, is he.' He placed a few more photographs on the table. *'I took the route the locals thought he'd come down and snapped these with my compact camera.'* He ordered the photographs into a rough sequence, shots from the top of the slope to the bottom. *'I found clear signs of what had happened. Look here. These are some of the rocks on the way down.'* He tapped them with his forefinger. *'These are blood stains. Quite large, some of them, you can see, so he must've been bleeding profusely from the first fall. And look here, this is high up.'* He moved two of the photographs to the side. *'Here you can see the footmarks where he slipped, clear signs in the scree, and here ... Right down to the bottom.'* He pointed to a large rock. *'He landed on this, head first, with the full weight of his body behind him, judging by the injuries. Then he fell further, hitting both arms and legs, but mostly'* – he went back to the first photograph – *'his head.'*

'But up there.' I pointed to the pictures at the top of the slope. 'Did you check to see if there were any other rocks there? Smaller ones that could've been used as a weapon?'

'No, nothing. I mean, of course I looked around for something like that. But there was nothing.'

'Nothing apart from the slide marks in the scree, blood on the rocks down the path and finally on that large rock?'

'No. There was nothing to suggest this was anything other than an accident.'

'The weapon I'm looking for could've been a smallish rock. It's easier to handle and can be thrown a long way from the path.'

He wore a sullen expression. *There were no signs of anything like that, I'm telling you.*'

I pondered. 'Was there an autopsy?'

'Yes, we sent the body to Bergen, of course. To ascertain the cause of death, if nothing else. If it'd been a heart attack, or a stroke, for example. But the report was clear on that point. It was the head injury and the massive damage it caused that was the most probable cause of death. They also found small particles in the wound from where his head had hit the rock, so there was no doubt the rock was the guilty party, if I can put it like that.'

'But I suppose you made enquiries about any relevant circumstances?'

'Yes, of course. I spoke to the bereaved party. The widow. Or, to be precise, his partner. They weren't married.'

'No, I know.'

'And to the two men who found her. I've got their names here.' He showed me the report.

'Yes, I've spoken to one of them.' After a moment's rumination, I continued: 'It's no secret that there are great schisms in Solvik, to do with fish farms – an old one and a current one – as well as the owners' various interests. Nor is it a secret that Klaus Krog, the deceased, was actively engaged in discussions about fish breeding. His opinions were so strong that someone might've wished to silence him.'

Hans Hosteland eyed me with concern. *'Surely the conflict wasn't so serious that someone would go that far? Sætenes didn't think so. Nor did the mayor.'*

'The mayor? What's he got to do with this case?'

'Well, for a start he's from Solvik. And he's also the brother of the bereaved woman. His name is Truls Hatlevik. He's still the mayor now.'

'What did you say? The brother of Betty Kleiva?'

'Yes. That's her name, I think. I've mentioned her here.' Again, he pointed to the typewritten sheets.

'And he thought it was nothing more than an accident?'

Now he was beginning to show clear signs of irritation. 'Yes, he did. Not that there's anything personal in this, of course, but...'

'But...?'

'You know how it is in small places. And it was his sister who was bereaved. Surely if he suspected something criminal, he wouldn't cover it up?'

'Well...' I said. 'In summary, then, the case was put down to misadventure and no further investigation was undertaken.'

He nodded mutely, his lips pressed together tightly, as if he had decided he had said enough.

'I assume I'll find the mayor in the council building?'

He nodded again. 'On the southern side, as we say here. Across the fjord, in Masfjordnes. But...'

'Yes?'

'Well ... this isn't my case.'

'Because it's been shelved, you mean?'

He was wearing the same worried expression on his face again. 'What I meant to say was, I doubt the mayor will want to talk to you about this.'

'I can believe that. Time will tell though.'

With that we concluded our morning confab. He returned to his leisure activities. I pointed the car's nose towards Duesund and the cable ferry across the fjord to Masfjordnes.

22

Light rain was falling across the calm sea as I got into my car on the quay in Duesund and waited for the ferry to dock. There were two cars in front of me, three behind. Just off here, there had been a terrible drama during the war when the coastal steamer, the *Masfjord,* sank in stormy weather early one morning in February 1944. Eleven people lost their lives. In those times the sea was the highway that connected all the tiny places along the coast to Bergen. Now most people drove, and for a long time there had been calls for a bridge instead of the cable ferry.

During the short trip across the fjord to Masfjordnes I stayed in my car. It struck me as odd that Betty hadn't mentioned that her brother was the mayor of the local council. I supposed she had her reasons.

The town hall in Masfjorden was situated on the hill above the ferry terminal. It was long and white, with a series of prominent first-floor windows. Leading to the ground floor there was what I presumed was a covered external staircase in the shape of a tower with a point. It looked exotic, like some kind of shrunken minaret.

At reception I was met by a young man in a white shirt and tie, but no jacket. To my enquiry about the mayor, he answered as expected: the mayor was busy and had a tight schedule the whole of this Friday. I mentioned that I was here about his sister, Betty Kleiva, and when the young man made some enquiries, it turned out that the mayor was able to put aside a quarter of an hour after all.

Physically, Truls Hatlevik was not unlike his sister: medium height, thick set, with a firm handshake when we introduced ourselves. He showed me into his office. From there he could look across the fjord to 'Northern Solvik', as he called it when I commented on the view. I put him at somewhere in his forties.

His hair was thinning, though he tried to camouflage this with the classic comb-over, from east to west.

He parked himself in a high-backed chair behind a large desk, indicated a rather more mundane chair on the client side and got straight to the point. *'What's Betty up to now then?'*

'Have you spoken to her recently?'

He averted his gaze. *'No, not for … a while.'*

'Of course you know her son, Jonas, has been reported missing?'

He nodded. *'I've heard.'*

I left him space to comment, but as nothing was forthcoming, I continued. 'He took part in a demonstration outside Sunfjord Salmon, in Sørnes.'

He heaved a sigh and looked at me wearily. *'I know Sunfjord Salmon, or Sørnes Oppdrett as it was originally called. I hate this anglicisation of the Norwegian language.'*

'Whose side are you on?'

He leaned his head back and jutted out his chin. *'I represent Senterpartiet and we give full support to local industry, whether it is fish farming or any other activity. These demonstrators…!'* He snorted.

'Have you ever discussed this with your nephew?'

'Discussed? With Jonas? I haven't seen him since he was so high.' He held his hand at about knee height.

'No?'

He leaned forward. *'You know, Veum, Solvik's in the centre of what we call chapel country. Folk here are reliable and loyal, they thank God for all He's given them and they live decent lives. Betty soon parted company with the Church, to the great shame of both our parents and the rest of us. She married far too early, and was widowed after two or three years; however, it wasn't long before she had another man, but then she got divorced. Let me put it this way: I haven't spoken to Betty for about twenty years.'*

'Now I understand why she didn't mention you when I last spoke to her.'

All of a sudden, he looked a little uneasy. *'Get to the point. What's this about?'*

'So, you never met Klaus Krog, I take it?'

Again, he averted his eyes, as if trying to avoid answering. *'Klaus Krog? No, but I've heard the name.'*

'I bet you have. He lived with her until he met his death on the way down from the Marka farm around two years ago.'

'Yes, I remember. But what…?' He splayed his hands.

'Betty's asked me to investigate the circumstances surrounding his death, and in that connection I heard that the mayor of this municipality himself was her brother.'

'So? What have I got to do with an accident in the mountains?'

'Have you got a house there?'

'Me? A house? I've lived in Sandnes for the last twenty years. Before that, I studied in Bergen.'

'Studied what?'

'What did I study? Social studies. Comparative politics. I know what I'm doing, I can tell you.'

'But you go home now and then?'

'I go and visit my elderly parents, yes, when I have the time. But a month or two can elapse between visits. And then, of course, I sit on the board of … Sunfjord Salmon – representing the council, you understand.'

'On the board of Sunfjord? Then you probably didn't appreciate what Klaus Krog was doing, either.'

'And what was that?'

'He was collecting material for a book critical of fish breeding, amongst other things.'

Again, he leaned his head back and stuck out his chin, a pose he assumed whenever he had to say something he was proud of, I inferred. *'As I told you before, Veum, we in Senterpartiet support local industry. Fish farms and their spin-offs create work for folk out here. They produce tax revenue for the council and in this way secure welfare for the local area, as well as increasing income for the country. I have nothing bad to say about this fishing industry. So don't come here…!'* He thrust out his arm and stared demonstratively at his watch. *'I'm afraid your time has run out.'* He stood up and looked at me with an expression that strongly suggested I did the same. *'Good luck with … whatever you're doing for Betty. And thank you for your visit.'*

'Not at all,' I said, rising to my feet. 'Should I say hello to Betty from you?'

'No need.'

'No, right. And if Jonas should turn up, in the worst conceivable way, you won't come to the funeral, either?'

He blinked, several times in a row, as though, out of the blue, I had punched him in the stomach. *'To be quite honest, Veum, I don't know.'*

'OK. But don't forget that blood is thicker than water, even if there are not so many salmon lice in it.'

He sent me an uncomprehending look. Then he shook his head in resignation, pointed silently to the door and stood watching until I was out of the office and on my way to the exit. There were no calls from the minaret after I was outside, either. I sat behind the wheel of my car, set my brain to drive mode and prepared myself mentally for the long and winding road before I met the E39 at the exit from Eikefet tunnel.

Chapel country, and other places, had given me something to mull over.

23

It was Friday afternoon by the time I got back to Bergen. I parked the car in Øvre Blekevei and went to my flat in Telthussmuget to drop off my travel bag before strolling down to the office. After a chin-wag with the receptionist in the hotel, which had now taken over the whole building except for my room on the third floor, I took the stairs up to help offset my lack of movement earlier in the day.

I still had a landline in my office. The first thing I did was to see if there were any messages. There weren't. So I switched on the computer and checked my emails. There was a bit more activity there, even though it was mostly offers from websites from which I'd ordered items that were otherwise impossible to get hold of. I sat deleting most messages and was left with a handful of emails that were worth examining more closely. Potential jobs beckoned behind a couple of them. I made notes on the pad I kept on my desk.

The nicest message came from my son, Thomas, who asked if I had any plans for my birthday on Friday, when I would be sixty-two. Thomas had turned thirty-three now and with his wife, Mari, had produced my only grandchild so far, tiny Jakob, who was two. They lived in Ullevål Hageby, in Oslo, and Thomas had a permanent post at the university. The chances of a return to Bergen were small, and I had seen Jakob only a handful of times since he had been born. I answered that I didn't have any plans, as yet.

This email triggered some reflection on the stage I was at in my life. I was a grandfather, but not much more than that. Thomas's mother, Beate, lived in Stavanger with her partner, Regine, having announced her transition sometime in the nineties. The other queens of my life were either dead or had decamped. I was left, a single king, one move from being in check and with no mate to cling to. I could give Sølvi a call, of course, even though I had no reason to, other than to enquire how her daughter, Helene, was. But those conversations never put me in an especially good mood. Or I could ring…

She answered as quickly as the previous time. 'Torunn.'

'Varg.'

There was a tiny pause before she said: 'How nice, yet again. Are you still working on the fish-farm case?'

'Well, as I told you last time we spoke, this is definitely an environmental issue. By the way, there's a colleague of yours called Klaus Krog. Did you know him?'

'Past tense? Does that mean…?'

'Yes, he died two years ago, as the result of an accident, allegedly.'

'And by allegedly you mean…?'

'Yes, that's exactly what I mean. He was writing a book that was going to be critical of the entire fish-breeding industry. For all I know, exemplified by what he'd observed while in Solvik.'

'And he died before he'd finished his work?'

'Yes. Did you know him?'

'No. I recognise the name, but I can't place him.'

'He worked for a magazine called *Jakt & Fiske*.'

'I don't believe I've ever opened its covers.'

'I suppose not. By the way, I have a question I'd like to ask you. Is it easy to find a summary of who owns shares in Sunfjord Salmon?'

She chuckled. 'Easy peasy. You're only a click away. If you know the right short-cuts. Have you got a computer handy?'

'Ready and waiting.'

She gave me the instructions I needed, precise and fluent. After some dithering over the keyboard on my side, the Sunfjord Salmon website showed me a full overview of the company's shareholdings, the board of directors and the complete accounts for the previous year, 2003.

Fredrik Martens wasn't mentioned anywhere, but Torunn explained that Riverbank Invest and two other companies on the list were owned by him, his total shareholdings through these companies making up fifty-one per cent.

There were also a number of smaller holdings owned by a variety of concerns and banks, as well as some private investors. Among these I noticed Einar and Knut Sørnes held shares corresponding to a total of five per cent. Of equal interest was a company called Kleiva Invest, which had shares amounting to ten per cent.

'Now tell me,' I asked, 'this Kleiva Invest company, do you know anything about it?'

'No, but I can soon check it out.' Over the telephone line I could hear the rhythmic clicking on the keyboard of someone who had fully mastered touch-typing, interrupted only by a few pauses for reflection and a ping or two from her computer. Then she was back again. 'Kleiva Invest. Based in Bergen, branch address, Olav Kyrres gate, run by a man called Kåre Kleiva.' More clicking on her keyboard. 'Incidentally, he's on the board of Sunfjord.'

'Right!' I scrolled down the page until I came to the membership of the board. Yes, indeed. Kåre Kleiva, Einar Sørnes, Truls Hatlevik and two other names. After one of them, Ole Lavik, in brackets it said he was the director. 'Ole Lavik. Know anything about him, Torunn?'

'He's a kind of second-in-command to Fredrik Martens. Sits on various boards, deputising for him. CEO of Riverbank Invest. I've talked with him a couple of times on the phone, but never met him. Thirty-two and no family.'

'You're impressively well informed, I have to say.'

'It's just the way I am. Everything I could conceivably use in the future I store on the hard disk in my brain.'

'Hm.'

'Has that worried you?'

'Not really ... There's a fifth name here: Cecilie Tangen. Who's that?'

'An investor from Østland. She represents international interests.'

'This Kåre Kleiva, he's on the list of people I want to contact. In fact, he's the father of Jonas Kleiva, the young protester who went missing at the same time as Fredrik Martens' daughter drowned in the camper-van accident. If that's what it was. In all probability he was in the same vehicle, behind the wheel.'

'And he hasn't turned up yet?'

'No. Now, I don't know how long Jonas was in the whale's belly in the Bible, but...'

'I think it was three days.'

'Bible-savvy too?'

'Vestlander, you know. Bible belt.'

'But no, he hasn't turned up yet, and it's been quite a bit more than three days. On the face of it, he's lying, if not at the bottom of the sea, then somewhere in Skuggefjord, where of course he could appear at any moment too, but hardly as alive as Jonas was when he emerged from the whale.'

'Well, I still have plans to visit Solvik, Varg. The way things are for Fredrik Martens, with the death of his daughter, I doubt there's any hope of him agreeing to a chat. But Ole Lavik should be open to one, maybe. If I can agree a time to meet him over the weekend, I'll give you a buzz. Perhaps we can work on something together.'

'That would be nice.'

'That's what I think. You'll be hearing from me.'

I registered the conversation with Torunn Tafjord as a bit of a boost and approached the weekend in a much more cheerful mood. After dinner in Holbergstuen restaurant, I returned to Strandkaien 2 and had a protracted top-level conference with the bartender in red braces. On the agenda was lager and aquavit, and it was past midnight before I wended my way home to Telthussmuget.

Another October day had passed and bedded down for the night. I followed its example.

According to ancient Norwegian tradition, Saturday was bath day, time for the weekly full-body ablution. Sunday was sun day. This Saturday Bergensians only had to step outside to get washed, but there wasn't much sun to be seen on Sunday, so what they gained on the swings, they lost on the roundabouts.

On Saturday morning I walked down past Forstandersmuget in the hope of a casual encounter with either Marita Svanøy or Geir Gravdal. I still had a sense they had been holding something back when I last met them. But neither of them was anywhere to be seen. So I wandered on into town, spoiled myself with a few beers at the Saturday matinee at Sweet & Swing, the jazz club, and on my way home stopped off at the Lerøy supermarket in Galleriet to buy some lamb chops and then invited myself to a superior Sunday lunch. On Sunday evening I finished the Icelandic thriller and went to bed well before midnight. It had been one of those weekends. Two pages torn from the calendar without any trace.

Kleiva Invest resided in Olav Kyrres gate, walking distance from my office. The big fire of 1916 had left huge parts of Bergen centre in ruins. The reconstruction work had led to all the districts around Torgallmenningen, the main square, consisting of solid, stylish buildings from a time when quality of craftmanship and taste for select details both inside and out were still fashionable. The elegant lift rose in a visible shaft in the middle of the stairwell. I took the stairs and made it up as fast as the occupants of the lift.

Kleiva Invest was on the third floor. I entered a reception area where the timbers and hues of the original interior had been solemnly preserved. The front desk with computer and other devices belonged, however, to our times. The woman behind it definitely did, too. She was somewhere between forty and fifty, with well-groomed brown hair, a white shirt blouse, black jacket and skirt. She wore large, black-framed glasses, had a round face with gentle contours and a mouth that on more romantic occasions could be described as a rosebud. Here it functioned more as a doorbell, compact and firm.

I introduced myself and asked if Kåre Kleiva was available. The doorbell tensed visibly as she glanced at the screen in front of her. 'I can't see an appointment for you.'

'No, I don't have one, but is he in?'

She looked as if that required some mental calculation.

'Tell him it's about a family matter. I represent his ex-wife.'

'You're a lawyer?'

'Private investigator.'

That loosened the stiffness. Her judiciously plucked eyebrows rose in two elegant curves. 'Hm.' She got to her feet. 'Let me go and check.' She indicated a couple of chairs by a small table in front of the window looking out onto Olav Kyrres gate. 'You can wait there.' She took some papers with her, opened the door to a side corridor and disappeared into it.

I walked over to the window. The offices of Kleiva Invest were on the corner overlooking the past's two main communication centres in town: the post office and the telegraph building. Both had now been converted into shopping malls, as was the custom of the time. The post office had been banished to a corner in one of them; telegraph was history.

A door behind me opened. The same woman smiled formally and said: 'You can go in. It's the third door on the left.'

'Thank you very much.' I passed her on the way. She wore a discreet scent – autumn roses, naturally enough.

Kåre Kleiva stood up behind a large desk when I entered. He had a square face with strong, masculine features, thick eyebrows, blue eyes, swede-coloured hair in tight curls, cut short around his ears. He was wearing a dark suit, white shirt and a blue tie, and had a studied formality, like the woman in reception – a clear sign that it was worth investing here: wealth and added value awaited you.

He fixed his eyes on mine. 'And the name is…?'

'Veum. Varg Veum. I've been commissioned by your ex-wife, Betty, to carry out some investigative work.'

'I assume this is about Jonas. But surely the police are investigating that case?' Kåre Kleiva had dropped his Solvik dialect, probably for commercial reasons, and spoke a sober standard Norwegian, with only the odd word and some slurring of vowels revealing his origins. 'I'm afraid I have nothing to offer on that score.'

'That's not the case I'm working on.'

'Oh, no? What is then?'

'The death of Klaus Krog two years ago.'

'Klaus Krog? But that was an accident.'

'Most people think so.'

'Including the police, unless I'm much mistaken.'

'Nevertheless, Betty's asked me to investigate it.'

He blew out his cheeks. 'Betty! Are you her new bed pal perhaps?'

'New?'

'Yes, you heard what I said.'

'My relationship with your ex-wife is one hundred per cent professional.'

'Oh, yes?' He didn't seem to believe me. 'She likes to seize an opportunity if she gets one.'

'I can assure you I've stayed over in her annexe twice and I was allowed to sleep in total peace both times.'

'Then she's changed her style. Our marriage didn't end in divorce for no reason.'

'Perhaps she has other things on her mind, with Jonas still missing.'

'Yes, Jonas…' Kleiva still hadn't indicated that we could sit down.

'But what I've come here to talk about is Klaus Krog, and for that matter, Sunfjord Salmon.'

'Klaus Krog…' He shrugged as if to display his ignorance. 'But we can always discuss Sunfjord.' He pointed to a chair beside the wall. 'You'd better take a seat.'

I lifted the chair and moved it to a better position with respect to the desk. He sat down with his back to the window, placed his hands on the desk and folded them as if performing a silent prayer before the conversation.

'OK, we can start there,' I said. 'You have a sizeable shareholding in Sunfjord Salmon and you're on the board.'

He nodded.

'But originally you were involved with a very different fishing operation, in Markatangen.'

'That's true. But it was actually Betty's – she inherited it from her first husband. I tried to take over the reins when Betty and I got married. Mons Marken hadn't exactly run it in an exemplary manner, but he can be excused, of course. Those were the pioneer days, before we had any idea of the problems lice – and combating them – could cause.'

'There are claims that the fjord's dead around there because of it.'

'Yes, it probably is. It was a bit like the Klondike at the start. I had plans for a land-based farm there. There would've been no danger of a leak but … other things got in the way and they didn't come to anything.'

'And the other things were?'

'Work was started on a new fish farm in Sørneset, further out in the fjord.'

'Sørnes Oppdrett, yes. What is now Sunfjord Salmon.'

'Correct.'

'So now you've gone over to them. In a way you've joined the enemy?'

'The enemy? We had the same ideas. To secure jobs in the area. To generate income for the local council and the state.'

'But they never had plans for a land-based business.'

'No, the time wasn't right for that. And the area around Sørneset isn't suitable, either.'

'You could've offered them the land you had at your disposal in Markatangen.'

'At my disposal? First off, it was Betty's property. Second, I didn't join Sunfjord until I'd already moved away from the village and established myself in town with Kleiva Invest.'

'And after you left, Klaus Krog came into the picture.'

He grimaced. 'Yes, I never met him myself, but I heard about him. In all honesty, to me he seemed like a total nonentity.'

'Nevertheless, he was a robust critic of aquaculture in general. As a journalist he'd worked for a magazine called *Jakt & Fiske*. And after moving in with Betty, he was collecting material for a book about the topic.'

'I hear what you say.'

'And he died after falling on the mountain down from Lake Stølvannet two years ago.'

'Yes, and *I* didn't push him.'

'Someone else might've done, you mean?'

'It was a joke, Veum.'

'Oh, I see. Ha ha ha.'

'As I said, I never met him, dead or alive.' After some reflection, he added: 'He was a good deal younger than her, wasn't he?'

'You're relatively well informed then?'

'It's not that I've never been to Solvik since I left. My parents are in the old folks' home in the neighbouring village, and I have to attend board meetings at Sunfjord a few times a year.'

'Speaking of which, you were there the day of the recent demonstration, the twenty-first of September. You probably remember it.'

He looked somewhat displeased. 'I remember some chimps outside the gate when we turned up for the meeting, yes.'

'Was there a confrontation between you and them?'

'Not at all. It all went off without any trouble. Security guards were called in so that we could get into the premises without any bother.'

'One of these chimps, as you call them, was your own son. Another was Mona, the daughter of Fredrik Martens. I'm sure you're aware she was found dead in Jonas's camper van.'

'I am, yes.'

'Did you know that there was something between Jonas and Mona Martens?'

'I didn't. To my knowledge, she was engaged.'

'To whom?'

He regarded me with a condescending look. 'You're the detective, aren't you?' After a suitably dramatic pause, he added: 'To Ole Lavik, the CEO of Riverbank Invest.'

'And director of the board of Sunfjord Salmon.'

He nodded.

'He led the meeting on the twenty-first of September, didn't he?'

'He did.'

'So, in other words, Mona Martens was among the demonstrators against a company her father owns and where her own fiancé is the director of the board. That must've been an odd situation.'

'Ole wasn't with us that day, so I don't know if they saw each other or not.'

'I heard she'd been with Knut Sørnes as well.'

'You've got an interesting love triangle there, Veum, you

know,' he said sarcastically. 'Knut Sørnes, Ole Lavik and Mona Martens.'

'It's not the only one, it seems.'

'No?'

I decided to change tack. 'It's my understanding that you and Jonas didn't have much contact after the divorce?'

He grimaced.

'Not even after he moved to Bergen?'

'No.'

'I mean, I've experienced a lot of fiery father-son relationships in the course of my career as—'

He glared at me. 'So? He wasn't my son!'

That stopped me in my tracks for a few seconds. 'What? But Betty said…'

'I'm sure she did. It was something we never talked about.'

'But how can you be so sure?'

'It's just something I know. I can't father children. For reasons I have no intention of discussing with you.'

'So who is Jonas's father?'

'I'm afraid you'll have to ask Betty that. I wouldn't like to comment.'

An embarrassed silence ensued, as though he had suddenly realised how personal this conversation had become.

'Did Jonas know?' He didn't respond, so I became more specific. 'That you weren't his father?'

'*I* didn't tell him, anyway.'

'But Betty and you stayed together until he was fifteen.'

'Yes, that was just how things turned out.'

There was no getting away from the fact that I had been given a lot of food for thought, but whether it brought me any closer to what had happened to Klaus Krog was a moot point.

'Fredrik Martens – do you have any kind of relationship with him?'

He shook his head. 'He's the classic *éminence grise*. Keeps in the background and mostly lives abroad. It's Ole Lavik who runs the shop for him on a day-to-day basis. I've only ever said hello to him on a couple of occasions.' He got up from his chair. 'I'm afraid I no longer have any time for this. I don't understand why I let you in even. For me this has been a complete waste of time.'

'Not for me.' I got up slowly as well. 'Thank you for being so open with me ... about all sorts of things.'

'Thank you for the visit,' he said, to make it clear we had finished. He nodded me in the direction of the door.

'Thanks again,' I said, and left.

I thanked the receptionist for her help as I passed her. She offered no response, other than a withering rosebud, which then dropped to the ground. I noticed that neither Kleiva nor his receptionist expressed a desire to see me again.

That same afternoon there was a news flash, first on the radio, then in the online newspapers. On Sunday, around the middle of the day, a body had been found in the sea, not far from Solvik in Masfjorden municipality. The deceased had not been identified as yet, but the police announced that they considered it very likely it was the young man who had been missing in the area for almost three weeks.

25

It wasn't long before I had Betty on the line. Her voice was high-pitched from the first moment and cracked several times. *'Have you heard, Varg? They've found Jonas! In the sea by Markatangen. I know it's him. Oh, my poor boy.'*

'Yes, I've just heard on the radio. Have you received confirmation that it's really him?'

She was sobbing. *'It can't be anyone else. There's no one else reported missing. Surely you realise that? It's Jonas. He's dead!'*

'Who found him?'

'Someone out walking. They found him on the shore of the fjord.'

'Have the police been in touch?'

'No, not yet. But what can they do? Klara told me.'

'Klara Kyvik?'

'It was their neighbour who found him.'

'But has he been identified?'

'Identified? I imagine Harald recognised him.'

'Harald Eide?'

'Yes, that's what I said, didn't I?' Her sobbing transmuted into painful, inconsolable weeping so she wasn't able to speak for a moment.

I waited a little, then said: 'Listen, Betty. Isn't there someone you can talk to? Someone nearby?'

'Who? They all hate me – they gossip behind my back.'

'Your parents?'

'They're so old.'

'How ol—?'

'Mentally!' she interrupted.

After the conversation I'd had with her brother, I knew I couldn't suggest him. 'But you must have some woman friends in the village?'

She breathed in. The words came slowly, but she seemed to

have more control over her voice now. *'I don't know who now. You don't understand the power Louise Sørnes has in the village, Varg.'*

'But—'

'I told you what it's about. Just the same old stuff. The argument about fish farming.'

'Yes, but in a situation like this ... It must be possible to rise above disputes when confronted with such a tragedy.'

'You don't know how deep-seated enmity can be in a village like this, Varg. The village doesn't lie on its back and wag its tail at you when a young man's found dead in the fjord. Deep down, a lot of folk will be pleased. They'll look at each other, nod and say: "The whale's spat him out, but this Jonah didn't survive. He's dead!"'

'Well, let's wait to see what the police have to say. With respect to identifying the body. They're bound to contact you. It's their duty, to all relatives.'

'If you say so...'

After a pause, I said: 'Do you still want me to see what I can find out about Klaus's death?'

Her voice was stronger now. *'Yes, I certainly do. There could be a connection. You mustn't ignore that possibility.'*

'Have you got something particular in mind?'

'The hatred between folk, Varg. Hatred and enmity over generations. I know what I'm talking about. I'm a victim of it myself. And now...' Her voice cracked. *'Yet again.'*

I had a question at the back of my mind, based on Kåre Kleiva's flat denial that he was Jonas's father. But this certainly wasn't the right moment to bring the matter up. 'Let's stay in contact, Betty. I'll continue my investigations, for the time being from Bergen, but I'll come up to Solvik as soon as I consider it necessary. In the meantime, try to find someone to talk to.'

She heaved a sigh. *'Alright then. I'll see who I can come up with. Thank you for listening to what I had to say. Talking to you helped, anyway.'*

With that, we rang off.

I went onto the Net to see if I could find anything there. The news had spread, but there were no further details, just that a body had been found in Masfjorden, near Solvik, and they assumed it was the same man who had been missing in the area for at least two weeks. Beyond that, the police were unwilling to make a public announcement until the relatives had been informed.

I definitely wasn't a relative, but I took a risk and rang the police anyway. Signe Moland was busy, I was told. When I asked if I could leave a message for her, they answered: 'What's this call about?' 'The dead body in Masfjorden.' The woman on the switchboard said she'd leave my message, and after that there was not a lot more I could do.

Moland took her time answering. It was nine in the evening when a message appeared on my mobile phone from her: Hi Varg. Could you drop by the station early tomorrow at 9.30? Ask for Solheim.

Bjarne Solheim? That didn't bode well. I permitted myself a glass of Simers to give myself strength. When I had drunk it, I had another. But I drew the line there. One for each leg, that was the rule. There was no reason to go over the top.

26

Inspector Bjarne Solheim and I had a chequered relationship. I had known him since the early 1990s. The first years had been relatively easy. Solheim had been a keen young police officer with spiky hair that made him look as if he suffered from chronic fright. Now, around forty years of age and an inspector of some years, he had shaved his head to the scalp and adopted a far tougher style. After I had escaped from custody at the police station on his watch a few years ago, I had been about as popular with him as a blood-soaked beefsteak with a vegetarian.

There was still a tinge of reserve about the way he received me, but it appeared he had calmed down. Sparks no longer flew when he caught sight of me. He proffered a wry smile when he met me at the entrance downstairs and asked me to go with him to his office on the third floor. I followed, nodding to Helleve in passing. As we entered his office, Solheim thanked me for coming in for 'an informal chat', and I noted that he didn't call it a formal interview, at least.

'About what?' I asked.

'I'm sure you've heard that a body was found in the sea in Masfjorden, near Solvik. It'll hardly come as any surprise to you when I tell you that the body's been identified. It turned out to be the missing Jonas Kleiva, whom you contacted us about earlier when he was reported missing.'

'That's good then. That he's been found, I mean. His relatives will have less to brood over.'

'Exactly.' He waited for me to follow up, but as I didn't, he went on. 'We've been given to believe that you've been investigating this case off your own bat. Could that be true?'

'No, it isn't. Who said that?'

'It's been reported by the Masfjorden police station.'

'Ah … Masfjorden police station. Well, I can disabuse you of that. What I can say is that I've been asked to undertake some enquiries regarding a different death, an incident that happened near Solvik two years ago. On the face of it, an accident. The deceased was the partner of Jonas Kleiva's mother. There were circumstances around the accident that led to this woman, Betty Kleiva, commissioning me to have a closer look.'

'I see. So you haven't been investigating the case of the woman drowned in Jonas Kleiva's camper van, or his disappearance, in any way at all?'

'I was only a casual witness. But I will admit that right at the beginning, when it was just a missing-person case, I did call on a couple of people who attended the demonstration to hear their version of things – not that anything came of it. After all, it was Edvard Aga and I who found the camper van in the water, and it was quite a shock when we heard there was a dead woman in it. A woman, it transpired later, I'd seen living and breathing only a couple of weeks before.'

He leafed through some of the papers on his desk, found the one he was looking for and looked up at me. 'On the bus from Førde, wasn't it?'

'Yes.'

'With a girlfriend.'

'Marita Svanøy.'

'You have all the details in order, I see. But you weren't investigating the case?'

'No. Although of course I've done some thinking about it. About what might be behind all this. And there are a few leads. There's a controversial fish farm in the area. The one that Jonas and his friends were demonstrating against and the subject of a critical book Klaus Krog was working on.'

'Klaus Krog?'

'The victim of the accident two years ago.'

'So, what have you found out?'

'About the case? Nothing special, so far. But as you can imagine … This fish farm, Sunfjord Salmon, is definitely an important business for parts of the local population. Solvik is a small place and people's lives criss-cross in so many ways there – family, work etc.'

He nodded slowly. 'I can believe that.' Again he shuffled through his pile of papers. 'Let me put it like this, Veum. Without going into any detail, there's now a full murder investigation under way there.'

'Really. Based on what?'

'I can't go into that, but some circumstances surrounding the body point in that direction.'

'Signs of violence?'

He looked at me with resignation in his eyes. 'As I said – no comment. But this means you – and possibly others – have to keep your distance from the work we, led officially by the chief of police in Masfjorden, will carry out.'

He interposed a pregnant pause, then continued:

'We cannot, of course, prevent you from investigating the accident you just mentioned, but should anything emerge with even the slightest connection to what happened to Jonas Kleiva and Mona Martens, you must report it to us at once. Is that understood?'

'Crystal clear.'

He eyed me sceptically. 'We know our old friends have their quirks, if you catch my drift. If I see you near any of the people we're investigating, there's a good chance you'll be arrested and driven back to Bergen in a police car.'

'Can you give me a list of the people I should avoid?' I grinned.

'Very droll.'

'It's not so unlikely that I'll contact some of the head honchos at Sunfjord Salmon again. If any of them are on your radar—'

He interrupted me. 'The whole village may be on the radar from what we know so far. It would be best if you kept right away from Solvik until the case is solved.'

'And how long will that be?'

'The Masfjorden police are already firing on all cylinders. We have forensics and detectives working in Solvik, with my colleague Signe Moland in charge. I'll join them in the course of the day, after doing some investigative work from here, so … You have been warned, Veum. Try to take on board what we've told you this time.'

He didn't say *Not like before*, but I could read it in his eyes. That was what he meant.

27

Back in my office, I sat wondering what my position now was. On the one hand, I had been given what was tantamount to a professional embargo on the issue of what had happened to Mona Mertens and Jonas Kleiva. On the other ... that embargo didn't stop me letting my thoughts run free.

The police had started a full-scale murder enquiry. They hadn't done that after finding Mona Mertens. That suggested there were unmistakeable signs of violence on Jonas Kleiva's body. Furthermore, ten days had passed between finding the camper van with Mona inside and Jonas turning up. According to Betty, Jonas had been found in the same area and on the shore of the fjord. He could have clambered out of the camper but drowned anyway. In which case, there would hardly be external traces of violence on his body, unless he had been assaulted before the vehicle plunged into the sea. Could there have been a fight between Mona and Jonas while they were inside? And had they been alone? Could there have been more passengers with them going to Markatangen? This was doubtless the question the police were asking themselves now too, with a far better awareness of the facts than I possessed.

One detail that lay grumbling away at the back of my mind was the evidence Edvard Aga and I had discovered in the Marka farmhouse, evidence that someone had stayed there overnight. Was it at all conceivable that Jonas could have survived the accident, then gone up to the house and hidden there? Were his injuries caused by more recent violence or were they from the fateful day he and Mona ended up in the sea?

I could ring the pathologist in Haukeland, of course, Tor Flaten, whom I knew peripherally from previous cases. But I also knew that he was one hundred per cent professional and wouldn't answer any questions in connection with a specific case. I didn't have any reliable sources in the police, either. The national newspapers in Oslo normally did though – unofficially, mind you, and with a fat wallet as a go-between.

What if I concentrated on what I called with a smile 'my' case? Was there anything at all that suggested what befell Klaus Krog was something other than an accident? Was there someone who wished him dead, apart from Sunfjord Salmon, about whom he was collecting damning material? A jilted lover maybe? If Betty really was as frivolous as most who mentioned her name claimed, was that a place to start looking? And if so: how discreetly? How directly?

There was yet another question thrumming away at the back of my head; one put there by my conversation with Kåre Kleiva: who was the real father of Jonas Kleiva? The challenge here was the same: how discreetly should I proceed? How directly? I still wasn't ready to confront Betty with this claim. Nonetheless, this was probably the route I would have to take in the end.

In a way I recognised in this situation something of my own position nine months ago, when I had opened a letter from the Public Health Institute and read a DNA report confirming that my biological father was the saxophonist Leif Pedersen, who was unknown to me, and not the tram conductor Anders Veum, who I had grown up with. At the age of sixty, I had a new father. It appeared that my own mother had carried this secret for all the years I had been alive and she had never confided in *me*; and barely to my father, I guessed. Whatever the truth of the situation, I had grown up with Anders Veum. In my head, he would always be my father, even if I had many of this Leif Pedersen's genes in my body.

For Jonas this was all too late, but you never knew. Could this matter of unknown paternity have played a role in what took place in Solvik – either with him, or, for that matter, with Klaus Krog?

Was there anyone else I could contact with respect to Klaus Krog? Someone who could give me a description of what he was

like as a person, beyond what I already knew? I could go to
Bergen's public library and ask if they had any old *Jakt & Fiske*
magazines available. If they had, I could go through the last ten
years' worth to gain a perspective of what he stood for, and to
see whether there were any important personalities he had interviewed over the last few years before he resigned and moved
to Solvik to write a book.

The position I found myself in was therefore still shrouded
in mist. I had no clear images of Jonas Kleiva or Klaus Krog as
people. They both seemed as vague and difficult to approach as
the third misty figure, Fredrik Martens.

I just had to admit it – I was stuck. I tried as hard as I could
to concentrate on Klaus Krog, but my mind was drawn to Mona
Martens and Jonas Kleiva and what had led to their deaths.

My ruminations were interrupted by the sudden ringing of
my phone. I quickly checked the screen before I answered. 'Hi,
Torunn.'

'Hi, Varg. Listen, is there any chance you can drive me to
Solvik tomorrow?'

'Yes, I haven't been given a travel ban yet, so…'

'What do you mean?'

'Jonas Kleiva's body has turned up.'

'Really? In the sea?'

'Yes.' I gave her a rapid summary of what I knew before con-
cluding: 'But yes, I can drive you to Solvik. What are you going
to do there?'

'Well, as expected, I had to give up trying to reach Fredrik
Martens. He's shut himself off. But I've got an appointment with
Ole Lavik. He insists we meet in Solvik, on their premises. He's
looking forward to showing me round, he says. He's convinced
that it'll give me a more nuanced view of what they're doing than
the way he thinks I see things now.'

'Mhm. And the appointment is tomorrow?'

'At twelve. They've organised a board meeting for one, but he wanted to welcome me there ahead of it. I've already booked the flight and a room in a hotel in Bergen. I could make it to Solvik under my own steam, but it would be nicer if you drove me.'

'By all means. There's someone there I'd like to talk to anyway. The police have a full-scale murder investigation under way in the village. For all I know, they also have an appointment with Ole Lavik.'

'Really?'

'He was engaged to Mona Martens.'

'I see. But…' She cleared her throat. 'When we made the arrangement, he insisted I come alone. The demonstration during the board meeting a few weeks ago has made them tighten up their security measures. They've heard rumours there are more actions planned against them, maybe even out-and-out sabotage.'

'Rumours?'

'That was the word he used.'

'Well, we'd better keep ourselves informed. Which hotel have you booked a room in?'

'The one where your office is.'

'And when do you arrive?'

'Last flight of the evening. I won't be at the hotel before ten-thirty, I fear.'

'Still time to grab a glass of wine at the bar.'

'I think that will have to wait until the next time, Varg. We have to leave by nine at the latest, and I need all the hours of sleep I can get.'

'I don't intend to deprive you of your beauty sleep.'

'No?' She paused, then rounded off: 'See you at nine then. Is that a deal?'

'It's a deal,' I said, and held the phone for a while as if not wishing to break the connection, even though she had rung off some time before.

28

She gave me a hug before we got into the car. In the nine years that had elapsed since I last saw her, in Vigra, near Ålesund, her facial features had become sharper and her hair had turned grey. But she looked both alert and supple, and radiated a kind of concentrated energy. She was wearing tight blue jeans, a black leather jacket and a tartan shawl in brown and green, so big that she could pull it over her head and even hang out with Islamic extremists, if she should meet any in Masfjorden.

'You haven't changed, Varg,' she said with a smile.

'Hmm,' I said, stroking my hair, which was also quite grey now.

She slung a rucksack onto the back seat. 'Emergency rations, in case we get caught out by the weather,' she grinned.

'I have my own in the boot,' I replied.

We both got into the front. I indicated and then pulled out. For traffic reasons we bypassed the Møhlenpris district and the Fløyfjell tunnel and then headed for Solvik and the valleys beyond. I followed the E39 via Romarheim and turned off for Solvik at the same intersection where I had seen Jonas, Mona and Marita a good three weeks ago now.

During the journey we updated each other on what had happened since we were last together. We established that we were both single – 'for the moment' – as she expressed it. It didn't take long before another kind of togetherness developed on the front seat. That was the strange thing. With some people years can pass between the times you meet and yet it is as if it has only been a few days.

It wasn't that, however, which currently occupied her attention. 'A source has told me it could be a heated meeting there today.'

'A source?'

'Yes, apparently Kåre Kleiva has some pretty stern criticism of the way the fish farm is run, and the meeting is likely to see a real showdown between the main shareholders.'

'But Fredrik Martens and his companies hold the majority of the shares.'

'Yes, but on crucial decisions they need at least a two-thirds majority, and it's a moot point whether they have that. Kåre Kleiva's companies have ten per cent. Masfjorden council has five. Cecile Tangen holds twenty per cent, and the others have fourteen. Among them are the ex-owner and the CEO, Einar and Knut Sørnes.'

'Nice. I've had the dubious pleasure of meeting the Sørneses myself, both father and son, and they're definitely on Fredrik Martens' side. I've also met Kåre Kleiva. He's been at logger-heads with the company before. But they all say how important the development of the industry is for all our futures.'

'Mmm,' she commented. 'It can't be denied that there's an acute need for increased food production around the world. And most people agree that food from the sea is more sustainable than from cattle, for example. So it shouldn't come as a surprise that the seafood business is one of the world's fastest-growing indus-tries, setting up shop everywhere that's feasible. But it comes with its own problems. One of them is that fish need feed, and where does that come from? From natural resources that otherwise would have been used for humans, of course. For example, one of the main ingredients in fish feed is soya, and growing soya de-stroys the rain forest and the savannah in Brazil. And that has serious consequences for the climate across the whole globe.'

'They claim that the fish industry is what we'll live off when oil is gradually phased out.'

'Yeah, great. They also claim they're maintaining *and* creating new jobs. And, of course, they are. But that'll lead to the destruc-tion of other jobs. If aquaculture is sited in areas that are spawning

grounds for wild fish, there'll be smaller catches for the sea fisher-
men, who've provided the main source of Norway's nutrition
since the dawn of time. Look how the shrimp stocks have fallen.
Not to mention how many fish die while they're being bred. The
animal welfare has been abysmal. If you look at the percentage of
dead fish and think of all the feed they've had while growing,
we're talking about an enormous waste of resources that could
otherwise have been used for human consumption.'

'I see you've come well armed with arguments for the
meeting with Ole Lavik.'

'Oh, yes, but I'm trying to think constructively too. If the
seafood industry is to be sustainable, it has to become more circular. They're working to develop feed from the insects and sand
hoppers produced by food waste, and from the yeast protein
grown on wood off-cuts, or even microalgae living on climate
gases. If they're successful, production from aquaculture will
have achieved a balance. And there's another thing – all these
new farms are only being built to increase the companies'
income even further. Not to provide more food. With the profit
the seafood industry makes now, they could lean back and enjoy
the status quo. But this is where the laws of capitalism kick in.
Every arm of the fjord has to be filled with new farms, and the
result is over-production, which does not bode well for anyone
except those with the right shares on the stock exchange.'

'Fredrik Martens and the like, based in tax havens outside any
national borders.'

'For example.'

After we had branched off the E39, she fell silent. A few times
she moved closer to the windscreen and peered up at the mountainsides. 'Fantastic views,' she said.

'And down there you can see the fjord. On the headland there
is Sunfjord Salmon.' I glanced at the clock on the dashboard.
'Time's getting a bit tight.'

Through Solvik a morning stillness prevailed. Not a soul around. I turned off for Sørnes. After five minutes I parked outside the gate to the fish farm. There were more cars than when I was last here. The gate was open and guarded by two uniformed men. Inside there were two more cars, a black Mercedes Benz and a military-green van.

I turned to Torunn. 'Sure you don't want to have a bodyguard with you?'

She smiled wryly. 'I'll just have to hope I emerge with my brain intact.'

'In that case I'm going back to Solvik to chat with some people there, if I can find them. Text me when you've been given the boot.'

'You have great faith in my diplomatic abilities, I can see.' After a pause she added: 'I'm here to listen, primarily. Listen and take notes.' She plucked a notebook from her jacket pocket and held it up in front of me.'

'That's usually my method as well.'

'Ah, so maybe we're twin souls in the way we work too.' She leaned forward and brushed her lips against my cheek. 'Thanks for the lift. See you.'

She opened the door and swung her legs onto the tarmac. I watched her leave. After she showed her ID to the guards, one of them pointed her in the direction of the office building, and with a little wave to me she walked off.

Once she was in the building, I drove out of the car park and back the way we had come. The plan was to pay a call on Betty. But I stopped somewhere else first.

29

The red sign outside the local store reminded me that this was also Solvik's post office. Inside, it wasn't very busy this Wednesday in the middle of October. The only person there was the owner himself, who popped out from the back room like a mole from under the ground to see what was going on.

'Ah, our man from Bergen's back in Solvik, is he? Cup of coffee, Veum?'

'That'd be wonderful.'

'Bite to eat, too, perhaps?'

'There was nothing wrong with the rolls you served last time I was here.'

He nodded contentedly. *'Take a pew by the window and I'll serve coffee first and the rest afterwards.'*

I sat down at the same table as before. Outside, it was as quiet as when I drove through half an hour ago. But if I craned my neck, I could see some heads bobbing up and down in the schoolyard, where I thought I could also see Louise Sørnes, a giraffe-head higher than the others, probably checking that everything was as it should be during the break.

Stein Solvik arrived with a cup of steaming coffee. *'It's been quite eventful since you were here last.'*

'So I understand. Do you know any more details about what they found?'

'Mm ... It was one of the young fellas in the village who was on a Sunday hike. Harald Eide.'

'Isn't he the one who found Klaus Krog too, along with Nils Kyvik?'

'That's right, but this time Harald was alone.'

'The police have launched a full-scale murder investigation. I suppose that means there was something about the state of the body that alerted them?'

He stared at me with concern on his face. *'Yes, that's how I interpreted it. I saw the chief of police here, too. Doesn't sound like a pleasant business.'*

'No.'

A thoughtful silence arose, as though we were both wondering what the body looked like. Then he clapped his hands and exclaimed: *'Food's on the way. I'll make you your rolls.'* With that, he disappeared behind the counter and into the back room.

When he returned, he was carrying a plate with two rolls cut in half, two halves with brown cheese on and two with ham. In his other hand, he was holding a flask of coffee. *'Refill?'*

'Yes, please. Do you know what the police are doing?'

'They're making house-to-house enquiries. Officers from Masfjorden and detectives from Bergen. They've turned the chapel into their HQ, so if there's a queue outside as you walk past, they're not the faithful, but potential witnesses.' He looked at me with curiosity in his eyes. *'Are you investigating the case, too?'*

'No, no. That's a police job. I'm still looking into what happened to Klaus Krog. By the way, it would be useful to have a chat with Harald Eide. Is he still on leave from the North Sea?'

'I'm sure he is. I saw him yesterday, coming out of Betty's place.'

'Betty's place?'

'Yes, he's an electrician by trade, you know. If anyone has a problem with their electricity or anything electrical, Harald's their first port of call.'

'Apropos Betty – the first time I came here, you made a pretty brazen comment about her. You said she ate men for breakfast.'

'Yes, well…' He did look a little ashamed of himself. *'That's the way I am. Open my mouth first and think afterwards.'*

'But I suppose you had a reason for saying that, all the same?'

He hesitated. *'It's the rate she gets through men. It's a bit more frequent than is usual in this area.'*

'OK. But to be fair, the first was a natural death, even though he was young. The second was a divorce, which is not exactly uncommon in our times, either. In some circles far more natural than death, dare I say. And the third was apparently an accident, with a wavy line under *accident*.'

He was still not quite on my wavelength. '*Alright, seen from Bergen it might not be so unusual, but...*'

'Are there others on the list?'

I could see he was dying to tell me more. His lips were quivering and his tongue protruded between his front teeth like an inquisitive rodent. Although there was no one but the two us there, he lowered his voice to a remarkably low, confidential level, as if to protect himself against anyone within earshot. '*You know, in a little village like this you can't go anywhere without someone noticing, however late at night. Especially then, you could say. It wouldn't be a huge lie to say that after Mons Marken died, Einar Sørnes paid Betty regular evening visits.*'

'But hadn't they fallen out?'

'*Fallen in, more like – into bed with each other,*' he said, chuckling at his own wordplay. He hastened to add: '*Yes, officially they were on opposing sides in the great village dispute, but they knew each other from before too, even if Einar got the short straw when Mons appeared on the scene...*'

'Yes, I remember you mentioned that.'

'*Perhaps what they were doing was a form of negotiation? But it stopped abruptly once Louise heard the rumours. There hasn't been a louder proclamation in the village since the doomsday priest spoke at the chapel in the early 1970s. After that Einar stayed at home in the evenings, and Louise and Betty haven't exchanged a word since, to my knowledge. They walk past each other as if each of them were air.*'

'Any other candidates?'

'*No. You know, there have never been many places to stay in Solvik. I have my cabins here, and she has her rooms over there.*

Staying with Betty is more appealing than at mine, I know – she has meals and red wine, even if it's a weekday, whereas the service here is little more low-key, if I can put it like that. Some of her guests come back year after year, I think.'

'And what type of guests are we talking about?'

'Travellers of various kinds, from sales reps to tourists. Anglers, for as long as there was life in the fjord.'

'And she ate them all for breakfast?'

Now his eyes went walkabout. *'Well, what do I know? It was just a rumour going round. And I suppose Kåre Kleiva didn't get fed up for no reason.'*

'I have a very different impression of Betty, regardless of what you or Kåre Kleiva may think of her.'

'Have you spoken to Kåre, too?'

'I met him a couple of days ago, yes.'

The door opened. And in walked Edvard Aga. He nodded to me. 'Right. I thought I saw your car parked outside. Any new developments?'

'Not really. But so much is happening here.'

'You know Betty from way back, don't you, Edvard?' Stein Solvik interceded.

'Betty? Why do you ask?'

'Well, this detective here is making enquiries.'

Aga looked at me. 'Not that well. She lived in a room at my parents' place in Bergen when she went to the agricultural college in Stend, so I said hi a few times. Even then I was keen on fishing, and it was her who lured me up here, telling me how much fish there was in the fjord. But several years passed before I actually came, and a lot had happened in her life in the meantime. Then I rented a room in Betty and Kåre's house until I bought a plot up here and built my own cabin.'

'Around 1985, wasn't it?'

'Yes.'

'I remember we talked about that. But neither of you told me her brother was the mayor of the municipality.'

'Mayor?' Aga said, looking at Solvik. 'Betty's brother?'

'Yes, you must know that, after all the years you've lived here? It's true he and Betty aren't on speaking terms, but it's general knowledge in these parts.'

'Well, it's news to me. I barely know his name.'

'Truls Hatlevik,' I said.

'Have you spoken to him, too?' Solvik asked.

I chose to answer that question with a mute smile, otherwise the gossip would have probably spread around the village faster than a cold around a nursery.

'I take it you'd like a cup of coffee and two rolls as well, Edvard?'

Aga nodded and Solvik left to carry out his order.

Aga sat down at my table and looked at me again. 'What's on the agenda then?'

'Not much except I'm trying to get an idea of Betty Kleiva's circle of acquaintances, inasmuch as they may have some bearing on my investigations into Klaus Krog's death.'

'Have you got any further?'

'Not much further than when I last saw you. I've spoken to the police officer who investigated the accident at the time, and I've met Betty's brother, who's the local mayor, not that I learned much more than what Solvik just said. They haven't spoken for the last twenty years, according to him.'

'Twenty years? Is it any wonder then that I've never heard of him? Must be an odd family.'

'Everyone tells me that Betty is the black sheep. Is that your impression, too?'

'Black sheep? Because of what, exactly?'

'Well, that's the point. Even Solvik here casts her as some kind of *femme fatale*, as they say in nynorsk.'

'A *femme fatale*?' He seemed to be chewing on the words and they appeared to leave him with a bitter taste in his mouth. 'That's never been my impression.'

'Nor mine.'

'When I met her at my parents', she seemed modest and reserved, if you ask me. But, you know, in places like this ... the small-town mentality we Norwegians know as the village beast never sleeps, and especially not at night. Neither Kåre nor Betty were regular chapel-goers. Let's put it like that.'

'Betty said something similar when I spoke to her at the weekend.'

Stein Solvik re-emerged from the back room, with coffee and rolls for Aga and a refill for me. He stood leaning against the wall while looking out of the window, as though spying for more customers.

'You heard that they'd found Jonas, did you?' I said to Aga as he rounded on the first half of a roll.

'Oh, yes. Harald Eide says hi and told me to tell you they had. I just met him in the street.'

'Oh?' I glanced at Solvik. 'What did he have to say?'

'Well...' Aga hesitated. 'It was him who found Jonas in the fjord.'

'And now the police have launched a full-scale murder investigation.'

'Yes, can't miss that. Half the village has been turned upside down.'

'Not without reason.'

'No. If Harald Eide's word is to be trusted, Jonas had a nasty gash on his forehead, as if someone had hit him with a rock. And one more thing: it didn't look as if he'd been in the water for weeks, he said.'

'Then I can understand why the police have reacted the way they have. That makes me wonder ... We both saw that someone had been staying in the Marka farmhouse when we were there

on Thursday last week. We both felt – I did anyway – Jonas
could've been hiding there, for some reason.'

Aga nodded and swallowed without answering.

'There can be two explanations for that. One is that another
person, or other persons, may have pushed the camper van into
the water, but Jonas managed to clamber out and swim ashore.
Then he went up to the house and hid there, away from possible
enemies.'

'*Sounds very dramatic,*' Solvik commented.

'The other is that Jonas himself was responsible for driving
into the sea and then lay low, either suffering from a guilty conscience or because he would have to answer for what he'd
done.'

'*Responsible? What do you mean? That he just drove into the sea
with the girl beside him?*'

Aga took a mouthful of his coffee. 'Do you know if the
vehicle had been tampered with – something technical, I mean
– that would've led to him losing control of it, or if the brakes
had failed?'

'No idea. The police might know, but they've said nothing to
the press. I doubt they would though, for strategic reasons.'

'*The girl who died, she was the daughter of Fredrik Martens,
wasn't she?*' Solvik said. '*If in some way Jonas was the cause of her
death, he'd be in real trouble – for several reasons.*'

'Enough for him to keep a low profile, you mean?'

'He couldn't hide for ever, though,' Aga said, setting about
the second roll.

'No, and we don't know, of course, if it *was* him staying up
there.'

'Have you told the police what we found?'

'No, but I should. Someone should check the house for fingerprints at least.' I stared out of the window. 'Does either of you
know where they are now?'

'Try the chapel, Veum,' Solvik said. 'I'm sure you'll see some of them there.'

'If you don't, I will,' Aga said.

'No, I'll do it.' I drained my coffee cup and stood up. 'I'm used to getting hauled over the coals by them, so one more time won't make any difference.'

30

The chapel was classically furnished. At one end of the room there was a simple lectern. On the wall to the left there was a large picture of Jesus welcoming his flock with open arms. At the front the pews had been moved aside and the police had assembled some kitchen tables in a kind of square. Officers were sitting on both sides of the tables, their laptops in front of them.

As I entered, three faces turned to me. Chief of Police Sætenes remained seated, but both Hans Hosteland and Signe Moland stood up. Signe said something to the other two and came to meet me, while Hosteland sat back down behind his computer. Both men from Masfjorden police station watched Signe make her way over and seemed to be silently following our conversation, as far as they were able.

'Varg, what are you doing here?'

'I'm here on a case. I thought Solheim had informed you.'

'He did say, yes. But he also said he'd told you to keep well away from our investigation.'

'And I really intended to do that. But he also told me to inform you if anything came up that had any relevance to what you were doing.'

'And you have something to give us?'

'Yes. That is ... there was something I'd forgotten to mention when he and I were talking yesterday.'

'Uhuh,' she replied with an ironic undertone. 'And what was it you forgot to mention?'

'I have an idea that when Jonas was found, there was no indication that he'd been in the water long.'

'Really? And where did you get this idea?'

'Well, there have been rumours ... And then I remembered: in connection with the case I've been asked to look into – a death that occurred two years ago – Edvard Aga, whom you met last time you were here, took me up to a farmhouse in the mountains further down the fjord. There was no one inside, but there were clear signs that someone had been staying there very recently. Both Aga and I suspected that the person or persons staying there was, or were, hiding from us. We both had a feeling we were being watched as we left.'

'Mhm?' She was the very model of taciturnity, and I knew very well why.

'So when I heard Jonas had been found, and it was clear he hadn't died along with Mona Mertens but later, it struck me it could've been him staying in the house.'

'And what would his motive have been?'

'Well, you tell me.' I smiled disarmingly. 'I'll leave that to the official enquiry to answer. If I were in charge, I'd send someone up to the farmhouse and check it for prints. If you should find some matching Jonas's, at least you'll know he's been there.'

She nodded slowly as she scrutinised me with narrowing eyes. 'Anything else you've forgotten to tell us?'

'Not that I can recall,' I said, essaying another tentative smile.

She watched me with a resigned expression on her face. 'Right, thank you for coming here. I'll have to get back to what we were doing when you decided to pay us a call.'

I looked around. 'You know, there's something about chapels. I think I have some genes from them, too. My mother came from that kind of milieu, down in Ryfylke, many, many years ago.'

'We can have that conversation at our next family reunion, Varg.'

'I'm afraid it'll have to be you and me doing the invitations, Signe.'

She smiled politely, nodded towards the door, turned and went back to the two Masfjorden officers. The looks they sent me made me feel like the townie who'd had a whirl on the dance floor with the prettiest girl in the village and now knew what I had coming to me once I was outside and they had me 'round the back', as they put it in these parts.

31

I didn't want to risk being subjected to that, so I crossed the street from the chapel and headed for the house opposite the school, where I had spoken to Nils Kyvik the last time I was in Solvik. I was told Harald Eide lived next door. But when I looked at the nameplate on that house, one along from the local store, I saw a different name. Across the street, however, I struck gold. Its nameplate bore a single name: *Eide*.

I rang the doorbell. After a while I heard footsteps inside. The door opened and a young man stood in the doorway. He was wearing what I would call a track suit. It was black with white stripes down the sleeves and legs. On his chest was a logo, *SIL*, which I assumed stood for Solvik Idrettslag – Solvik Sports Club. He looked to be in relatively good shape too – a strong guy, with a broad face and such a short haircut that it bordered on shaven.

'Harald Eide?'

'That's me.' There was something tense about him, as though he feared an unpleasant message or something he couldn't say no to.

'My name's Veum. Varg Veum. I'm looking into what happened to Klaus Krog two years ago.'

'OK.' For some reason he seemed relieved. *'What ... Who are you? Are you from the police?'*

'No, I'm a private investigator, commissioned by Betty Kleiva.'

'Betty?'

'Yes, she was living with him when he ... died. You were at hers yesterday, I gather.'

He looked at me in surprise. *'Who told you that?'*

I shrugged.

'It was just an outside light she wanted fixing before the winter

darkness sets in, and I'm an electrician, so folk ring me if there is any-thing needs doing.'

'Is there somewhere we can sit and chat?'

His shoulders twitched. *'Chat? Erm…'* He cast a long look in both directions before opening the door wider. *'You'd better come into the sitting room. It's only me at home. My mother had to take my dad to the doctor in Bergen.'*

'Nothing serious, I hope.'

'Mm. Some investigations. He's been better, let me put it like that.'

I followed him in. He stopped in the hallway and looked down at my shoes. I removed them and placed them tidily before carrying on in. He was wearing classic West Norwegian bootie slippers.

We came into a room with an obvious parlour feel, as though in this house they mainly stayed in the kitchen, as so many others like them did. A dark, shiny wooden dining table was sur-rounded by six high-backed chairs in the same wood, with rose-pattern upholstery on the seat and back. On the walls there were home-woven rugs, also in patterns reminiscent of old, tra-ditional craftsmanship. On one wall there was a tastefully arranged collection of family photos, many of them in black, oval frames and with a sepia tone, which gave them a special patina. In one corner there were two golden-brown armchairs either side of a small table with a red azalea in a dark-brown vase on a rosette mat crocheted in a Hardanger pattern.

Harald Eide showed me to this corner. He pointed to one chair and sat down in the other.

'What would you like to ask about?'

'I spoke to your neighbour, Nils Kyvik, last time I was here. You were together when you found Klaus Krog, he said.'

'Yes, we were. That's right.'

'Please tell me what happened.'

'What happened? It all started when Betty came to the door

and said that Krog had gone missing, and she wondered whether anyone from the village could help search for him. It was a Sunday, I remember. Well, both Nils and I are volunteer firefighters for the village, and she'd already spoken to him, she said. Could we go up to Lake Stølsvatnet and look for him? It's a steep climb up there and back down, and she was scared he might've had a fall and hurt himself, she said. And that appeared to be exactly what'd happened.'

'OK.'

'We found him at the bottom of the steep slope up to the lake, with a nasty injury to his forehead, where he'd hit a rock, we guessed.'

'Did you see the rock?'

'There's no shortage of rocks. So it was a strong possibility. I've done a first-aid course, so I thought I should try to do whatever I could, but we saw at once that he was dead. We told Betty first and then the emergency doctor. They sent an ambulance, but all they could do was confirm that he was dead and call the police, and an hour later an officer by the name of Hosteland showed up.'

'Yes, I've met him.'

'I see. Why have you come to see me then?'

'You might think it's a bit funny, but first impressions count for so much. Was there anything that caught your eye?'

'No ... What sort of thing? It was dramatic enough finding a body. From what we could see it looked like it was a tragic accident.'

'Hosteland said the two of you had moved the body.'

'Moved? We turned him over in the hope that we could help him, but that was when we saw the ugly gash to his head. That was all we did.'

'And you didn't meet anyone on the way up?'

'Meet anyone? Who for example?'

'Well ... anyone who was out searching for him, maybe?'

'No, we didn't see anyone. And there were no parked cars. There's

just the one path up to Markatangen and further on, so if anyone had been there, we would've seen them.'

I nodded and ruminated. 'This is not the only body you've found though.'

He clenched his lips and breathed audibly through his nose. After a moment of thought, he opened his mouth again. *'You're referring to the events on Sunday?'*

I nodded.

'I don't know what I can say about that. The police told me not to say anything to anyone.'

'They're undoubtedly thinking about the press and suchlike,' I said, crystal clear in my own mind that I myself would be included in the 'suchlike'. 'But this time you were alone?'

'Yes.' With a suspicious look in his eye, he said: *'Have you heard any different?'*

'Not at all. I only know he was found in the sea.'

'Yes,' he said sullenly, firmly pressing his lips together.

'Did you know him? Jonas, I mean.'

It was taking him time to answer, I could see. *'...I knew who he was. But he was a bit younger than me, and of course he'd moved to Bergen, so he was only at home during the summer, I think.'*

'Or to demonstrate against the farm on Sørneset.'

He rolled his shoulders as if to express what he thought about that.

'Where do you stand in the debate?'

'What debate?'

'For or against Sunfjord Salmon.'

'I don't give a shit what these townie kids think about it. I myself work in an industry they would close down as soon as they could. Without a thought for how this country would've been if we hadn't found oil at the bottom of the sea thirty years ago. Surely it's the same with the fishing industry? That's what we're going to live off when the oil runs out, isn't it.'

'That's what they say, and they're laughing all the way to the bank, I've heard.' As he didn't react, I carried on: 'So you weren't exactly on the same wavelength as Jonas then.'

'I don't give a flying fart about Jonas! He was six or seven years younger than me and I don't think I've ever spoken to him, from what I can remember.'

'Mona Martens then. Did you know her?'

He sent me an uncomprehending look. *'The girl in the van that Jonas drove into the sea? Where would I know her from?'*

'Marita Svanøy?'

'What the hell is this? Some kind of quiz? What are you chuntering on about?'

'Well, you know what it's like with us townies. Gobs always open. He hadn't been in the water long, I was told.'

'No, he hadn't. He was lying on the shore, like he'd just fallen asleep in the water. Face down.'

'Did you turn him over as well?'

'We did, yes, but we saw at once…' he bit his tongue before finishing the sentence: *'…that he was dead.'*

I let this hang in the air between us before querying: 'We?'

'I, I mean,' he snarled, the top of his cheeks flushed.

'Who were you with?'

He made a move to get up. *'I was alone. I told you! Didn't you hear what I said?'*

'I heard you say it, yes. That the two of you found him in the sea, as though he'd only just washed up.'

This time he did get to his feet. He turned to me, puffing himself up to his full height, and breadth, flexing his biceps in my face. *'I don't think you and I have anything more to talk about, Ve— … whatever your name is.'*

'Veum.'

'The door's over there.' He pointed.

I slowly rose to my feet. 'I can see it is.'

While I put on my shoes in the hallway, I looked up at him. 'I assume you've told the police?'

'Told the police what?' he barked.

'Who you were with when you two found him.'

'You're asking for it now, Veum.'

'"It" is what's waiting for you, if they find out before you tell them.' And I flexed my muscles too, as far as I was able. I could see that he was on the point of exploding.

He opened the door for me, and I walked past, on my guard in case he thought it a good opportunity to wallop me in the back on my way out.

As I walked from the gate to the road, Knut Sørnes came running up at full speed. On seeing me, he stopped. He stood glaring furiously at me as I approached.

'What the hell are you doing here?'

'I might ask you the same.'

'Harald and I are old school pals.'

'So you're the person he was with when you found Jonas?'

His face tautened. Then he shifted his gaze to Harald Eide, who was standing in the doorway with an irresolute expression on his face. Sørnes opened his mouth to speak, but held back. Finally, he said: 'I have no idea what you're talking about.'

'Shouldn't you be at the board meeting?'

'I'm not on the board.'

'Is it still going on? I have a friend there.'

'The newspaper woman? She's waiting for the meeting to finish so that she can interview anyone who wants to talk. I had the pleasure of showing her around, together with Ole Lavik. I think she was impressed by what she saw.'

I had my own view on that. However, I knew Torunn Tafjord better than he did.

He hesitated. Then he walked past me. Before he reached Harald Eide, I heard him say something. As he had his back to me, I couldn't make out what it was, but the intonation sounded aggressive. My guess was something along the lines of: *What the hell did you tell him?*

For an instant or two I wondered if I should amble back to the chapel to tip off the detectives about the new information. But it struck me that I should keep a low profile around anything connected with Jonas Kleiva, so I decided to continue up the street to Betty's. I had more than enough to fill my time with while Torunn was in Sørneset waiting for the board meeting to finish.

Betty saw me coming from the kitchen window and was standing in the doorway when I arrived. I had barely crossed the threshold when she wrapped her arms around me and leaned against my chest. *'Oh, Varg! I'm so glad you've come.'*

At least here there was no doubt that I was welcome.

32

She sobbed into my shirt. I held her tight and stroked her back, waiting for her to calm down.

'I can see this is a heavy blow for you,' I said into her hair. The old social worker was awakened in me. 'Let's sit down and talk about it. Talking always helps.'

Eventually her crying subsided and she released me from her firm grip. Warily, I let her go, still holding her upper arm as I looked down into her tear-stained face. It was puffy from crying. Her lips were trembling, and she had dark bags under her eyes.

In a voice racked with tiny sobs she said: *'I don't know what I'm going to do. I have nothing left now.'*

I chose the parish-priest approach. 'Let's make a cup of coffee. Then we can have a chat about it.'

She nodded and wriggled free. *'I've got some freshly brewed coffee in the pot.'*

I followed her into the kitchen. She had half a cup by the chair where she had been sitting when she saw me through the window. On a plate there was a slice of half-eaten buttered bread. She looked up at me apologetically. *'I tried to eat something, but could only get down a couple of mouthfuls.'*

She took a cup from the cupboard, put it in front of the chair on the opposite side of the table, fetched the Thermos from the worktop and filled my cup. *'Are you hungry?'*

'No, thanks. It can wait.'

She plodded back to her chair and sat down. I did the same.

'Everything seems so black. Jonas is all I can think about, lying there in the fjord, as if spat up by the sea, lifeless, destroyed.'

'I've just come from Harald Eide. As I'm sure you know, he's the one who found him.'

'Harald's a good lad. He was here yesterday fixing the outside light for me.'

'Did he tell you anything about what he saw?'

'Yes and no. Not in detail. He wanted to spare me, he said. But the police have been here and … My understanding is Jonas had a head injury, just like…' She sobbed. *'Klaus.'*

'Yes, and that's still the death I'm investigating. Or I am allowed to investigate, to be precise. What happened to Jonas is police business.'

She looked at me. *'But it's strange, don't you think, that they were both killed in the same way?'*

'It's food for thought, certainly. I hope the police see it that way, too.'

'If they find out who did this to Jonas, they should ask them where they were when Klaus died.'

'Them?'

'Well, him then!'

'Did Harald say anything about why he was down by the fjord?'

'He was just out on a Sunday walk, to get some air to his brain, as he put it. Then he caught sight of something – or someone – bobbing up and down by the shore, and it was…' Again her voice broke. *'Jonas.'*

'And he was alone when he found him?'

'That was my understanding. What are you getting at?'

'Nothing in particular. It's my nature. I get fixated on details. I like to have everything at my fingertips.'

'But worst of all is that we parted on such bad terms. We never really had a chance to talk things through properly.'

'You're thinking about Jonas now?'

'Yes. I'll admit one thing: I've not been completely honest with you, Varg. I didn't tell you what happened when Jonas came here that day. With the girl, Mona Martens.'

'Oh?'

'I think … no, I know, that he wanted to show her off to me, in a

way, because I'd nagged him so much to get a girlfriend. But it just led to a row in the end.'

'Why was that?'

'I . . . I don't want to talk about that. It was private.'

'You've commissioned me to do a job, Betty. That means you mustn't keep things back from me. At least not if they have any significance for the case you've asked me to look into.'

'It was between Jonas and me – and barely that. We didn't talk it through properly, him and me, and I don't see why I should tell you what we argued about.'

'Sure?'

She shrugged and sent me a melancholy look. Like two synchronised swimmers we raised our cups of coffee to our mouths and drank, she slightly faster than I, so the illusion was broken when we put them back down again.

After a short pause I chose a new angle. 'I spoke to your ex-husband, Kåre, a few days ago.'

She watched me and waited.

'He'd never met Klaus Krog, he said.'

'No, that may well be true.'

'But he was up here a good deal, as he sits on the board of Sunfjord Salmon.'

'Yes, I know. He joined the enemy after we split up.'

'On the same board as the mayor of Masfjorden. Your brother, Truls Hatlevik.'

'I know his name,' she almost barked.

'But you aren't in contact, I understand.'

'Haven't been for many years. They broke contact with me, my parents and Truls, a long time ago.'

'Do you know why?'

'Well, for my mother and father I wasn't religious enough, but what was in Truls's mind, I don't know. You'll have to ask him, if you're curious.'

'I've met him already, and ... well, he's probably in agreement with your parents.'

'I suppose he is, for all the good that may do him. They don't have much property. I'm sure they've disinherited me.'

'I doubt that's possible under today's laws, so far as I know. You definitely have a right to an obligatory inheritance. But with regard to that...'

'Yes?' She sent me a provocative glare. 'Are you wondering who will inherit from me, now that my heir's dead?'

'I'm no lawyer – by any stretch of the imagination – but I assume that Kåre and you changed your wills when you divorced?'

'There wasn't much to change. I had all the assets I'd inherited when Mons died. We had separate estates, so he didn't get much ... Poor soul.' I could see a smile playing on her lips.

'But if you haven't written a will, it'll go to your brother and parents, perhaps?'

'You can bet your life I'm going to write a will. If for no one else, then for the Association of the Blind, all of it. So they can put that in their pipes and smoke it.' After another tense silence, she added: 'Was there anything else you wanted to know?'

'We-ell, your ex-husband came out with a pretty bold and un-equivocal statement when we spoke.'

Her face tautened again. The short outburst of unbridled emotion was over. 'Oh, yes? And that was...?'

'He said he definitely was not Jonas's father.'

Her eyes wandered and she paled. Then she refocused on me. 'So he said that, did he? To you?'

'He didn't mince his words. And he didn't go into detail, but he asserted it was impossible for him to father children.'

'And you believed him?' she countered.

'Erm, I had no reason to believe he was making it up. It explained his lack of contact with Jonas after he moved out. Are you saying he was lying to me?'

She stared into the distance as though reflecting. In the end, she said in a low voice, *'No, I don't suppose he was.'*

I hesitated before continuing. 'But I imagine you have a clear idea who the real father is?'

Her voice crackled with anger and sarcasm: *'Yes, I do. Fancy that. I wasn't sleeping with half the village as some folk like to believe.'*

'But it was someone from the village?'

As she didn't answer at once, I added gently: 'Someone told me Einar Sørnes was courting you here for a while.'

She went both white and red at the same time, as though someone was flicking a switch on and off inside her. *'Who the …? Has that Louise been spouting off again? I could kill her.'*

'No, it wasn't her.'

'I know what they say about me in the village. And it's absolutely true that Einar Sørnes was hanging about around here at one point. At first, I had my own ideas about why, because I doubted he got much action in bed with that stiff old baggage of his. But I soon discovered that wasn't why he came. This was after Mons had died, so what he was after was Markatangen and all the property there. And it wasn't peanuts he was offering, either, I can tell you. But I refused point blank. With Mons barely in his grave, I couldn't have lived with my conscience if I'd sold the land to his worst enemy. So that's the explanation for that, Varg.'

'But when—'

Then the dam burst. *'Why do you think I argued with Jonas that day? It wasn't over nothing. He came here with that girl, and I tried to restrain myself for as long as she was here. But just as they were about to go, I asked him to stay a bit longer, on his own. It had given me such a jolt when he told me her name, so … Anyway, once she was outside, I told him he should keep as far away from her as possible. He went crazy. I'd never seen him like it before. The situation got totally out of control. One word led to another. "Why?" he kept* saying again and again. I really hadn't intended to tell him like this, in the middle of a terrible row, but in the end it just came out ... As he left, he told me I should forget any ideas I had about ruling his life – he was free of me, once and for all. And then he slammed the door and that ... that was the last I saw of him. Those were the last words we exchanged before he ... well, you know.'

'If I've interpreted you correctly, Jonas's father was...'

She met my gaze with a defiant stare, like a small child who has finally got her way. Then with a tiny nod of her head she said: 'Fredrik Martens.'

33

I said gently: 'I think you'll have to explain this to me.'

She looked at me with resignation in her eyes. *'There's not that much to explain. It only happened once, but that was enough to make me ... pregnant.'*

'But how did you meet him?'

'It was the summer of 1983. You've already met Edvard. Edvard Aga. He rented a room here with Kåre and me before he built his own cabin, which was finished a few years later. He and Fredrik Martens were friends from their schooldays, apparently. That summer he came here with Fredrik to try the fishing by Storfossen. The first time they were both here, but some weeks later Fredrik came here again – on his own. Kåre was travelling, and one evening, after a little too much red wine, what should never have happened, of course happened. It did. And some months later, when I realised the condition I was in, I contacted him. But he brushed me off and said it must be a mistake. He was married and already had a daughter, so I shouldn't try anything because he was well connected. Yes – that daughter! I wonder if you can imagine how I felt, how ashamed I was? I just had to put on a brave face, as folk say. Then I told Kåre that I was pregnant ... That was when he told me how things were with him. And when he heard who the father was...'

'Yes, I'd like to hear a bit more about that.'

'Well, he seemed to calm down. At the beginning I was afraid he would contact Fredrik himself, but I don't think he ever did. It was as if he accepted the situation. And then when Jonas was born, it was his turn to put on a brave face.'

'So who's registered as the official father?'

'Kåre.'

'In other words, there's no documentation in black and white, and of course no DNA test, to confirm who the biological father is.'

'Of course not. That's how it was. There was no doubt. When I looked at Jonas, not only when he was small, but also later, I could always see who he reminded me of – Fredrik.'

'That must've been hard for you to live with.'

'It was worse for Kåre, and … That's probably why things went as they did between us – our getting divorced.'

'And the two of you kept this secret from Jonas, until now?'

'Secret? Mmm…'

'It's not altogether a surprise, then, that he reacted as he did when you told him the *real* truth. And it was a particularly difficult situation, with Mona Martens waiting for him outside.'

She looked down. '*Mm.*'

'It's on such occasions I ask myself the same question Henrik Ibsen did. How important is it to tell the whole truth? And at what price?'

Her eyes flashed again. '*So you think I should've just let them get on with it – as lovers? Two half-siblings, with all the consequences that could have?*'

'The consequences turned out to be the worst possible, anyway.'

'*You don't have to tell me that,*' she snapped, then leaned forward, hid her face in her hands and burst into floods of tears again.

I let her cry. The coffee had gone cold long ago, but I drank up and poured myself another, then another for her, without asking if she wanted any.

That Tuesday in September must have been an unusually harrowing day for Jonas Kleiva. I could just imagine the atmosphere on the front seat of the camper van as they drove into Markatangen after visiting Betty. It could well have been the cause of the vehicle driving straight into the sea without leaving any brake marks. But did it also explain why only one person was left dead inside, while the other appeared a few weeks later with a head injury not unlike the one Klaus Krog had received two years earlier?

Betty raised her head. She grabbed a box of tissues from the worktop behind her, took a small handful and wiped away the tears from around her eyes and from both cheeks. *'I'm sorry, Varg. I didn't mean to sit here weeping, but I'm sure you understand.'*

'I do. There was one last matter I wanted to take up with you though…'

Immediately the sarcasm was back. *'More local gossip about my lovers?'*

'The manuscript Klaus Krog was working on. I believe you said it was in Jonas's bedroom?'

'Yes, it is.'

'Could I possibly have a flick through it? You never know, a working document can throw up the odd clue or two.'

She shrugged. *'That's fine. It has great sentimental value for me, so you'll have to take good care of it. When I read it now, it's as if I can hear his voice, how he used to sit with me in the evening, talking, the way he was totally committed.'* She got up and went towards the door. *'I'll find it for you.'*

I remained at the kitchen table. I looked at the clock. It was getting on for three hours since I had left Torunn at Sørneset and I hadn't heard a peep from her yet.

I looked out of the window. It was still light, but the tall mountains and the low clouds formed a kind of dusk over the road outside and the nearest houses with their lit windows.

Betty returned. Under her arm she was carrying a brown document wallet, the kind you can tie at the front. She placed it on the table, undid the dark-brown lace and showed me the pile of papers inside. She took out a few sheets and examined them before handing them to me.

I cast a quick eye over them and nodded. 'This looks really

interesting. Is it alright if I take them back to Bergen? I don't
think I'll be able to read anything while I'm here.'

'Aren't you staying over till tomorrow? I can make dinner for you.'

'I doubt it. I suspect I'll have to go home today. I'm the driver
for a journalist who's in Sørneset now but will probably have to
be back in town by tonight.'

She nodded slowly. *'I see.'*

'Thank you for the offer though.'

She put the manuscript back carefully, tied the lace and
passed the wallet to me.

'Thank you. I'll take good care of it … Edvard Aga – his cabin
is on the other side of the fjord, isn't it?'

'That's right. You can't get there without a boat.'

'Then I'll head down to the store and see if he's still there.
There's something I have to ask him.'

'So you're still doing the job for me?'

'Yes, of course. But I have to admit it isn't easy finding information two years after the fact. Especially now that Mona and
Jonas are occupying centre-stage.'

'I'll pay you for your time.'

'Noted. Thank you very much.'

I stood up and thanked her for the coffee. She accompanied
me to the door. Before I left, she gave me an irresolute little hug,
as if out of obligation. I stroked her shoulder and wished her the
very best in the days to come. Tears poured from her eyes, and
the smile she sent me was like a salmon leaping out of the water,
its dorsal fin erect, and then it was gone again.

34

The fixed ritual repeated itself. I opened the store door, the invisible bell jangled, a chair in the back room scraped, and Stein Solvik appeared in the doorway.

'Is my coffee so addictive, Veum? You'll soon be the most loyal customer I have.'

The store was otherwise empty.

'Actually, I was looking for your other regular customer, Edvard. Has he gone back to his cabin?'

'I guess so.' He walked past me and peered through the window. *'I can see his boat isn't moored at the quay. So he won't be back today, at any rate.'* He angled a glance at me. *'You did want a cup of coffee, didn't you?'*

'One cup more or less won't make any difference. Yes, please.'

I strolled over to the window table and sat down. There was a copy of the *Nordhordland* newspaper on it, open at the page about the Solvik murder enquiry. There was a photograph of the chief of police, Sætenes, in front of the chapel with the caption, 'Police Make HQ in Chapel'. I skimmed through the article, but it didn't contain anything I didn't know.

Stein Solvik returned with a cup of coffee, which he carefully placed in front of me. He looked at the open newspaper. *'Have you heard the latest?'*

'What's that?'

'I've just heard it on the radio. The police are looking for a car in connection with the accident that led to Jonas and Mona ending up in the sea.'

'Really? Any details?'

'They just say a black or a dark-coloured car of unknown make. Not a lot to go on, in other words.'

'Where have the police got this from, do you know?'

He hesitated before answering. *'Guri Leitet's supposed to be the police source. She lives in the last house in the village, on the road to Markatangen. But she's eighty-seven years old, so she doesn't have much of an eye for makes of cars.'*

'Or a head for the right date, now that it's a few weeks later?'

'Yeah, maybe. She remembers the day well enough, though, because of the demonstration in Sørneset – one she fully supported.'

'You're impressively well informed, I must say.'

'Guri's one of my most loyal customers. I deliver goods to her several times a week, and I often sit down for a chin-wag with her.'

'Wow. Good, old-fashioned customer service.'

I made a mental note: Leitet. Another person I wasn't allowed to talk to. But could I ask her some questions about Klaus Krog and still stay on the right side of the murder investigation?

'So, are there any unofficial theories in the village about who the black or dark-coloured car might belong to?'

He smiled thinly. *'I'm sure there are. But it doesn't have to be a car from this area.'*

'No, of course not.'

'You were asking after Edvard. Is there anything I can be of help with, maybe?'

'Hm. There's been talk of something that happened more than twenty years ago. When Edvard started to come here and rented a room with Kåre and Betty, in the summer of 1983, he had a pal with him from Bergen. Do you remember him?'

His gaze turned reflective. *'A pal of Edvard's? Mm, now you say it, there was a guy who came with him a few times in those days. Whether it was 1983 or not, I couldn't say. But I think they came to the store and did a bit of shopping. I didn't know either of them then. To me they were just two run-of-the-mill townies on a fishing trip in Masfjorden. It was only when Edvard built himself a cabin here that I got to know him better.'*

'And the other guy? Do you remember his name?'

'No idea. And I haven't seen him since.'

I nodded and let it go, without telling Stein Solvik I knew very well who it was. If the name got out, it would spread through the district like an epidemic, I feared. And if people looked around for the carrier, there was a not insignificant risk the finger would point at me, to the additional annoyance of the police.

'Have you got Edvard's phone number?'

'Yes, I have.'

I took out my mobile phone and I scrolled my way through to his number. But before I had got as far as deciding whether to ring him or not, a text came through. It was from Torunn:

Hi, I've finished here now. Ole Lavik's offered to drive me to Bergen but I said no. He'll drop me off in the village. Where are you?

I answered in brief: In the local store. You'll see my car outside.

She responded: Leaving now.

I looked up at Solvik again. 'Someone I've been waiting for is coming.'

He raised his eyebrows.

'A journalist who's been covering the board meeting at Sunfjord Salmon. Have you got any rolls handy in case she's peckish?'

He smiled sagely. 'I never run out of rolls, Veum.'

I drained my cup and went outside. I stood leaning against a fence post. The weather was clear and cold. The sun had receded behind the tall mountains some time ago, but it was still a while before dusk would fall. It wasn't long before a mini-cortege of four cars turned in from Sørnesvegen. Three of them carried on while the fourth – a black Mercedes – pulled in by the store. Through the reflections in the windows I could make out Torunn in the passenger seat and a dark-haired man behind the wheel, whom I vaguely recognised from the pictures I had found on the Net. They exchanged a few words, then Torunn opened the door and stepped out. Ole Lavik glanced in my direction, his expression blank, not evincing much interest. Torunn walked around the back of the car and by the time she was with me, he had already set off towards the main road.

She gave me a quick hug. 'I think you're better company than he is.'

I gently grasped her shoulder and squeezed. 'Thank you. If you want a bite to eat before we go, I've ordered some rolls in there.'

Heartened, she glanced over at the store. 'A store and a café? Thank you. At Sunfjord Salmon they didn't even give me a coffee from the machine.'

'Not so much as a bit of salmon?'

She grinned. 'No, Varg.'

We headed to the entrance.

'I'm looking forward to hearing what interesting things you found out on the headland.'

Seeing us coming, Stein Solvik opened the door. He introduced himself to Torunn and welcomed her to his modest café, as he termed it. After enquiring whether we wanted coffee and rolls, he disappeared into the back room while Torunn and I sat down at the window table.

She looked around. 'Snug, but not such a big selection of items?'

'No, I'm afraid business is a little on the slack side, but I've realised that it's a useful place to pop into. You get a pretty good overview of what's going on in the village.'

'So, did you make any progress while you were waiting?'

'I've got the answers to some things, and some new questions have emerged, as always happens when you leave no stone un-turned.'

'And you find all sorts of oddities?'

'You could say that. But listen, did you get a decent tour around the place?'

'Oh, yes. Ole Lavik was nice enough, professionally speaking. And the organisation itself was quite impressive. But with the same inbuilt weaknesses all these offshore farms have. Exposed to all kinds of weather, and vulnerable to damage when the well-boats come to collect fish. This is when accidents happen. One tear in the cage and the whole fjord is full of escaping farmed salmon. That's a catastrophe in itself, of course, but when many of them also carry disease, it's obvious it's not good for the fjords. But I didn't want to argue with him about it. I was interested in maintaining a good rapport and squeezing as much information out of him as possible.'

'And the board meeting?'

'It was behind closed doors – not exactly unexpected. But they said I could wait until it was over if I wanted to ask any of the board members a question.'

'And did you?'

'I waited – but to no avail. Not one of them would answer so much as a single question about who they were. But I'd done my homework, so I recognised the lot of them: Kåre Kleiva, Truls Hatlevik, Einar Sørnes, Cecilie Tangen and Ole Lavik.'

'And none of them would say anything?'

'They all pointed to Ole Lavik. Said he's the director and therefore responsible for statements to the public.'

'And what did he say to that?'

Again she grinned. 'He'd already said all he had to say. If I had any criticisms or questions that needed some reflection on his part, I had to send them in writing. Then he would – he said with a smile – answer them as well as he was able.'

'Right. They're doing their level best to protect themselves from prying eyes.'

'Nothing new there, Varg. But I promise you they were quite embarrassed, most of them. In the car park I saw Kåre Kleiva and Cecilie Tangen with their heads together, while Einar Sørnes stood alone by the entrance scowling at them.'

'And Mr Mayor?'

'Truls Hatlevik? He looked out of his depth. He could barely find his car.'

Stein Solvik coughed loudly as he came from the back room, to warn us he was approaching. A tray of rolls was put down before us, a cup of coffee for Torunn and a refill for me, and then he went to fetch the coffee pot, just in case. He had really gone to town this time, for the lady. The ham was dressed with beetroot, the roast beef with pickled cucumber, and on the cheese there were slices of red pepper. What was more, he had put prawn salad and smoked salmon on some of the rolls, so we definitely weren't going to starve on our journey home from Solvik. The freshly brewed coffee was excellent as well.

'*Just say if you need anything,*' he said with an elegant bow, before discreetly retiring into his back room and leaving the stage to us, as if we were a mature Romeo and Juliet fleeing from Verona.

Torunn watched him, the lines around her eyes smiling. 'Nice.'

'Yes, isn't he?'

We pounced on the rolls – I was hungry despite having eaten here earlier in the day.

Between swallowing one mouthful and taking another, she said: 'One of the first things I did, before he showed me round – Ole Lavik that is – was to offer my condolences on the loss of his fiancée.'

'How did he react?'

'Well, he thanked me. But there was no time for any more chat as we had to get into his car to go to a far corner of the farm.

I did venture a question about how he had reacted to his fiancée being in Solvik to demonstrate against his company on the day she died.'

'To which he replied?'

'Bit ambivalent, I'd say. Perhaps she had her reasons, he said, without looking at me.'

'Really?'

'Exactly. But it must've been strange, mustn't it, I said, going to a board meeting while your fiancée is demonstrating outside the gate. "*There were far worse things that happened that day than that*," he said. But then we reached our next stop, so I didn't get to hear any more about how he'd reacted.'

'Perhaps you should've accepted his offer after all. To drive you all the way back to Bergen?'

'Then I would've missed all this,' she said, spreading out her arms and helping herself to one of the roast-beef rolls.

'So you didn't touch on the evidence pointing to Mona and Jonas Kleiva having got together? And how she'd even been with Jonas to visit his mother?'

'No.'

'I wonder when this transfer of affection occurred and who knew about it.'

'You can say that again.'

'He had a top, top car. A different class from Jonas's VW camper van. It was black, too.'

'What's the significance of that?'

I briefly told her about the search the police had initiated for the car that had been seen on the way to Markatangen on that fateful September day.

'Hm,' she commented. 'But there are lots of dark-coloured or black cars, aren't there?'

'Absolutely. In other words, it's just circumstantial evidence. Or another unanswered question.'

Night was beginning to fall when we took our leave. Torunn insisted it was her turn to pay. We said our goodbyes to Stein Solvik, left and got into the car.

She looked at her watch. 'An hour and a half to two hours and we're back in Bergen. Is that right?'

'More or less. Are you going back to Oslo tonight?'

'No, I've got the room until tomorrow.'

I started the car. When we passed Betty's house, I looked across. There was a light on in the kitchen, but no other evidence of life.

After passing the enclosure with the goats, which Betty had told me belonged to her parents, the ascent began in earnest. It was pitch-black, now, and I had my eyes glued to the road in front of me when I suddenly felt a palpable vibration running through the car. I lowered my speed and leaned towards the windscreen. A powerful rumbling sound filled the side of the mountain and I had to squint to make out the contours of the terrain above us.

'What's happening, Varg?' Torunn cried next to me. She pressed her face against the side window and looked up.

We both heard it at the same time. It was as though the whole mountain was on the move. It was sliding down towards the road, and us, as black and immense as the night itself.

35

A large, black, amorphous mass came tumbling down the mountainside above us. Sparks flew in the darkness, and I only just managed to reverse the car a few metres before the landslide hit the road ahead of us. A colossal rock landed with a crash that made the whole car shake and the tarmac disintegrate into long fissures, some of them coming straight towards us, until the boulder settled like a solid barrier in front of us. At the same time smaller, and not so small, rocks, bushes and trees fell around and above us like a gigantic hailstorm.

'Oh, Vaaarg!' Torunn tore off her safety belt, grabbed my arm and clung to me. I sat staring ahead, shocked, tensing my entire body in an instinctive attempt to fend off whatever might come our way.

We sat in a bubble of deafening silence. Now, only a few small rocks came bounding down the mountain and over our heads. The massive, black boulder blocking off the road lay like the severed head of a mountain troll, its jaws still thirsting for Christian blood.

Torunn squeezed even closer to me. 'My God. If we'd been a few metres further on, it would've hit us!'

'We would've been history,' I said. I opened the door. 'Let me have a look.'

Slowly she let go of me and watched me step out of the car. I stood holding the door as I took in the sight.

There were rocks all around us, but behind us it wasn't so bad that the road could not be cleared. On the roof of the car there was a sprinkling of small stones. The bodywork was pockmarked with dents. A largish tree had settled partly across the rear and one of the branches stretched over to where I was standing. When I looked up the mountainside I saw the trail of the landslide, like a gaping wound in the terrain. Turning in the other direction, I looked down on the lights in Solvik and right out to Sørneset. The main fall seemed to have stopped close to us, but some sections had continued down to the bottom of the valley. It seemed to me that the colossal boulder in front of us had triggered the slide.

Torunn was out of the car as well now. 'How does it look?'

'For the moment we're safe, but if we can get some help from the village, I reckon it should be possible to get back down without too much trouble.'

'Is the car in a driveable state?'

'I presume so. Just a superficial rash, not so bad that some skincare won't cure it.' I took out my phone. 'I'll report what's happened.'

I rang 112 and gave the operator our position and the details of the incident. The first thing she asked me was if anyone was hurt and if there were any other vehicles involved.

'We didn't see anyone in front of us, so I don't think so. But we're hemmed in and can't move forward or backward. Just for your information, the Masfjorden chief of police and several detectives are in the area.'

'Really? Then I'll contact the chief so he can organise whatever measures and assistance are needed. I'll also ring the Highways Division to come and clear the road. They'll probably call in geologists to examine the terrain to make sure there's no risk of any further landslips. Stay where you are until help arrives.'

'Yes, well, we don't exactly have much choice,' I answered before I rang off.

I met Torunn's gaze. She snuggled up to me again. 'Are you aware how close we were to being killed, Varg?'

'All too aware. If you don't think I'm taking this seriously enough … it's the Vestlander in me, to quote a long-deceased poet. Landslides and avalanches are something we, consciously or unconsciously, are prepared for as we move from place to place in this part of the country. In Østland they make four-lane highways. Here, at best, they bore a tunnel through the worst parts, and by that I do mean the worst. All the other areas are vulnerable to landslides and avalanches. It goes to show that people moved around more safely in the days when the sea was what connected us. At least they didn't have experiences like this.'

I looked down over Solvik. It seemed as though my report had been received, if the landslide hadn't already been observed from down there. I could see the headlights of four or five vehicles on their way up. Further down there were heavier and larger ones, hopefully a tractor with a front loader. It was highly unlikely this was the first time there had been a rockfall on this stretch.

'I've been in some dangerous situations in my career,' Torunn said. 'Usually it was other people who constituted the greatest danger, and I've been in trouble at sea a couple of times, too. But I've never experienced something like this. I'm still shaking.'

'Looks as though we'll have to stay in Solvik until tomorrow, at least, if we're lucky. It'll take the Highways Agency time to reopen the road. We'd better get a roof over our heads.'

'Yes, I suppose we had,' she said, more confident of this than anything else.

'And we may have to fight with the police over any available accommodation. I think I should make another call.'

When I dialled Betty's number, she answered after one ring, as though she had been sitting, waiting. *'Yes? Who's that?'*

'Hi, Varg again. I don't know if you've heard, but we were almost swept away by a rockfall up here, so I wonder whether you still have the two rooms in the annexe free.'

'Both of them?'

'Yes, I've got someone with me. The journalist I mentioned earlier today.'

'I see. Yes, no one else has booked them, so that's fine.'

'Great. I've no idea when we'll be back down, but…'

'I'm making a red deer stew, so I'll warm it up when you come.'

'Thank you very much.'

We rang off, and I turned to Torunn. 'We've got both a room and a meal as soon as we get back down, hopefully this evening.'

The procession from the village was closer now. I could distinguish the vehicles and saw that the last one was lagging behind now, because of its weight. While we waited for them to arrive, I started to tidy up a bit myself. The tree was easy to pick up and throw into the roadside ditch, so that the branch lying across the car roof now stood in the air, at an angle. I walked around the rear of the car. Some of the rocks were small enough for me to pick up and throw to the side. Others were bigger, but with a few kicks or by crouching down and using both hands, I was able to move them. But some were so big they would need a machine. We both kicked at the smaller rocks while we waited for help to arrive.

By now the first car had come up as far as it could, prevented from approaching any nearer by the obstructions between us. It was no more than ten to fifteen metres away, certainly within what I reckoned was shouting distance.

Chief of Police Sætenes, and his sidekick, Hans Hosteland, stepped out of the front car. Behind them the second car had arrived. Out of it stepped Signe Moland and Bjarne Solheim. A third car turned out to contain Knut Sørnes, Harald Eide and two other men I didn't recognise. From the fourth came Nils Kyvik and three other unknown men, all summoned as a rescue crew, I assumed. They were already grabbing pickaxes, spades and shovels from their vehicles.

'Veum,' Sætenes shouted. *'Is everything OK?'*

'As you can see, we've survived.'

'It'll all be fine. It's not the first time there's been a rockfall from Mount Fossenuten.'

'No, that's what I thought.'

'Down the road from you, there are no insurmountable problems,
so we'll have you out in no time. We've got a guy coming with a front
loader. I reckon he can do the heavy stuff and the others can tidy up
around him. I gather your car's unscathed?'

'Unscathed is an overstatement, but it's certainly driveable. I
think.'

Now the huge digger with the road-scraper blade had joined
the other cars. Those that hadn't already done so, had to move
their cars to the side so that the digger could rumble through.
Then the big man behind the wheel manoeuvred it into position.
After exchanging opinions with Sætenes and sending us a re-
assuring wave, he got down to work. Twenty minutes later he
had cleared most of the road while the local guys walked behind
him with shovels and spades, tidying up the remaining debris.
The four police officers brought up the rear, inspecting the road.

The way they greeted us when they were up close varied from
person to person. The warmest welcome came from Signe, who
hugged me and said: 'This could've turned out very badly, Varg!'

'Weeds have a habit of thriving,' Solheim commented, not
without a friendly pat on the shoulder and a follow-up: 'Good
to see you alive and well, Veum.'

They both greeted Torunn. Knut Sørnes nodded in recogni-
tion and mumbled something about him thinking she was going
to Bergen with Ole Lavik.

Several of the local men shouted comments when they
caught sight of the massive boulder blocking the road. *'Bugger*
me, if that isn't Trolleye!' one of those I hadn't met before said.

'We've waited years for this,' Nils Kyvik said.

'We've talked about levering it loose so many times,' Knut Sørnes
added. *'But oh, no, it was part of our cultural heritage, someone in-*
sisted.'

'Cultural heritage?' Torunn repeated.

'It was claimed that it was the eye of a petrified troll, blinded by the sun.'

'Just as I thought,' I said, to which no one made a comment.

'Well,' Sætenes said. 'We can't do any more until the geologists from the Highways Division have been here, and that won't be before tomorrow morning. They have to give the green light before we can clear the rest of the road, and from what I can see, a bit of tarmac will be required too, so…' He glanced at Torunn, me and the two detectives from Bergen. 'You can all prepare yourselves for a little autumn holiday here in Solvik.'

'We've already arranged accommodation,' I said.

'So have we,' Signe said. 'And we'll probably have to claim for a ferry ticket if the reopening of the road takes too long.'

'So…' Sætenes looked at me again. 'Are you ready to turn your car round or do you need some help?'

I stared down past the parked cars. 'There's a place to pull in down there, isn't there?'

'Yes. It's a bit tight, but…' He called Hosteland. 'Hans, give Veum a hand with turning round down there. The rest of us had better have a closer look up here before we go back.'

'Do you need us?' Signe asked.

'No, you can go, too.'

'I'll wait until you've turned,' Torunn said, joining Hosteland as I started the car.

Using my mirrors, I reversed down past the other vehicles and, with Hosteland's help, completed the manoeuvre. Once I was facing the right direction, Torunn got in and fastened her belt.

'Two steps forward and one step back,' I said. 'If you'd taken up Ole Lavik on his offer, you'd be in Bergen by now.'

'Maybe…' she mused. 'If he hasn't been hit by another landslide.'

'Let's hope not. But this is Vestland, as I said. Nothing is completely safe, as we know. Out of our hands, I'm afraid.'

Then we set off. I have to admit I took extra care driving down, regularly glancing sideways at the mountain until we were back down in Solvik.

Betty eyed Torunn sceptically when she opened the door to us, as though she hadn't been informed that the journalist I had with me was female. But after the introductions she was clearly on board, even if she spoke in rather more measured tones to Torunn than to me.

After giving us each a key, she added that I knew where the rooms were and we could drop off our things. Once we had done that, the stew was ready to be served.

'A glass of red wine with your meal?' she asked when we were back, and neither of us said no.

'You'll have a glass with us, won't you,' I said.

'Don't you want to be alone?'

'Not at all. It'd be lovely if you joined us,' Torunn smiled. With that, the atmosphere relaxed, and we ended up having two or three glasses each.

The conversation was primarily about the landslide, and Betty was alarmed when she heard how close we had been to being killed. She sent me a look that spoke volumes. It was as though I could read her mind: *Remember what I said? Pursued by death…*

'I was told there are often landslides up there.'

'Yes, that's true, but it's quite a few years since there's been such a big one.'

'They said it was Trolleye itself that had fallen.'

'Trolleye! There's definitely a curse on that one.'

'A curse?'

'Yes, it's an old story, of course. There was a mountain troll on this side of the fjord who was so in love with a troll maiden on the other side that he was in a kind of trance. He watched her until the sun suddenly went down and he was turned to stone. But he still had one eye open and stared across the fjord into all eternity.' Grinning, she added: 'Now he has his peace at last and his eye's closed for good.'

The rest of the conversation skirted round Betty's personal tragedies and only tangentially touched on the sensitive subject of aquaculture. Before we retired for the night, I checked the Net to see if there was any news about when the Highways Agency estimated the road would be open again. The closest they came to anything definitive was 'in all probability during Thursday afternoon', so we reckoned one stayover in Solvik would do it this time.

Walking across the yard, Torunn said: 'I've got half a bottle of Jameson in my emergency rations. It's a habit I acquired when I lived in Dublin. Are you up for a little nightcap?'

'Yes, I think we can allow ourselves that after such an experience. Yours or mine?'

'Yours, if you don't mind.'

'Bring your own toothmug. There's only one in each room, it seems.'

Before going into our separate rooms, I glanced across the yard at Betty's house. I guessed she would be watching, but the legal paragraph banning cohabitation had been scrapped more than thirty years ago, and besides, the deal – so far – was a nightcap, an English concept Norwegians had warmed to. I left the door ajar and it wasn't long before we were each sitting, toothmug in hand, toasting our lucky escape with Irish whiskey, her in the room's only chair, me on the edge of the bed. She knocked back the first mug fairly swiftly, probably something she had also learned in Dublin. I followed suit, and she filled our mugs again.

'We got our explanation for why it was called the Trolleye then,' I said.

'And how dangerous it is to fall in love.'

'But it's a long time before tomorrow's sunset.'

'Yes,' she said, drawing her chair closer. 'You're absolutely right about that. Let's have a closer look at your eye.'

Whether you believe in fate or not, you could say this was an anticipated joy, something that just had to happen. She gave herself to me with both eyes open, as clear and precise in bed as she was in her journalism. An hour later she was lying on her side in the narrow bed, leaning on her elbow and looking at me. 'It struck me when I realised how close we'd been to being killed up there that ... Well, I was reminded of the old proverb: Don't put off till tomorrow what you can do today.'

'Right now, that seems like an extremely good axiom,' I answered.

When I awoke a few hours later, I was alone. I vaguely remembered her getting up and putting her clothes on, leaning down, kissing me on the mouth and tiptoeing back to her own room so as to wake up decent the following morning.

36

When I knocked on her door on Thursday morning, she opened it a fraction and peered at me with a sly grin. I took that as a sign there were no major regrets and said I was going across the yard for breakfast.

'I'm having a shower and will be right there,' she said, raising a hand and blowing me a kiss.

Betty had set the kitchen table for both of us and asked without any form of undertone if I had slept well. I had to confess that I had, but I didn't say how many hours. To the question of whether I wanted eggs and bacon, I answered yes. When Torunn joined us ten minutes later, she said a soft-boiled egg would be enough for her. In a way there was something very normal about the situation, as though we were just two casual tourists who had rented a room before moving on.

'They said on the radio they hoped the road would be open this afternoon,' Betty said.

'Yes, I saw that on the Net,' I replied.

Torunn asked: 'Would it be possible for me to stay in the room during the day? I have to try and write down what I saw at Sunfjord Salmon yesterday while it's still fresh in my mind.'

'That's fine. I'm not expecting any other guests.' She turned to me. 'And you, Varg?'

'There's a couple of matters I want to follow up. Do you know Guri Leitet?'

'Guri? Yes and no. She's a bit special. And she's … what age? Close on ninety, I'd say. What do you want with her?'

'Well, she's supposed to be the police's source regarding the sighting of the black or dark-coloured car the day Jonas and Mona drove into the sea.'

'Yes, I heard the news bulletin. That makes sense. She's still alert and writes down much of what goes on here in her diary. What the *weather is like, who visits her and who passes by outside. I remember chuckling at what she used to tell me. And she collected car registration numbers, like a little boy. She noted down all the numbers of the cars that passed in the same diary.'*

'Did she really?' I sent her an eloquent look. 'When I heard about her, I thought about the job I'm doing for you. Whether she might remember if anything happened in September two years ago. Perhaps there'll be something interesting in Guri Leitet's notes in that regard too.'

She nodded gently. *'Yes, maybe. So you want to visit her at home then?'*

'I thought I would. Does she live alone?'

'Yes. August, her husband, died twenty years ago, and her children moved to Bergen, as far as I know. They don't come back here that often, but she's been strange all her life, so maybe it's not so surprising.'

'Do you think she'll talk to me?'

'No idea. Not sure it'll help if you pass on my regards, either. You can try. Good luck anyway.'

'Thank you. And I'll have to see if I can have another chat with Edvard Aga.' I looked at Torunn. 'He may be able to help us contact Fredrik Martens.'

Betty stiffened. *'What's that about?'*

'It's in connection with an article I'm writing about Sunfjord Salmon,' Torunn said.

Betty glanced at me and whispered: *'I hope you haven't…'*

'No, no,' I said quickly.

Torunn observed all this with an ironic glint in her eye, but without making any comment.

We finished breakfast without any further drama. Walking across the yard, Torunn asked: 'What was that about Fredrik Martens?'

'We can come back to that later. Nothing to do with fish farming.'

'Right.' She wryly arched her eyebrows and a sardonic little smile played on her lips.

In the passage between the two rooms, which was visible from the kitchen window, we kept a discreet distance, but the warmth in her eyes still promised better times. We agreed to text each other if anything unexpected happened, and decided we would leave as soon as the road was open again. 'I ought to be back in Oslo by this evening,' she said.

'Let's cross our fingers the Highways Agency has one of its better days.'

I fetched my outdoor jacket and notebook and dropped in on Betty again. I reassured her that all the personal stuff she had told me would remain between her and me. I didn't share that kind of information. She thanked me and gave me a kiss on the cheek before I left. I was beginning to feel a tiny bit popular as I strolled down to the centre of Solvik, if that was the right term for the crossroads to Sørnes, the store, the quay, the school, the chapel and the rest of the buildings along the Markatangen road.

In front of the chapel, there were a police saloon and two ci-vilian cars, one of which was a grey Suzuki Alto I thought belonged to Bjarne Solheim. I saw Klara Kyvik outside her house in earnest conversation with another woman I couldn't re-member having seen before. As I passed, with a little nod to Klara, the conversation stopped. Klara nodded back mutely, and they watched me come to a halt by the last house in the village, open the gate and go in.

The house was white, but it had been painted several years ago. In many places the most recent coat was peeling, to reveal the previous one underneath. The garden around the house was overgrown, and the tall, yellowing grass couldn't have been cut since early summer. Around an apple tree lay the remains of the fallen fruit, much of it pecked at and eaten by birds and other animals. Above the doorbell was a bit of cardboard bearing the name *August Leitet* in a plastic sleeve and fixed with drawing pins. Over the plastic someone had put a blue line through the Christian name.

I pressed the bell and heard it ring inside. No reaction. I tried again while stepping back from the brown door and looking at the windows on the ground floor and at the gable above.

I cast around. Over by the neighbouring house Klara Kyvik and the other woman were silently watching what I was doing. When I met their eyes, it was as though a magnetic force was driving them towards me. I walked back to the garden fence and met them there. The other woman was slimmer than Klara, physically and facially. On her head she was wearing an old-fashioned light-brown hat that made her look older than she was.

'Is it Guri you want to see?' Klara asked.

'That was the idea. Do you know if she's home?'

'She's always at home. She doesn't go anywhere, Guri doesn't. She has her shopping delivered, a home help to clean a couple of times a month and nurses from the council two days a week.'

'I see. Do you know which days?'

'Tuesday and Friday, I think,' the other woman said, then introduced herself: 'Anna Eide.'

'Varg Veum. You wouldn't be Harald's mother, would you?'

She measured me with her eyes. 'Yes. Klara just told me it was you who came to our house yesterday. Harald was pretty angry about all your questions.'

'Well…'

Klara studied the house. 'Have you tried the door? I doubt it's locked. We don't usually lock doors here.'

'No, I haven't.' I moved back towards the door. Halfway there, I turned round. 'Do you want to come in with me?'

They didn't need to be asked twice. We went to the door together. I pressed down the handle and pushed. The door opened without a sound.

As a matter of form, I rang the bell again. The ringing was louder now, but the reaction inside was as silent and inert as before.

Klara Kyvik and Anna Eide peered inquisitively into the house.

'*Ages since I've been in here,*' Klara said.

'*Yes, I haven't been here since August's seventieth and that must be more than twenty years ago now,*' Anna said.

It didn't seem as if anything in those twenty years plus had been done, either. Even if it looked clean and tidy, there was something strangely abandoned about everything, as though it were a relic of another era, a life that had passed and would never return.

'*Hello! Guri!*' Klara had taken charge now. She led us through the small porch and into the kitchen. On the table there was a cup and a plate, but they didn't seem to have been used, as though everything had been set for breakfast but things hadn't got that far. Through the window we gazed straight out onto the road. This was probably where Guri sat, keeping stats on passing cars, weather conditions and whatever else she might have written down.

Anna peeped through the door to the sitting room. '*No one here, either.*'

'*I think the bedroom's to the right,*' Klara said.

I passed them both and walked to the door to the right of the sitting room. It was closed. I knocked and stood listening. Not a sound inside.

I looked at Klara, who was standing close by now, then shrugged as if to say there was only one thing to do. I opened the door.

The stench that hit us told its own story.

'*Oh, Guri!*' Klara exclaimed.

'*God bless her,*' Anna said.

The old lady was lying in the middle of her broad bed, staring up at the ceiling, with her mouth wide open and her tongue showing. The profile of her face was silhouetted against the wall behind her. Her white hair was spread out on the pillow and the colour of her face a sickly grey with blue patches, as if she was turning to ice. There was no reason to go any closer. It was one hundred per cent clear that she was dead.

'Poor thing,' Klara said.

'Her time had come,' Anna said.

'Who should we ring? Do you know where her children live?'

'No.'

I took charge. 'First we have to report this to the police. I'll do that. After all, they're here anyway. Let's go out, nice and calm, and then we can leave the rest to them.'

Klara gawped at me. 'Will they contact her family?'

'Sure. But as we three found her, they'll want to speak to us as well.'

'Surely you don't think … someone did this to Guri?'

'Yet another death,' Anna said. 'It's enough to scare the living daylights out of you.'

'I think we're going to have to start locking our doors now.'

'First, let's get out of here without touching anything. As it was me who opened the doors, it's best I close it again now.'

'Fingerprints,' Klara said to Anna, in case she hadn't already twigged.

Outside, I thanked the women for accompanying me inside and made a beeline across the road to the chapel.

37

This time it was Sætenes and Signe Moland who were holding the fort, each sitting in front of a computer.

The chief of police didn't look overjoyed about the disruption.

Signe got up. 'Varg ... How are things?'

'Fine, thanks. Close shave last night.'

'Yes, that was quite a rockfall. But I hear they're trying to reopen the road this afternoon.'

'Yes. In the meantime, I've stumbled across another dead body.'

'What!' Sætenes reacted instantly and rose to his full height behind the computer. *'Who?'*

'Guri Leitet, across the street from here.'

'Guri Leitet,' Signe said. 'She was the one who...' She looked at Sætenes.

'Yes, that's her.'

She turned back to me. 'Where did you find her?'

'In her house. She was in bed.'

'But ... What were you doing there?'

'Exactly,' Sætenes said. *'I was wondering that myself.'*

'There was something I wanted to ask her.'

'But weren't you told not to interfere with this case?'

'Yes, I was, but this was about the other case – the one I have permission to investigate.'

'The accident a couple of years ago?'

'Yes. I heard Guri Leitet kept some sort of diary, logging whoever drove past her house, and that was the reason you've been searching for a black car from the day that was relevant to *you.*'

'Yes, Solheim and Hosteland are out—'

'Now, we mustn't pass on information to outsiders,' Sætenes interrupted. *'Must we, Inspector.'*

Signe bit her lip and looked at me with an expression that suggested I had lured her into a trap.

Sætenes came over to us and firmly planted himself in front of me, legs akimbo. *'Who gave you permission to go into Guri Leitet's house?'*

'I wasn't alone. As I said to Inspector Moland here, I had a question to ask her. I rang the bell and no one came out. But two neighbours – Klara Kyvik and Anna Eide – joined me, and we agreed we would go in to see if something had happened. For all we knew, Guri could've been lying on the bathroom floor, injured and in need of help.'

'That's what you thought, was it?'

'The door wasn't locked. When we entered, we couldn't see her in either the kitchen or the sitting room, but … she was in her bedroom, in bed, and she's no longer with us.'

'And you're sure?'

'Unfortunately, I've seen dead bodies before, so … Yes, she's dead.'

'Any signs of an assault?'

'Not obvious signs. When we saw the state of her, we beat a retreat at once and agreed we should report it to you.'

'And what had you intended to ask Guri Leitet?'

'I was going to ask her if I could see her diary for 2002, to check if she had noted anything down on the day Klaus Krog died.'

'But you didn't?'

'Well, obviously not.'

'I mean, you didn't use the opportunity to look for the book once you were inside the house?'

'No, I didn't, and I have both Klara Kyvik and Anna Eide as witnesses.'

'We'd better find out how reliable the women are. I don't take anything for granted. In the meantime…' He turned to Signe again. *'The forensics officers, have they gone home?'*

She nodded. 'Yesterday, before the landslide. But we can get them back as soon as the road has been cleared – or by boat.'

'Let's wait and see how they get on with the road. But tell me if we have another crime scene and another suspicious death to investigate.'

'The deceased will have to be autopsied, won't she?'

'Absolutely. But I'd prefer not to move her until the forensics people have been here.'

'It's definitely suspicious,' I said. 'Dying now, a couple of days after the bulletin about the black car was released, information I'm sure the whole village knows came from Guri Leitet. That's just how it is in small places like this. Did she see who was in the car?'

Sætenes glared at me and refused to answer. Behind him Signe signalled no with a slight shake of the head.

'My understanding is that she wasn't so hot on makes of car. But I assume she would still have recognised a car from the village and, yes, perhaps the driver too. The driver wouldn't want to risk being named, which may have led him – or her – to try to put an end to any speculation. Again, you probably don't have to move very far in this village before several people have seen you and are working out where you're heading. Muzzling the source might have felt like a necessity for someone with a bad conscience. It's a good enough reason to silence Guri Leitet once and for all, isn't it?'

Sætenes turned back to Signe. *'I don't like it. It's extremely unusual for a small village like this to have so many suspicious deaths.'*

'Shouldn't we…?' She gestured towards the door.

'Yes. We'll have to go over and see whether what our master detective here tells us is true, and then we'll have to secure the scene until the forensics team gets here. Once that's done, we'll have to transfer the body to Bergen for an autopsy, and then we'll most probably have

to come to terms with the fact that we have yet another case to investigate.' He sighed deeply and pointedly.

'And me?'

'You can await further developments, Veum. We'll get back to you.'

'Does that mean I have to stay in Solvik?'

'Preferably not,' he growled. 'We know where we can find you, don't we?' The latter was directed more to Signe than me.

We nodded, both of us.

'Can I just ask you one thing? Those diaries – have you confiscated them?'

'Only the one for this year,' Sætenes said.

I looked at Signe. 'Could you do me a favour and flick through the diaries and see if you can find the one for 2002?'

The chief of police gave a loud snort. 'Any reason why it wouldn't be there?'

'Maybe not. But if it's gone, I'd guess that would be a very persuasive clue. Guri Leitet might simply be the key – not only to what happened in September but also to the accident two years ago.'

'Well…' Once again he looked at Signe. 'They were in a cupboard in the kitchen, weren't they?'

'In one of the drawers in a kitchen cupboard, yes.'

'It's up to you, if you want to do something to help this joker. I'm washing my hands, as the scriptures say.'

'And that's what Pontius Pilate did,' I said. 'He was a sort of police chief, too.'

'Let's go,' Sætenes said. 'Will you lock the door after us?' he asked Signe. 'Seems there are too many meddlers in this village for us to leave all this open.' From the look he sent me, I gathered he included me in that category.

'You've got my phone number,' I said to Signe. 'I'd appreciate a call.'

She didn't answer, but she did nod, briefly.

They crossed the road and opened the gate to Guri Leitet's house. Klara Kyvik and Anna Eide were still standing by the entrance so as not to miss anything.

As for me, I didn't go where Pontius Pilate sent Jesus, but back to Stein Solvik and his store.

38

Laurel and Hardy were both there, it transpired. Stein Solvik was leaning against the counter with his arms crossed; Edvard Aga was sitting at the window table, but so far back that I hadn't seen him from outside. He had a coffee cup in front of him.

Aga raised his eyebrows and inclined his head in welcome. Solvik said: *'Suppose I don't need to ask anymore. Cup of coffee, Veum?'*

'Please,' I said, and he was off into the back room.

I strolled over to Aga and sat down at the table, too. 'I was hoping to see you. If I hadn't, I would've had to ring you.'

'Shoot. I have nothing to hide.'

'Who was your fishing pal in the early eighties? You forgot to say.'

'Fishing pal? I had several.'

'Yes, but here – and staying over at Betty Kleiva's.'

He looked slightly disgruntled. 'Ah, you're thinking of…'

'Yes.'

'Fredrik Martens,' he mumbled in such a low voice that Solvik didn't hear when he appeared, cup of coffee in hand.

'What did you say?' he asked as he placed the cup on the table where I was now sitting.

Aga didn't answer.

I said: 'You were old schoolfriends, I understand.'

'Yes, that's right.'

Solvik retreated, but not so far away that he couldn't follow the conversation. The oracle of Solvik knew his role.

'I think I told you that a pal and I bought up apartment blocks, restored them and made a good whack when we sold them on. In the end, I sold my part and settled down here.'

'Yes, you said. But you didn't mention the name of your pal. Or what he did after you went your separate ways.' As Aga didn't say anything, I carried on: 'I don't suppose you were wild about him moving into fish farming.'

'You can say that again.'

'Are you still in contact with him?'

He shook his head. 'Not at all. Haven't been for many years.'

'But before that – during the summer of 1983, you both stayed at Betty and Kåre's.'

'Yes. It must've been that year, I suppose.'

I turned to the window in an attempt to prevent Solvik from hearing what I said: 'Kåre wasn't there at the time. He was on his travels.'

Aga kept his voice low too. 'No, I don't think he was. Not that I can recall anyway.'

'But you and Fredrik. You both courted the landlady, I gather.'

His face darkened. 'You gather, do you? What the hell are you insinuating?'

'But it was probably only one of you who – how shall I put it? – "hooked the fish" seems like a suitable image.'

He pursed his lips and remained silent. Over by the counter I could swear I saw Stein Solvik's ears flapping, but he had his gaze fixed on the door, taking a sip of his coffee and acting as though nothing was happening.

'Jonas was born the following April.' Again, I faced the window and lowered my voice. 'Kåre Kleiva told me he can't have children.'

Now Aga lost his composure. 'What? You don't mean … Fredrik Martens is the…?'

'It wouldn't take much more than a DNA test to have paternity confirmed. Or ruled out.'

'And who would ask for the test? You?'

'The mother maybe?'

His eyes went walkabout. 'But what … what's it got to do with all this other stuff?'

'All the stuff that has happened? First to Klaus Krog, then Mona Martens, and finally to Jonas?'

'Yes. It's all so meaningless. None of it makes sense.'

'It just seems as if there's a kind of pattern to it. I can make out the outlines of several love triangles, if not quadrangles. If they're left to rub up against each other, it's like tectonic plates causing regular violent earthquakes.'

'Well, I don't see any pattern in this. You'll have to explain it to me.'

'I didn't say I see the whole thing clearly. I can just make out the outlines.'

'More coffee, boys?' Solvik had come over, Thermos in hand.

'Yes, please,' we said, in unison, like a reborn 1950s Bergen pop duo.

After giving us top-ups, Solvik stood looking through the window. *'There's a conspicuous amount of police activity outside Guri Leitet's house, I can see. The two officers who came round checking for black cars in the village are back.'*

'So that's what they've been doing.'

'But they haven't been here yet.'

'There's a dark-grey Opel outside, if that's what you're thinking.'

'That's mine,' Aga said. 'I leave it here at the camping site. I only use it when I have to go to Bergen.'

'Wonder if something's happened to Guri,' Solvik said. *'Do you know anything, Veum? You came from that direction, I saw.'*

I gave it to him straight. 'She's dead.'

'What! Guri?'

I nodded.

'Another death?' Aga said.

'It could be from natural causes. She was very old.'

'Possibly. It's the police's job to find out,' I said. 'That'll be why they're there.'

As if on cue, my phone rang. I looked at the screen. It was Signe. I motioned to Solvik and Aga, got up and walked to the other end of the store, by the freezer counter.

'Yes?'

'Signe here. I'd like a few words with you.'

'Fire away, Signe.'

'Face to face.'

'Oh, right. I'll come over. Did you find out—?'

She cut me off: 'Preferably this minute.'

'Fine.'

We rang off. I turned to the other two. 'I have to go.' I looked at Aga. 'I'd like to have a chat with your old fishing pal. But I guess you're not really in a position to put in a good word for me?'

He slowly shook his head with a weary smile. 'Not really.'

'Well, then, boys, thanks for today and see you again.'

'*You're not staying over?*' Solvik asked.

'Not this time.' With that, I nodded to both of them and left the establishment.

Signe was like a cat on hot bricks outside the chapel when I arrived. I didn't even manage to open my mouth before she spoke. 'Take this as a piece of wise advice from a distant relative, Varg. The police have now clear leads to follow. The best thing you can do for us is to keep your distance from anyone who might have anything to do with this until the police investigation's over and we've taken the necessary measures.'

'Does that mean you're close to an arrest?'

'My personal advice is that you go back to Bergen and wait before you do anything at all connected with this case until we're home and dry. And I say this to you in all confidentiality. There are others in the force who want to deal much more severely with you.'

'The chief?'

She didn't answer.

'If I'm right, I'm used to it. And I have to conclude that this death is now considered suspicious?'

She didn't answer this time, either.

'But did you check the diaries? Was the one for 2002 there?'

She studied me in silence for several seconds before answering. 'No, it wasn't.'

I shrugged and held my palms out. 'QED. *Quod erat demonstrandum.*'

'And for those of us who didn't have Latin at school?'

'Which was to be demonstrated.'

'But not by you, Varg.'

'No,' I said, unconvinced. 'Not by me.'

39

'Is it true what they're saying?'

I was no longer surprised by how quickly news travelled in this village. Betty was standing in the doorway, pale around the gills, having seen me approach through her kitchen window.

'About Guri Leitet?' she added.

I nodded. 'I was there when she was found.'

'Yes, Anna Eide rang me.'

'But Guri was old,' I said without any conviction. 'We can't discount the possibility that she died of natural causes. It's been a lot of hullabaloo for her, too, you know.'

'Do you believe that?'

'Well ... the police are there now, anyway. We'll hear what they have to say.'

'She was in bed, Anna said.'

'Yes.' I looked past her. 'Should we go inside?'

She cleared her throat. *'Yes, of course. I was just so shocked.'* She stepped aside and let me in.

I followed her into the kitchen.

'But no visible signs of violence?'

'Not that I could see. But I wasn't there long. I made sure we left the place as quickly as possible and informed the police.'

'Yet another death,' she said, with a telling expression on her face.

Unbidden, she poured me a cup of coffee and placed it on the table in front of one chair. If I stayed much longer in Solvik, my insides would be black.

'And, of course, you didn't find out if she'd seen anything the day Klaus died.'

'No.'

'Do you think it's still possible to get to the bottom of this case?'

I envisioned the 2002 pocket diary. If it turned up, then, yes, maybe. But how likely was that? 'Hard to say. It's up to you whether you still want me on the case. My hourly rate is all it'll cost you.'

'With everything that's going on now – and that went on back then – and still so many unanswered questions, we can't stop now.'

'No. I have to confess I don't think I can let go of either case. But the police want to keep me as far away as possible, and Torunn has to travel to Oslo, she says, so we'll probably drive back to Bergen today. Have you seen anything of her?'

'I took her a pot of coffee an hour ago. She was sitting at her computer.'

I finished my coffee and stood up. 'Then I'll go over and see how she's getting on.'

As I made for the door, she grabbed my arm and held me back. I turned to her. She sent me an imploring look.

'I don't regret employing you for a second, Varg. There's something scary going on here. Poor old Guri. You have to put a stop to all this.'

I smiled apologetically. 'I'm afraid I can't do it on my own, Betty. The police said they were following specific leads. They wouldn't have said that if they didn't mean it.'

She glanced at the window. *'It's all so frightening. I don't just lock the front door any more, I lock my bedroom door, too. And I keep my mobile on the bedside table.'*

I patted her reassuringly on the shoulder. 'Then you should feel safe. And at the moment the police are not far away, either.'

She pulled me closer and gave me a hug, then let me go with a slightly ashamed expression on her face. I sent her a smile, then carried on out into the yard and walked across it.

I didn't even manage this without being observed. This time it was by Torunn. She was sitting at the table by the window with her laptop open and a mobile in her hand, talking to someone. She beckoned me over. I stepped into the passageway between the two rooms and opened her door.

She was rounding off her conversation. 'We've got a deal then. Great. Thank you very much.' After ringing off, she gave me a thumbs-up and said: 'Change of plans. Now we have an appointment in Bergen this evening, Varg.'

'We?'

'I told him it was you who found the camper van in which Mona Martens died, and they both said they'd like to meet you.'

'And who are we talking about here?'

She grinned. 'I was speaking to Ole Lavik. We're invited to a meeting with Fredrik Martens at nine tonight.'

'Right. That's impressive…'

'They've booked a conference room in Hotel Norge.'

'And how on earth did you manage to fix that?'

'Fredrik Martens will be there in a private capacity, as Lavik put it. I had to promise not to write anything about meeting him personally and not to quote him on anything. If anyone is to be quoted, it's Ole Lavik. But apparently Martens wants to guide the press in the right direction, but indirectly, as it were, and, for whatever reason, he's chosen me to do it with.'

'That can of course be interpreted in a variety of ways, but I'd view it positively, if I were you.'

'Let's wait and see,' she said in that neutral tone I had gradually begun to recognise.

When we went back to see Betty in the kitchen, she refused to let Torunn pay for the overnight stay. 'Anyone who's a friend of Varg's, is a friend of mine,' Betty said, and Torunn mounted one of her reflective smiles, which were always hard to decipher.

Not long afterwards, we were on our way. The rocks had been cleared; but the huge boulder, Trolleye, still lay at the side of the road. We reached Bergen without any further mishaps, neither from nature's side nor from unexpected telephone calls.

40

Ole Lavik met us in the reception area of the hotel and accompanied us up four floors in the lift. Then he guided us along a corridor to a furnished conference room with a view of the City Park and the Music Pavilion.

From 1885, Hotel Norge had been one of Bergen's most sophisticated hotels. The old, timbered building had survived the great conflagration of 1916, the fire having been extinguished when it was midway through the building. But it hadn't survived modern times. In 1961 the magnificent old hotel was razed to the ground and a new and far sleeker one was erected on the site. For many years it had been a favourite meeting place for the town's upper echelon, if they wanted either splendidly discreet isolation or a more sociable atmosphere, on festive occasions.

For Fredrik Martens there was no doubt that discretion was his guiding principle in life. Having searched once again for information about him online, I had found not one single picture earlier than a Norwegian School of Economics orchestra photograph dated 17th May, 1969. I reminded myself that Riverbank Invest had its HQ in Jersey, at a comfortable distance from the Norwegian tax authorities, and that the office in Kokstad was, from what I could see, no more than a branch.

Indeed, the man who rose to his feet behind the dark, shiny mahogany table looked as discreet as a dyed-in-the-wool accountant. Nevertheless, from the very first moment, he radiated the power a fortune of several billions lent him. The cut of his grey suit revealed that it had been sewn by a far more exclusive tailor than I would ever be able to afford. The royal-blue tie was held in place with a stickpin of white gold, and on his lapel he wore a cryptic pin denoting membership of an association with much stricter acceptance criteria than the Rotary Club or the

Lions Club. However, his face was strangely anonymous: lean, colourless, his grey hair neatly parted and combed backward on both sides. His nose was pointed, his mouth rigid, and he wore a pair of narrow, rectangular glasses that only partly camouflaged his sharp, flinty eyes.

Ole Lavik did the introductions. Martens remained behind the table, eschewing walking round and shaking hands. But he confirmed his presence with a slight nod, once again more accountant-like than magisterial.

He gestured to two chairs on our side of the table. Ole Lavik pulled one out for Torunn and left me to grapple with the other. He then walked back around the table and stood beside Martens, who in the meantime had taken the weight off his feet.

Lavik leaned forward and pushed a few sheets of paper across the smooth table top in our direction. 'Before a word is said, you must sign this non-disclosure agreement.'

Torunn raised her eyebrows and studied the two gentlemen across the table. For my part, I said: 'Really? For what reason?'

'CEO Martens never gives interviews, on principle. He's invited frøken Tafjord for a conversation in order to give her the best possible overview of the situation, but it is a private conversation that can neither be reproduced in the public media nor cited.'

Torunn's face stiffened even further, if that was possible.

Lavik looked at me. 'As far as you're concerned, Veum…'

'Now I am curious.'

'CEO Martens has invited you because you were the individual who found the vehicle in which his daughter died on Friday, 1st October. He's interested in hearing your side of the story.'

'And for that I need to sign this non-disclosure agreement?'

'It covers everything that may be discussed around the table today.'

Torun turned to me, angled her head and shrugged. 'We have

no choice, Varg.' But I saw from her expression that she was see-thing inside.

'That's correct,' Ole Lavik added. 'It's take-it-or-leave-it time.'

We each picked up the three sheets and read them carefully. I was thinking that broken agreements are a daily feature of business life, and signed the third sheet with a wry smile – mentally, of course. Ole Lavik told me to add my initials to the first two sheets as well, and with a heartfelt sigh I completed this part of the proce-dure, too. I noted that Torunn was doing the same, tight-lipped and with such daggers in her eyes it wasn't safe to be near her.

His Master's Voice reached out for both sets of signed docu-ments and nodded contentedly.

'I assume we can have a copy,' Torunn said.

'You can after the meeting.'

'Shall we get started then?'

Ole Lavik turned to Fredrik Martens, who leaned slightly forward and castled his fingers, like some esoteric ritual he had brought with him from his masonic lodge, perhaps.

He coughed thinly, and for the first time we heard him say something. His voice was conspicuously high-pitched, some-where between choirboy and castrato. But, musically speaking, he maintained the same register throughout, an unvarying monotone. And like an echo from the 1950s he used the formal mode of address when he spoke to us. It created a distance that was bizarrely difficult to neutralise.

'I've read most of your reports with interest, frøken Tafjord. Strangely, they lack nuance, like most of what is written in the press and elsewhere about our line of business. I'll leave it to others to correct you, where necessary. Personally, I will set forth why I think this industry is so vital, not only for our own country, but for the whole world.'

Torunn smiled acidly and leaned back in her chair, as if to demonstrate that she'd heard this before – it was such a *yaaawn*.

'In Norway, aquaculture is in fact no more than around thirty years old, but over the last decade it has seen a marked increase in growth, thanks to technological advances in the fight against what at the outset was a challenge: salmon lice and other parasites.'

He took a little pause and shifted his gaze from Torunn to me and back again, as if to emphasise that he included the likes of us in 'other parasites'.

'Historically speaking, fish farming goes back to long before the Christian era, with the breeding of carp in China and tilapia in Egypt several millennia ago, while up here in the north we were still in the Stone Age. In Norway, there were trout hatcheries in the 1800s, but this was to supplement the stock of freshwater fish. What we characterise as modern salmon farming started in the 1960s and 1970s; in other words, at about the same time as oil was discovered in the North Sea, with all that implied for our country.'

I was dangerously close to yawning myself.

'Today there has been such accelerated growth in aquaculture that it looks very much like the industry this country will live off when oil comes to an end, either because the reserves are drained or because the development of climate politics demands it.' He parted his fingers and pressed his splayed hand hard against the table, as if to keep his balance. 'Obviously fish farming is a more natural business than extracting oil from the sea bed. Man has always reared livestock for slaughter and meat processing. We've lived on fish in Norway, well, from the Stone Age. And currently the world population is increasing year on year. The need for food is greater than ever. The majority of the globe is covered in water, so what would be more natural than to regard the seas as the most natural pantry for us all? This is what we're investing in, and are personally committed to, and with ever-improving technology, this bodes well, both for our own country and the rest of the world. It is all the more regrettable that it has become fashionable to protest against this development, with on occasion dramatic consequences for some of us.'

Now it was his turn to lean back and observe us in the same distanced way as before.

Torunn trod warily. 'Yes, it was terrible what happened to your daughter.' She chose the informal form of address. As she didn't receive an instant response, she continued: 'All these arguments you've mentioned are very familiar, and I don't see any reason to sign a non-disclosure agreement to prevent them from being heard. I assume there are other sides of the issue you wish to elucidate.'

Martens didn't visibly react. Instead, he focused on me. 'I've been informed that it was you who found the vehicle Mona was in, herr Veum.'

'Yes, I'm afraid so.'

'Under what circumstances?'

'Erm ... haven't the police told you?' I also used the informal form.

For the first time, he showed some temperament. His expression stiffened and he exclaimed: 'No, they have not. I have my information from other quarters. My experience has been that the police almost consider me a suspect in the case!'

'A suspect? On what basis?'

'Well, your guess is as good as mine, herr Veum.'

For a moment, there was a silence between us. I cast a glance at Ole Lavik, who had been sitting at the table, listening, stony-faced.

Torunn said: 'It must've been unpleasant for you to find out that your own daughter was participating in the demonstration against Sunfjord Salmon?'

Martens met her gaze. 'Unpleasant? Yes, it was. But from

there to … It's absurd. Every family has disagreements. The young want to rebel, but Mona was clever enough to be able to see the issue from both sides. There was no enmity between her and me.'

'And from what I've been told,' I broke in, looking at Ole Lavik, 'you two were engaged to be married?'

Martens looked at his intended son-in-law with a slight inclination of his head, which could have been viewed both as confirmation and a form of sympathy.

Ole Lavik said: 'Yes, we were. No one – apart from her father, I mean – has grieved more over what happened than I.'

I made a mental note that I had to find out if there was a mother in the picture, too. Martens was sharp-eyed enough to read the situation and said: 'My wife passed away almost ten years ago.'

'I see.'

He carried on: 'And now we're back to why you were invited to this conversation, herr Veum. As the police are refusing to tell me what happened, I would very much like to hear your version of events that September day when she … died.'

'As you yourself know, she wasn't alone in the camper van.'

He nodded briefly.

'And, to tell the truth, I don't know anything at all about what happened on the day she went missing, along with Jonas Kleiva.' I tried to discern some kind of reaction to the name, but he seemed as unmoved as before.

'How did you come across them?'

'A cabin-owner living in the district, Edvard Aga, wanted to show me the disused fish farm in Markatangen. I believe Aga's an old acquaintance of yours, isn't he?'

'That is correct. But it's years since we've seen each other.' He now seemed a trifle taken aback.

'So you had no idea he was with me when we found the van?'

'None at all.'

'Well, that's how it was. We drove out there, he and I, and by chance we spotted the van under the water, just off the end of the quay. We rang the police, who arrived with a team of Fire & Rescue Service divers from Bergen, so in that sense neither Aga nor I found her. The divers did. But I had, of course, seen her before.'

In brief I told him about my enforced bus journey from Førde on the day the demonstration against Sunfjord Salmon took place, and how I had seen Mona and Marita when they got off the bus and met Jonas.

'Marita…?'

'Svanøy. A friend of Mona's – and one of the tenants in Forstandersmuget.'

He nodded slowly. 'You are a private investigator, I understand.'

'Mm … yes.'

'So what did you find out as a result of your investigations?'

'I haven't investigated this case at all, herr Martens. The police are doing that.'

'But I've been informed you've been carrying out an extensive investigation.'

'I don't know where you've been getting your information, but I've been looking into quite a different case from the Solvik one. Klaus Krog – does that name mean anything to you?'

He nodded pensively while looking at Torunn and then glancing at Ole Lavik. 'There was an accident that ended fatally, wasn't there?'

'Yes. And Klaus Krog was – like Torunn here – someone who wrote critical articles about fish farming. In other words, there is a clear connection.' I looked at Ole Lavik. 'Perhaps he paid a call on you too?'

'Klaus Krog? Not that I can remember.'

'No?'

'No.'

I fixed my eyes on Fredrik Martens again. 'Not only that, he lived with Betty Kleiva, whom – I believe – you also knew.'

He met my stare and once again I became aware of how adept he was at reading others. A few tiny facial details – his eyes narrowing a fraction, his lips perceptibly tightening, though barely, the corners of his mouth stretching into the ghost of a smile – confirmed that he knew what I was saying. And he knew intuitively what I knew. Immediately his eyes fell onto the non-disclosure agreement, then he glanced at me again and answered: 'For as long as it lasted.'

'But you would never admit that.'

A strange atmosphere had developed in the room. The only matter of any significance now was the covert exchange between Fredrik Martens and me, with Torunn and Ole Lavik observers on the sidelines, relegated to the bench by the coach, as it were.

'There's nothing to admit.'

My response was to gape at him and pull a wry grimace. Then I turned to Ole Lavik. 'Did you know your fiancée was involved with Jonas Kleiva?'

He sent me a cold stare. 'Involved? I very much doubt that.'

'They were in the same vehicle on that fateful Tuesday in September.'

'She was going back to Bergen with him, I've been told.'

'Yes, it would've been a little strange if she'd been going back with her fiancé after just taking part in a demonstration against the company where he was the director of the board.'

'Don't you believe … It's not how it looks to … people like you.'

Fredrik Martens cleared his throat. Ole Lavik looked at him, received the silent rebuke, turned to face me and leaned back in his chair. 'I have no more to say on this matter.'

'No, of course not. But you've given me an idea,' I said, to give them some food for thought, too.

'If we can get back to what we should be talking about,' Torunn broke in. 'I have a clear sense that there's a sizeable internal conflict at Sunfjord Salmon. With Kåre Kleiva and the Østland investors, represented by Cecilie Tangen, on one side – and others too, perhaps – and you two on the other.'

'With the majority of the shares on our side, I think we should add,' said Martens.

'But without two-thirds of the shareholders, I'd say you'd had your wings clipped, wouldn't you?'

Martens regarded her with condescension. 'A passing cyclone. We'll sort it out. An extraordinary board meeting has been called for Monday, with myself in attendance, and then all will be resolved.'

'On Monday. So soon? It's that precarious?'

'This was what I wanted to make clear to you, frøken Tafjord.'

With a little smile, I noticed how annoyed Torunn became at being addressed in that fashion, but she swallowed it and sat listening.

'In principle, there is no internal conflict at Sunfjord Salmon. This issue has nothing to do with the way the farm is run, or the future of the business. Kåre Kleiva bought his way into the company to cause maximum mischief, because he's still bitter about what happened when we set up a farm in Sørneset that is ten times better than what he had further down Skuggefjorden. Cecile Tangen's an opportunist who follows the herd. I have myself been in direct contact with several of those she represents and her position is already hanging by a thread. We'll clear up all of this on Monday.'

Suddenly it was as if Fredrik Martens' voice had become louder and deeper; it was a style that was easily recognisable. This was the voice of power, the sound of someone who knew he was in total control. Ole Lavik sat beside him, nodding at regular intervals to show that he agreed with every word that was said.

'Will it be possible to speak to someone after the board meeting?'

'There'll be a press release. That will be enough.'

'This non-disclosure agreement,' Torunn said. 'Does it also apply to the news that there'll be an extraordinary board meeting on Monday?'

He leaned slightly forward and said in the same uncompromising tone: 'It applies to *everything* that's been said at this table this evening. Everything!'

With that, the conversation was at an end. Fredrik Martens rose to his feet before we left, but, again, there was no suggestion that he was going to come around and shake hands. Power sets the rules. Power decides who it will favour with the niceties.

Before departing, I said to him: 'Let's hope the police find out what befell Jonas and Mona.' I looked at Ole Lavik. 'Apparently they're looking for a black car.'

'Have you solved your own case, herr Veum?'

'The Klaus Krog case? No, I'm afraid not. Not yet.'

'Then perhaps we'd better wish each other luck,' Fredrik Martens said before demonstratively sitting back down at the table and taking a wad of papers from the briefcase on the chair next to him. From then on, we were invisible. He didn't so much as raise his eyes as we walked to the door, and he pretended he didn't hear when Torunn wished him a pleasant evening.

Ole Lavik accompanied us down to reception and thanked us formally for the meeting. We said there was nothing to thank us for, which was the truth.

Outside, in Ole Bulls plass, in the shadow of Stephan Sinding's bronze monument to the composer, with Ole Bull himself playing the violin, inspired by a male water sprite,

Torunn looked at me and asked: 'What on earth was that all about?'

'Good question. He seemed to be more concerned about being suspected of having had something to do with his daughter's death than the outcome of the board meeting on Monday.'

'Looks like I might have to cross the mountains from Oslo again for that. But what were you alluding to with your comment about Betty Kleiva?'

'I can tell you that over a glass of nectar. Shall we go and see the barman with the red braces or go to my place?'

She angled a glance at me. 'Let's stay at the hotel. Then it's not so far to bed.'

'It doesn't need to be that far at mine, either.'

She smiled sweetly, but we walked to the hotel. It turned out that the bar was closed for the evening, but there was a solution. As I passed reception at two a.m., the receptionist sent me a knowing look. On my way home it struck me that the old rule had been confirmed once again. The second time was always better. And now her bottle of Jameson was empty. Completely empty.

41

On Friday morning I was woken by Thomas ringing me from Oslo. 'You awake?'

I blinked. 'Yup. Sort of.'

'Here's Jakob for you.'

'Right.' I pushed myself back in bed, sat up and leaned against the bedhead. I heard some diffuse sounds from my two-year-old grandchild, which I interpreted as something like *gagagaga-da*. 'Hello, Jakob,' I said. 'This is Grandad.' Again the response was unclear, but considerably easier to understand: 'Ganda'. It gave me an acute attack of lump-in-the-throat. I missed seeing them more often.

Then it was Thomas again. 'You understood what he said, of course?'

'Well…'

'Happy birthday!'

I looked at the screen on my phone. 'Oh, heck. Actually I'd forgotten.'

'You're not planning a celebration, in other words?'

In fact, I'd been celebrating until half past one in the morning, but I kept that one to myself. 'I guess it'll be a trip down to see the man in the red braces. We'll have to see. No plans beyond that.'

'I can give you some good news anyway.'

'Really?'

'You're going to be a grandad twice over sometime over Christmas or early in the New Year.'

'Really!' I repeated. 'That's great to hear. Then I'm looking forward to a trip across the mountains when it's spring.'

'But we'll see you for Christmas, won't we?'

'Yes, yes, I'm sure we will.' In my head, it was still a long time to Christmas.

'Mari sends her love. And you've already spoken to Jakob.'

I chuckled. We chatted for a bit longer: some updates on academic life in Ullevål Hageby and so on; relatively discreet descriptions of life in Masfjorden municipality. We wrapped up the conversation in the most congenial style: Enjoy the day, Dad, and Thanks for calling, Son.

'See you soon,' he said.

'See you,' I replied. But as I always reflected after we had rung off: at my age and with my profession you were never absolutely sure what life had in store for you.

Suddenly waking up, as I had, set in motion a process in me. There was a time for everything, even for birthdays. With regard to which, I had kept a low profile for years, and I had no intention of hoisting a flag over the front door this year, either. But I did allow myself a generous portion of eggs and bacon and lingered over the first cups of coffee.

The conversation with Jakob and Thomas had triggered a merry-go-round of memories and images. I remembered Thomas when he was two years old and how relations between Beate and me had already started to go wrong: the conflict over my irregular working hours in social services and her need for a more stable life to make her working day easier too. I hoped Thomas and Mari managed to balance that side of their lives better than we had. But I envied them the feeling of closeness they had with their little child, at the start of what would hopefully be a long life without too many problems. This phase of life was one that would never return.

After breakfast I made myself comfortable in the best chair I had, with a view of the rooftops on the other side of Telthussmuget. In my lap I was holding Klaus Krog's manuscript, which I had brought with me from Solvik. I opened the brown wallet. The sheets were loose-leaf and typewritten, but there were a number of corrections in biro, some in the text, some as comments in the margin.

On the first sheet he had written a possible title for the book: *WILD FISH*. But he had crossed it out and inserted some alternatives beside it: *Dead Fjords*, *The Death of Wild Fish* and *The Catch in the Fjord*. He had drawn a large circle incorporating the original title and the alternatives. Outside the circle there was a big question mark, a clear sign that he hadn't reached a final decision.

I started reading. By way of an introduction, he mentioned a lot of the historical detail that Fredrik Martens had summarised during the meeting at Hotel Norge. Klaus Krog also referred to carp farming in European monasteries in the Middle Ages and early attempts on the west coast of the USA and Canada. However, he soon moved on to the pioneer days in Norway during the 1960s and 1970s. Problems had arisen from the very start. Farmed salmon escaped and lice spread down the fjords and up the rivers where the wild salmon spawned. The crossing of wild salmon with farmed salmon was a catastrophe for the wild stocks. There was a risk that the wild salmon would have to go on the Red List of threatened species before long. Krog picked out fish health and the effects on tourism as arguments against fish farming.

After this general introduction he went on to describe more personal details. He talked vividly about his own younger years in Skien in the seventies and eighties and how his father and uncle had taken him fishing in the Skien watershed, on mountain hikes in Telemark and over the Hardanger plateau. As a result of this, he himself had become a passionate hobby angler. He even managed to turn what was at first a leisure activity into his profession, as a journalist on *Jakt & Fiske*. Before he got that far, he had taken an MA in geography at the University of Oslo. He had travelled to Iceland and Scotland, always with research into river fishing as his driving force. And in Norway he had travelled across most of the country in search of the perfect fish, which he saw as a free, living creature, a national symbol that was far more important and, geographically speaking, more appropriate than the lions outside parliament in Oslo, and elsewhere in heraldic symbolism.

Gradually he began to turn his attention in particular to Solvik, Skuggefjorden and the development of aquaculture there, from the first farm by Markatangen to the one in Sørneset, which had been set up by Einar Sørnes and later renamed Sunfjord Salmon, which he excoriated in the most biting terms.

Thereafter the manuscript became something else. His love for Solvik itself and the countryside shone through. He described the hike to Storfossen waterfall, up to Lake Stølsvatnet and beyond to Bjørn West country. He wrote about experiences in nature, animal life, birds he heard and spotted, and fish he saw swimming through river watersheds. It all appeared to be a description of a paradise that was about to be lost, not because anyone had eaten from the Tree of Knowledge, but because they were in the process of chopping it down and digging up the roots.

He also gave intimate descriptions of people he had met and spoken to, most of them with a varying degree of irony. None of them was mentioned by name, but were labelled with a first letter or initials. I thought I could identify Einar Sørnes, his son Knut, and even Caesar, as well as Kåre Kleiva and Truls Hatlevik, the latter referred to as 'TH, B's brother'. The same 'B' was never mentioned directly, but as a marker, so that 'J, B's son with KK' was easy to see through.

The style here was critical, and he also mentioned – provisionally just as keywords – the schism the dispute over the fish farms had created in Solvik – within one family even, as he put it, without elaborating.

The last thing he had committed to paper was an account of how he had tried in vain to get a tour of the fish farm in Sørneset and how he had literally been shown the door by 'ES'.

On the last sheet there were some handwritten notes, which I construed as plans for what he would do next, among them a few interesting details, which I committed to memory. After flicking back to the start, there was also a table of contents, which suggested that what I was holding in my hand was about two thirds of a complete manuscript. Klaus Krog's posthumous writings, which would never amount to anything more than that.

I wondered if the Masfjorden police had bothered to read through this manuscript as thoroughly as I had, or if they had even had access to it. I jotted down a couple of things, which gave me some leads to follow, if the respective persons were willing to talk, that was, which I had grave misgivings about.

But there was another person I wanted to talk to. Something that both Ole Lavik and Fredrik Martens had alluded to during the previous evening had given me something to chew on. And I had a feeling that person wasn't so very far from me, in a geographical sense. Only a stone's throw or two down towards Vågen bay. I would have to accept that I was, once again, defying the police's clear instructions to leave the investigation into Mona Martens' and Jonas Kleiva's deaths to them. But then I wasn't going to investigate. I was just going to ask a couple of questions, as I told myself on the way down to Forstandersmuget, without even being able to convince myself.

42

It was around two o'clock in the afternoon when I rang the top bell beside the green door. I stepped back and looked up at the windows on the first floor. Behind one, to the left, I saw a movement – a blonde head lunging out of sight.

I gave her a minute or so. As nothing happened, I stepped forward and rang the bell again – a long, insistent ring.

This time she opened the window and stared down at me. *'What d'you want?'*

'There's something we have to talk about.'

She pursed her lips.

'It's important.'

She shook her head, annoyed. *'Alright then. I'll come down.'* Then she slammed the window shut.

Immediately afterwards I heard her footsteps clomping down the stairs. Then the door opened. She got straight to the point. *'What?'*

'May I invite you out for a cup of coffee? We can go to Kafe Løkten just down here – or somewhere else.'

She rolled her eyes. *'I haven't got the time. You'd better come in. But I can't offer you a drink or anything.'*

'If we can just have a little chat, that's more than enough for me.'

She led the way up the stairs. She was wearing a cotton sweater with blue and red stripes. Her blonde hair was gathered in a ponytail and held with a matching blue-and-red elastic band.

At the top of the stairs, she turned left, where the door to her part of the floor was open. I followed her into a room that was, if possible, even more cramped than Geir Gravdal's. It was considerably tidier, however. A sofa that probably doubled as a bed was by one wall. The table in front was low. There was an open iMac in the middle. Beside it, a pile of magazines. On the sofa a book was open, spine up. It was a textbook. In this room, instead of a bean bag, a single Jæren chair stood next to the table. Along the wall opposite there was a narrow writing desk with a bookshelf above. The books looked fairly well organised. I noticed she didn't have a TV or a decent hi-fi, but there was a combined radio and CD player on one end of the shelf. The only decoration on the wall was a large poster of the Kings of Convenience with a photograph of the two musicians and the title of their debut album: *Quiet Is the New Loud*. Through an open door I glimpsed a kitchenette, as tidy as the bookshelf and as compact as her sound system.

I stood in the middle of the room. 'Things ended rather abruptly last time we met,' I smiled.

She appeared somewhat uneasy. *'What did you expect? I was so frightened about what might've happened to them – Mona and Jonas – and when that policewoman phoned, it was all too much for me. I still feel numb inside. And you were just sitting there when you already knew!'* I was about to answer, but she was faster. *'It could've been me in that camper!'*

'Really?'

'But when Mona set her cap at a guy, she usually got what she wanted.' She stood staring ahead of her. *'There was so much going on.'* She focused on me again. *'We were ... we are young people. It's an emotional time, and we say and do things that are different from what we actually want.'*

'What do you mean?'

She glared at me defiantly. *'I don't want to talk about it.'*

I gestured towards the seats. 'Shall we sit down?'

She eyed me, still hanging back. Then she shrugged. She pointed to the traditional wooden chair.

'I'll sit here then,' I said, and did so.

She coiled up on the sofa, as far away from me as possible.

'Mona,' I continued, 'she must've been a rare bird in your

flock. Her father's a primary shareholder in Sunfjord Salmon, and she was engaged to Ole Lavik, who runs Riverbank, the investment company behind the whole business.'

'Engaged? Yes, I suppose she was. Not that that held her back once she'd made up her mind.'

'Have you met him?'

'Ole Lavik? Not to my knowledge.'

I waited a moment. Then I said: 'In Solvik there were rumours that there'd been something between her and a man called Knut Sørnes as well. The CEO of Sunfjord Salmon.'

'Oh? She never said anything about him to me.'

'I can see she wasn't short of suitors. I suspect we can add your neighbour, Geir Gravdal, to the list. How many fingers do we need to get an idea of how many men she had on the go?'

She looked quite unhappy now. 'Mm. Who knows. I don't. But Jonas was definitely new. They'd only been together since August.'

'Let me ask you one thing.'

'OK.'

'You were a bit taken by Jonas yourself, weren't you.'

She shrugged and nodded vaguely.

'Smitten perhaps?'

'... Maybe.' Then she nodded more firmly. 'I thought we were going somewhere. But then everything was turned upside down.'

'He got together with Mona?'

She nodded.

'Were you good friends, you and Mona?'

'Good ...? I'm not sure. But I thought we were equally committed to the environment, and we lived here, in the same house. And she went home with me to Førde to make the banners. But...'

She paused, so I interjected: 'You said "I thought". Was there any indication that she was play-acting?'

She hesitated. 'I wouldn't say that exactly. But there was always something strange and distant about her, as though you could never quite get close to her. Perhaps that was why things happened the way they did – later that day, I mean.'

'Can you elaborate?'

She glared at me. *I don't know if I want to. Not to you anyway.'*

I left a pause, then I said: 'And what about Jonas? What was he like? I've never got a real impression of him.'

Her eyes wandered. *'Hm, what should I say? Jonas was very special. A one-off. I suppose, in many ways, he was a lone wolf. I don't think he had an easy upbringing. His parents split up when he was fifteen, which is a vulnerable age, isn't it. During our classes he always sat at the back or as far away as he could from everyone else. In the breaks he didn't speak to many people, apart from me – eventually.'* She took a breath. *'It was me who took the first step and spoke to him. I just went up to him and asked him straight out: "Are you from Sogn og Fjordane, too?" He answered, "No, Masfjorden," and then we stood chatting for a while.'*

'But you became friends?'

'Yes, we did, eventually.' Then she quickly added: *'And he didn't seem to have any others. I don't think he had any girlfriends either.'*

'No, that's what I've heard. Did you go and visit him in his bedsit?'

'No, I didn't. But he was here a few times. Visiting. Nothing else.'

'Was that how he met Mona?'

She looked at me unhappily and pouted. *'I suppose so, yes.'*

'But you were all committed to the ecological movement – and especially involved in the debate around fish farms?'

She nodded her head enthusiastically. *'Yes, we were, all of us. I thought we were, anyway.'*

'But, again, Mona's commitment was the most incongruous, considering her background?'

'Yes, it was, but then Jonas also came from a family who had a fish farm.'

'Yes, of course, you're right. My understanding was that after his parents separated, he didn't have any contact with his father. Did he ever talk about that?'

'Never.'

'Never ever?'

'The only thing I can remember him saying was that he rarely saw his father. He didn't explain why. I thought it might have something to do with the divorce and how his father had behaved towards his mother. But he said nothing about that. It's something I've wondered about since.'

'The picture you've painted of Jonas is of a rather quiet, re-served young man. But he can't have been that reserved; he took part in demonstrations, such as the one against the farm in the area where he grew up. He clearly knew what he was doing.'

'Yes.'

'Last time I spoke to you and Geir Gravdal, you said there'd been a bit of a situation, which ended with Mona intending to come back here with Jonas.'

She hesitated. '...Yes, there'd been a row. Mona was in the middle of it.'

'Uhuh?'

'It had become clear to everyone that Geir was in love with her, too. You're right, he was another name on the list. It was so obvious – the puppy-dog eyes he was making...' She rolled her own eyes. 'But when we arrived in Solvik that day, Mona declared to the whole wide world that it was Jonas who had taken her fancy. It was as though she was clinging to him and giving him all the attention she could. Of course, I could see how jealous Geir was. It was just as obvious as his puppy-dog eyes. He was furious.'

'And it all blew up?'

'Yes, between Mona and Geir. A blistering row, I'd call it. He made the nastiest accusations. And he may've been right, for all I know. I mean, you couldn't ignore the fact that security was much tighter than we'd expected. In fact, there were more guards than demonstrators. Geir said it was because Mona had warned them that we were on our way. And he actually claimed he could back up everything he claimed. He said he'd been shown emails and that she'd been passing on all our plans to Sunfjord Salmon for months. When she said she was on our side, she was playing a role, she was a fake, he said. It all just poured out of him. Everyone heard it.'

'Wow, that's a completely new picture of ... well, a number of things.'

She scowled at me. 'If you say so.'

'What happened next?'

'We were all shaken up by their row. We stood there like a flock of ... yes, we were like sheep. Mona grabbed hold of Jonas and almost dragged him over to his van. "Come on, Jonas," she said. "We're leaving." She said nothing to me, and that hurt, I have to admit. We'd travelled together from Førde, and then she just left me standing there, without bothering about how I felt.'

'And you didn't object?'

'What good would it have done? Mona had a strong personality, and she had the security and confidence her upbringing had given her. Geir was still fuming, but what could he do? It was him who had caused the whole situation. Besides, at the back of our minds, we knew she was our landlady in Bergen. If we fell out, she might show us the door. So that was how we left it. I went off with another friend – Herdis, her name is. Mona and Jonas were still talking beside his van when we left.' All of a sudden, she had tears in her eyes. 'And that was the last I saw of them.'

'And Geir?'

'He went off to his car – seething...'

'Then you drove back home in a sort of convoy?'

'A convoy? No. Herdis drove pretty fast, I'd say, so we were back long before he was.'

'Do you know if he's home now?'

'Geir? I doubt it.' Now there was something new about her.

Her mouth tightened into a thin line. Her eyes wandered and I noticed how her upper body seemed to shrink as though she was trying to protect herself against a dangerous threat.

I leaned forward. 'What's the matter, Marita?'

She looked up abruptly and stared me straight in the eyes. *I've finished with them.'*

'Finished with whom?'

'The group. I don't want anything to do with them anymore.'

'You mean the other demonstrators?'

'Geir and the others anyway. Him and some of the boys. They said they're going to get tough this time.'

'What do you mean?'

'They've found out there's going to be another board meeting on Monday. Do you know if there is?'

'Yes ... Perhaps.'

'And they're planning some kind of action, bigger than ever before.'

'What kind of action?'

'I don't know.' She cast around, resting her gaze on the poster of the Kings of Convenience. *Quiet Is the New Loud*, resonated at the back of my head. *'I believe in non-violent protest. And I don't know what they're planning, but Geir's been a different person the last few weeks, after what happened to Mona and Jonas. He's furious. I don't know what he might be capable of.'*

'It's only Friday today. What—?'

'They're dangerous. Him and some of the other guys. They're lying low, I reckon. But I don't know where.'

'No idea at all?'

'None.'

I leaned towards her. 'You have to report this to the police.'

She looked at me in despair. *'What should I say? I don't know anything.'*

'If you won't, I will. They have to be warned that there's something brewing. There's been enough drama already.'

She shrugged and nodded slowly. I took that as a sign that she was leaving me to contact the police.

'Before I go: if Geir turns up, can you let me know? Give me your phone number and I'll send you mine.'

She hesitated, then grabbed the phone lying on the table in front of her. We exchanged numbers.

'So you're not going to Solvik on Monday?'

She shook her head firmly. *'Not even if they paid me a hundred thousand kroner.'*

I patted my inside pocket. 'I'm afraid I haven't got that much on me.'

That produced a fleeting smile, but you had to be eagle-eyed to catch it.

43

I tapped in Signe Moland's number, but only got a voicemail telling me to leave a message and she would get back to me as soon as she had an opportunity. I didn't have the patience for that. When I rang the police station, they said that she wasn't available. I asked if I could speak to Helleve instead. He was tied up in a meeting, the duty switchboard officer said.

'Can you tell him to call me when he's free? Tell him it's important. We're talking about a potentially violent protest here.'

'What? Then you'll have to contact the security services.'

'Just tell Helleve. Then he can evaluate what I have to tell him.'

'And your name is…?'

'Veum. Varg Veum.'

We finished the conversation, him with a little sniff, which I heard as loud as if he were sitting in the next room.

I wasn't sure what to do while I waited to hear from Helleve. Should I ring someone at Sunfjord Salmon and warn them? Knut or Einar Sørnes? Ole Lavik, to pass a message on to Fredrik Martens? On the other hand, would they take me seriously?

I couldn't celebrate my birthday with a few drams either, in case I suddenly needed the car. Besides, I didn't have anyone to celebrate it with, apart from the man with the red braces, and he had to tend the bar, so he couldn't let rip, either.

To my great surprise, Helleve rang back straight away. When he heard what I had to tell him, he asked if I was able to drop by the station. Fifteen minutes later we were sitting in his office. But he wasn't alone. He introduced me to a colleague I had never met before.

Hjalmar Høgelid was an inspector at PST, the security services, dressed in civvies for the occasion: dark-brown suit, white shirt and a slim-jim tie, blue with red stripes, to signal his political neutrality. He was around forty years of age, lean and by the look of him very fit. His face was long, his nose a modest snub. His hair was whitish blond, shaven round his ears and neck, and with a decorative quiff on top, which evoked an image of Tintin. He subjected me to a searching stare, as though assessing my enemy-of-society potential.

'I've invited Høgelid along so that he's fully appraised of what you've told me, Veum.' I noted the formal mode of address. When I met Helleve in town, we were generally on first-name terms.

I met Høgelid's gaze. 'I assume that groups like this are already on PST's radar.'

When he answered, I could hear that he was a Rogalander, most likely from the central districts of the county. 'You're thinking about the demonstrators in Solvik a few weeks ago?'

'On the twenty-first of September, to be absolutely precise.'

A smile flickered. 'We've never really regarded them as a serious threat. The environmental movement mainly operates within the rules when trying to get their opinions heard. But there are always exceptions that prove the rule. Such as the explosion of a bridge in Gulen a few years ago.'

'I was there when it happened.'

He raised his eyebrows and glanced at Helleve.

'Yes, that's true. He has a strange knack for getting himself caught up in dramatic events.' Høgelid turned back to me. 'So let's hear what you have to tell us once again, Veum.'

I concentrated on everything relevant to Sunfjord Salmon, made a passing mention of Klaus Krog and emphasised that the police, and not me, were investigating the deaths of Jonas Kleiva and Mona Martens.

'The case will soon be cracked,' Helleve said. 'We have some clear leads.'

'I see…' I said, sending him an enquiring look.

He raised his palms. 'But what they are, we're keeping to ourselves.'

'So Signe Moland and the others are still in Solvik?'

'Not necessarily,' he said with a meaningful glance from me to Høgelid.

'There may be a link?' the PST man asked.

'We can talk about that after Veum's gone.'

'But he's still here,' I said.

'Yes,' Høgelid nodded. 'Thank you for reporting this. We'll follow it up in our own way.'

'Which means…?' As he failed to answer, I added: 'But you're not going to say anything about that, either.'

After a couple more barren exchanges, we agreed I should go.

Helleve said: 'You can find your own way out, Veum.'

'I've managed it before.'

'You have,' he said brusquely, without exhibiting the slightest joy at my initiative.

The way out was where it always was.

I had done my social duty. What more could they expect?

That evening I felt precisely as old as I was, sixty-two in stockinged feet. There was no other celebration than the one I poured into a glass at home, to the accompaniment of some rock 'n' roll, for a change. '*It's all over now*,' sang the Rolling Stones, and that was pretty much how I felt too.

For the rest of the weekend, I found myself on life's waiting list. I passed my time reading through Klaus Krog's posthumous manuscript once again and made a few more notes. On Sunday evening Torunn rang from Oslo. She told me she had received an exclusive invitation from Ole Lavik to the extraordinary meeting in Sørneset on Monday morning at twelve o'clock and asked if I was still available as her personal chauffeur and companion.

'Into the meeting as well?' I asked, more in disbelief than expectation.

She laughed. 'Hardly. But he did promise me the exclusive right to report on the meeting's conclusions, and that could be interesting enough, no?'

'My goodness. Did he say anything else?'

'What are you referring to now?'

'There's supposed to be a demo planned there this time too, and according to my source to more telling effect.'

'Really?'

I told her what Marita had said and that PST had been notified.

'This is sounding more and more like a scoop, Varg. Great. I'll be on the first morning flight from Oslo.'

'I'll have to be up early, I can see.'

'I can meet you in town.'

'No, no. I'll meet you at Flesland Airport.'

She gave me the arrival time and we rang off.

Afterwards, I sat staring into the air. The police were close to solving the case, there was a climactic board meeting in the offing, and Geir Gravdal was threatening a tougher response. '*Let it bleed*,' the Stones sang, and I had an uncomfortable feeling in my stomach there was going to be bloodshed.

44

The Oslo flight was ten minutes late this Monday morning. Among the passengers arriving at the top of the stairs and coming down to the concourse I spotted Torunn. I waved. She waved back with a big smile. Reaching the bottom of the stairs, she whisked through the crowd, ran up to me, gave me a hug and said: 'We have to wait for my rucksack.'

'The one with our Irish friend in?'

She smiled mischievously. 'Mhm.'

We went to stand by the baggage carousel and were among the fortunate ones to get their bags off the first cart to arrive. Five minutes later we were in the car and on our way to Solvik. The traffic around Bergen was in early-morning snail mode, but as soon as we were through Åsane, the queues melted away. From Knarvik and to the north we had almost a free run.

On the way I gave a detailed summary of the conversation with Marita and the meeting at the police station. I posited a theory on what might have happened. Several times Torunn came back with objections or asked questions such as: 'But why did…?' and 'D'you think…?' Which weren't always easy to answer.

It rained the whole way north and the windscreen wipers were going hell for leather, as if they were being paid. On our descent to Solvik, the clouds were so low you couldn't see the tops of the surrounding mountains. The fjord was such a dark grey, it bordered on black, and in Sørneset we could barely make out the salmon cages in the sea and the two buildings on land. I drove slowly through Solvik and glanced to the right at Betty's house and to the left at the store straight after, without seeing a sign of life in either place. We didn't stop. We turned into the road to Sunfjord Salmon and whatever was awaiting us there.

A police car was stationed in a passing place just before

Sørneset. In the front seat an officer was holding a mobile phone to his mouth. I assumed he was reporting that a car was coming.

When we turned into the forecourt of Sunfjord Salmon, there were already several cars parked. A door opened and out stepped Signe. She looked over in our direction, but when she saw it was me, she pulled a resigned grimace and said something to a colleague in the car. But she didn't get back in. She leaned against the bonnet while keeping an eye on us.

There was a feeling of tension and expectation in the air. The number of demonstrators in attendance was strikingly modest. Eight people faced the gate, five of whom were young women. They were holding a banner that still hadn't been completely un-furled; all we could see were the letters O-R-D-E-N. There were considerably more guards and police officers. The guards were bare-headed and wore practical, dark uniforms with wide reflec-tive stripes down the edges of their jackets and round their ankles. They stood by the gate, ready to guide in permit holders. Inside the gate, Einar and Knut Sørnes stood as representatives of the local welcome committee, Knut holding Caesar on a chain beside him. In front of one of the police emergency vehicles were two officers in full kit with helmet, visor, bulletproof vest and a Heckler & Koch MP5 machine gun. Inside the vehicle I saw more officers with similar equipment, ready for action. There was no doubt that someone had taken the warnings seri-ously.

'You'll have to tread carefully here,' I said to Torunn, who was looking at the armed police officers with a wary expression. 'No sudden moves,' I added with a grin before opening the door slowly and stepping out of the car at a speed that clearly dem-onstrated I was taking heed of my own instructions. She followed suit on her side. I looked down towards the fish farm and noticed a patrol boat glide slowly past the perimeter of the cages with a fully armed police officer standing on the quarter-deck. They were leaving nothing to chance and were ready for whatever might come.

I gestured to Signe, asking if it was OK for us to join her. She tilted her head and wore an expression that I interpreted as a yes. Everyone around us watched as we crossed the car park to where she was leaning against the car. Inside, Bjarne Solheim sat with a mobile phone in his hand, staring blankly at us as we approached.

'We'll have to stop meeting like this, Signe,' I said.

'Fine by me.' She nodded to Torunn. 'Nice to see you again.'

'And the same to you,' she said with a little smile.

'Torunn's been invited to cover the scheduled board meeting inside,' I said, pointing in the direction of the gate.

'Really? Then you'll have to report to the guard, I'd guess.'

Torunn nodded, glanced at me and said: 'I'll do that then. Let's see what happens.'

'Good luck,' I replied.

We watched as she crossed the car park. The guards – ten of them, from what I could see – assembled in front of her, wearing grim expressions, as though this unaccompanied woman constituted a grave threat to the salmon-farming industry. After she had explained why she was there, they opened a path for her, like the Red Sea opening for Moses, and let her through.

By the gate there was another guard, who hadn't heard her explanation. After a little negotiation she beckoned Einar and Knut Sørnes over, apparently to vouch for her. Clearly a little more negotiation and a word from Knut on his mobile were required before Einar motioned to the guard to open the gate. While this was going on, the eight demonstrators had the guards' undivided attention and had now fully unfurled their banner. *REDD FJORDEN!* It said in capitals: 'Save the fjord', although there was a lot of evidence to suggest it was already too late.

On the premises now, Torunn stood beside Sørnes father and son, who just shrugged in response to her questions. It struck me how small and thin she looked next to those two big, strapping guys.

Signe's phone rang. 'Yes? That's fine. We'll accompany them.' I looked down at her. 'More on the way?'

She didn't need to answer. At relatively short intervals all the expected board members arrived for the meeting. Every single car was thoroughly checked by the guards, all while maintaining their focus on the demonstrators.

At the sight of the board members, they erupted into life. In high-pitched voices they screamed their protests: 'Don't kill the fjord! Let the fish live!' The board members ignored them completely as they passed.

We watched from a distance as the few privileged vehicles were allowed inside the fence and the passengers got out. Mayor Truls Hatlevik drove a white Toyota Corolla of the same vintage as my own. He was the only person to glance nervously towards the demonstrators and us on the outside.

Kåre Kleiva and Cecilia Tangen came in the same car – an Audi A4, which I assumed Kleiva, or more than likely Kleiva Invest, owned. Cecilia Tangen stood talking to Hatlevik while Kåre Kleiva walked with determined step over to Einar and Knut Sørnes and addressed them. The preliminary skirmishes were well under way.

Now a Mercedes Benz that I had seen before appeared. It was immediately guided through the Red Sea and past the guard before parking safely inside the gate, which was then closed and locked with unequivocal clarity. Ole Lavik stepped out of the car on the driver's side, strode round and opened the passenger door for Fredrik Martens. He stood examining his surroundings, as if it was the first time he had been here. He nodded with satisfaction towards the cages, then turned and met the gazes of the others on the inside. I noticed that Einar Sørnes quickly went over to welcome Martens while Knut stayed with Kåre Kleiva, whose body language was hard to decipher from where I was standing. But from what I could see, it didn't signal a surfeit of cordiality, more a kind of measured distance.

I wished I were closer and could hear what was being said. I assumed I would get a blow-by-blow account from Torunn later.

I saw Fredrik Martens turn directly to her before making an announcement to the others. When they started walking towards the administrative building, she joined them. On the way up the stairs, she glanced in my direction, but she didn't send me a wave. That was probably a wise move, as Knut Sørnes was right behind her, holding Caesar by his chain.

I looked at Signe. 'I talked to Helleve and PST on Friday.'

'So I heard.'

'Helleve said you were close to solving the case.'

'That's true.'

'Would you—?'

'We have clear forensic evidence.' She held up her mobile phone. 'I have the arrest warrant here.'

'Indeed?' I sent her an expectant look, but she didn't say anything else. Then I proposed a suggestion of my own. 'Geir Gravdal?'

She didn't have time to react. Her phone buzzed irritably. 'Yes? … What? … But … Have you tried to … I understand. Then we'll deal with it here.' She rang off and ran to the armed policemen by the emergency vehicle, shouting something at them as she went. They reacted instantly. The doors at the side of the vehicle sprang open and within a few seconds there were six armed officers in full gear heading for the gate.

From the Solvik road came the rumbling sound of something big and heavy. I looked in that direction and mouthed a vulgar expletive. Around the bend hove a gigantic crane truck – at high speed. It didn't show any signs of wanting to slow down; it just headed straight for the gate. Automatically, I backed away, staring at the windscreen. Behind the wheel was a man I didn't know; however, the one beside him, hunched forward, I did recognise. It was Geir Gravdal.

The guards around the gate scattered out of the way of the monster vehicle. The armed officers arrived too late to prevent the collision. The crane truck crashed through the gate with a thunderous roar that resounded between the mountains; the gate itself snapped with a shrill crack. Inside the grounds of Sunfjord Salmon, the crane truck headed straight for the administrative building, where it came to a grinding halt, sparks flying from its immense tyres. Once the truck had stopped moving, Geir Gravdal climbed through the side window of the cab and threw an object in a high arc through a window in the admin building.

'Fucking hell,' I breathed aloud.

One of the policemen was kneeling and had Gravdal in his sights, but he had already clambered back into the truck. For a second or two everyone seemed to hold their breath. Then there was a loud explosion inside the building, the walls shook, several windows were blown out and a tall, yellow-and-red flame shot out of the closest opening. From inside came the sounds of angry barking, screams of pain and a bedlam of unrecognisable human voices.

'Torunn!' was all I could say as I sprinted towards the mangled gate and the blazing building.

45

Running through the gateway, I tried to gain a perspective of the situation. It was chaotic. With ten guards and eight police officers, all kitted up, as well as Signe Moland and Bjarne Solheim, there was definitely no shortage of people who could pitch in to help. The commander of the Special Forces Unit pointed towards the crane truck and sent some of his men to immobilise it and others to the entrance of the bombed admin section to see what they could do.

I glanced at the group of demonstrators. They were as shocked as everyone else outside the gate. The broad banner had been lowered and lay in a bundle on the ground. Some of them were crying, some were clinging to each other and staring with wide eyes at what was going on inside the fence, as though the attack had been directed against them personally.

Signe shouted to the commander: 'I've spoken to the fire and rescue services. Initially, it'll be the local unit.'

'Have they got any smoke divers?'

'We'll have to hope so.'

Two police officers had trained their machine guns on the cab of the crane truck while a third climbed up onto the running board and tried to open the door. It was locked from the inside. He banged on the side window and yelled at them to open up. The driver hunkered down over the wheel and shook his head. With a roar the engine started up again and the vehicle jerked backward. The man on the running board leaped back down onto the tarmac, where he landed on all fours and threw himself to the side to avoid being struck by the front tyre.

The commander pointed to the enormous wheels and gave an order: 'Fire at the tyres!'

After a quick check to make sure no one was in the firing zone, two of the officers aimed their weapons at the front tyres

and released a salvo. Then the officers fanned out on each side
of the crane truck and fired in an equally controlled fashion at
the rear tyres. One of the tyres exploded with a bang; the other
three were punctured and sank with a slow hiss until the wheel
rims were flat on the ground.

The driver tried to reverse, and the truck skidded towards the
quay, where the police patrol boat was about to moor and Hans
Hosteland, in his special-forces uniform, was standing ready to
jump ashore. One of the truck's rear wheels hung over the edge
of the quay and when the driver changed gear to move the truck
forward, the wheel spun round in the air while the other three
rims ground into the concrete. The truck was going nowhere.
Hosteland pulled himself ashore, took out his service pistol and
crept alongside the truck on the driver's side.

At the same time, some of the guards and the remaining
Special Forces Unit officers had entered the building. Bjarne
Solheim followed the last man and I stuck to his tail.

'Varg, be careful!' Signe shouted.

The screams inside had been partly drowned out by the
racket the truck had been making, but now they cut through the
general noise, accompanied by Caesar's barking. One of the
guards came stumbling towards us with the big dog on its chain.
But it was the dog leading. It snarled and snapped and raced
towards the exit with the guard hanging on behind like a ragdoll.

'Oh, shit!' Solheim shouted as he glanced behind and saw
me.

Black smoke was billowing through the corridor. The door
to the conference room had been blown out and down. Through
the doorway we saw the flames inside and were able to make out
a table that had toppled over, chairs that had been hurled aside
and people, bent double, stumbling round with their arms raised
above their heads to protect themselves. One of the officers was
right by the door and shouted to those inside. Many of the hazy

figures followed the sound and made for the door. The police officer grabbed them, pulled them into the corridor and shoved them backward, where another officer and two guards stood ready to receive them.

The first casualties were led out of the building. I squinted ahead of me in an attempt to see through the sea of flames. In front of me Solheim was seized with a fit of coughing, turned round and said: 'We've got to get out, Veum. Otherwise the smoke will overpower us.'

He pushed me back. I could feel a tickle in my throat, but I craned my neck to see past him. 'Torunn?' I shouted into the room, but before I got an answer, I felt my chest explode and a bout of coughing forced me onto my knees on the floor. Solheim and one of the guards grabbed me by the arms, lifted me up and led me back to the door and out into the fresh air. I stood gasping for breath and stared at the door in despair as I tried to see who was being helped out.

From the road we heard sirens. The local fire engine from Solvik swung in through the gate. It screamed to a halt and two men jumped out. One was Nils Kyvik and behind him came Harald Eide. He was carrying an oxygen cylinder and a mask. While Kyvik was pulling out a hose and directing the first jet of water at the flames, Harald Eide was shouting: *'I've got the smoke-diving gear. Let me through.'* Before going into the building, he attached the oxygen cylinder and pulled the mask over his head. Overhead, I heard the *thwump, thwump* of a helicopter. I looked up. It was an air ambulance, called from Bergen.

Now the rescue shifted into top gear. The helicopter was guided down to the car park and its crew ran into the premises with all the requisite equipment in their hands.

Truls Hatlevik and Cecilie Tangen were the first to be helped out. The mayor was shaking his head in despair, as if to signal that he couldn't understand how such a thing could happen in his municipality. Cecilie Tangen was pale with shock. She was gasping for air with long, shuddering breaths as tears ran freely from her eyes. Both bore the marks of the fire on their hands and faces.

Then came Knut Sørnes, largely without assistance, but accompanied by one of the police officers, who was loosely holding him under the arm. Out in the daylight, he held a hand in front of his eyes and had to be helped to find his bearings before he was resolutely sat down and received treatment from the air-ambulance doctor.

Einar Sørnes was carried out by two guards; he also bore visible burns and gasped for air in short, abrupt bursts. He was laid on a stretcher and moved away from the building, where another paramedic took care of him. An ambulance had now arrived with its crew and, in the distance, sirens could be heard, probably a fire engine on its way from another station in the municipality.

Three more men staggered through the door: Ole Lavik and Harald Eide, with Fredrik Martens between them. Martens was unconscious; most of Lavik's hair had been singed off and his face was covered with burns.

Harald Eide said something through his mask, then turned and went back into the building.

Signe came up alongside me. 'Have you any idea who's still inside?'

'Kåre Kleiva ... and Torunn.'

As I spoke, I made up my mind. Without a second thought, I sprinted back into the building.

Behind me I heard Signe shout: 'Someone stop him!'

But I was already well down the corridor. The smoke under the ceiling was now thick. Nevertheless, the fire was still only burning in the large conference room and the intensity of the flames seemed to have decreased.

I hunched down to stay below the smoke and suddenly I saw something. Under the door that had been blown out I glimpsed an arm and the palm of a hand. I knelt down, grabbed hold of the door and tried to raise it.

Solheim appeared beside me. He grabbed my shoulder. 'Veum! Out!'

'Look…' I pointed to the door. 'There's someone underneath. Give me a hand to lift it.'

Solheim followed where I was pointing, knelt and gave a nod of confirmation. Together we forced the door upward. With a jerk it came off its hinges and we managed to push it up lengthways and away from the opening. Now we could see who had been under the door. It was Torunn. She was lying in a distorted position, eyes closed, partly on a chair that had fallen, but, from what I could see, without any burns. I gestured to Solheim to keep holding the door. I then bent down, grabbed Torunn under her arms and tried to manoeuvre her out of the chair. I managed it by kicking one of the legs away.

'Careful,' Solheim shouted. 'She may have some spinal damage.'

'Doesn't look like it. The back of the chair will have protected her.'

But I still tried to keep her neck supported as I pulled her from under the ravaged door and into the corridor. 'Let's get her outside.'

I held her under the arms while Solheim gripped her round the legs, and between us we got her out of the building, to where the ambulance crew were standing. One of them – a young woman – said: 'We'll take over now. Let me see how she is.'

We moved as far from the conflagration as we could. Torunn was laid down gently, and the paramedic quickly checked that her airways were open, felt for her pulse, rolled her into the safety position and started her first-aid treatment.

I stood looking down on them, somewhat helpless. Torunn's eyes were still closed, but her eyelids were trembling and she was breathing. There were no visible signs of injury to her body. From what I could judge, she must have been sitting on her own in the corridor outside the conference room because she hadn't been allowed to attend the meeting. This is what had saved her, just like Caesar, who had been in Knut Sørnes's office.

The air-ambulance doctor arrived. He knelt down, exchanged a few words with the young paramedic, held Torunn's hand, leaned forward and said something to her.

She opened her eyes. The doctor place a hand under her neck to support her while she sat up and looked around in bewilderment.

Now I squatted beside her. 'Torunn, it's so good to see you.'

'Va-Varg? What happened?'

'A home-made bomb was thrown into the board meeting.'

'What?!'

She scanned her surroundings and fixed her gaze on the huge crane truck, which the police appeared to have under full control now. They had smashed the window on the driver's side and opened the door. Protesting violently, the driver had been dragged out, laid flat on the ground and handcuffed.

Geir Gravdal was clinging to the door handle on his side and kicking at the policemen trying to remove him. It finally took two men to pull him out by the legs and down, where he was firmly held on the ground and subjected to the same treatment as his companion.

From his prone position he raised his head and looked around. With a big grin, he watched the frenetic activity around the blaze. An apparently lifeless Kåre Kleiva was carried out by Harald Eide and two police officers, the last person to be rescued. There were extensive burns to his face and body, and smoke was rising from his clothes. He was placed on a stretcher and, after a brief examination by the doctor, ordered onto the air ambulance to be flown with the utmost haste to Haukeland hospital and the burns department. The same went for Fredrik Martens. The others were considered well enough to travel in an ambulance or a police car.

Another fire engine arrived. The hose was attached to a tap on the site and the flames seemed to be brought under control.

Bjarne Solheim stood looking down at Geir Gravdal and the truck driver while talking to the commander of the Special Forces Unit.

I was standing with Signe. I gestured towards Geir Gravdal. 'You can hand him your arrest warrant now.'

'Doesn't look as if it will be necessary. He's got enough to answer for as it is.'

'It was Gravdal you were after, though, wasn't it?'

Her eyes lingered on mine, as though she had to consider my question. Then she decided to answer. 'It was, yes.'

46

It wasn't over yet. There were still some details that hadn't quite fallen into place, at least not for me.

The drama at Sunfjord Salmon had made a splash in the press and received a lot of attention in other media too. The very next day it was announced that one person had died after what most were calling a terrorist action. Two days later the name of the deceased was made public. It was Kåre Kleiva. The cause of death was given as fatal injuries as a result of an explosion and fire at his workplace. Even though it was an ex-husband who was struck down this time, Betty could add another name to the list of sudden deaths in her circle of close acquaintances.

Fredrik Martens was also seriously hurt, but his injuries weren't life-threatening. He was discharged from hospital after six days and transferred to a private clinic in Jersey. He steadfastly refused to talk about the case.

Ole Lavik, however, did not. He was interviewed on television and in some of the country's biggest newspapers, photographed with his face and head wreathed in bandages. On behalf of Riverbank Invest and Sunfjord Salmon, he asserted that what he called terrorists would never stop the companies' business activities, neither in Sørneset, nor anywhere else. He expected the guilty parties to be convicted of terrorism and murder, and that they would receive the severest punishment the law could mete out for their misdeeds.

Spokespersons for the demonstrators on that Monday disassociated themselves from the attack in the strongest possible terms. As did all the conservation and environmental organisations. Everyone emphasised that this course of action was completely indefensible. One un-named representative for the demonstrators in Sørneset, however, characterised what happened as an example of how far despair on a personal level and as a result of the environmental situation could drive unbalanced individuals.

Neither Geir Gravdal nor the man behind the wheel of the crane truck had been named so far, but both were in prison with access to their families, friends and the media denied. Commentators assumed that both would be charged with involuntary manslaughter and acts of terrorism, including arson, detonating explosive devices, bomb-making and irresponsible use of a motor vehicle.

Everyone who had been in the building during the explosion and the resultant fire had various degrees of injury, both physical and psychological. The only person, apart from Ole Lavik, who had agreed to be interviewed about the incident was Truls Hatlevik. He condemned in the strongest possible terms people who resorted to such means to promote their own views. He let it be known that the municipality would be giving every possible support to the community of Solvik and the owners of the fish farm in Sørneset to maintain local jobs in what he termed an important, indeed, essential industry for the country, the region and the county.

Those on more neutral ground claimed that the actions of Gravdal et al had set back the fight against fish farming and against what this industry had done to the fjords and the local environment by at least ten years. The representatives of the various environmental organisations had to concede this, and did so in interviews, articles and public debates. They stressed, however, that the political fight against the worst features of aquaculture would continue, within the democratic framework and by peaceful means.

Several obituaries stated that KK had died as a 'martyr' in the cause of sustainable fish farming. It was also pointed out that the Kleiva family were among those hardest hit by the tragedy, as Kåre Kleiva's son Jonas had also died earlier this autumn, again in connection with demonstrations against Sunfjord Salmon. The fact that Jonas had been among the demonstrators was a point many commentators referred to as an irony of fate.

Torunn came out of the whole business with no serious physical injuries. She was stiff and bruised, but she had no fractures or burns. What surprised her most was her loss of memory. She told me with some astonishment in her eyes that the last thing she remembered was looking at me as she entered the building. Later she had a few vague, dream-like impressions from when she came to afterwards, the air-ambulance doctor's voice and face, the drive back to Bergen, then waking up in Haukeland hospital with a completely different doctor at her bedside, with such dark skin that for a moment she thought she was in a foreign country. Then he spoke to her in broad Bergensian and she realised where she was.

When, after a thorough examination, she was discharged from the hospital two days later, I picked her up in my car and drove her – at her own request – to Flesland Airport, where I parked and accompanied her to security control. We had another *Casablanca* moment and she gave me a hug.

Later we chatted on the telephone. She was busy finishing what she was going to write about Sunfjord Salmon, even if, naturally enough, the perspective would have to be different now from what she had first imagined. On the plus side, she could feel confident that it would not be a problem getting the report published when it was ready. We agreed that we would see each other again, 'in the not-too-distant future'.

✳

Towards the end of the week, I rang Signe to hear how what I called 'the other case' was going.

'The other case?'

'You had an arrest warrant ready, you said, but not because you already knew what Geir Gravdal was planning to do.'

'You know I can't talk about that with you, Varg.'

'Why not? I may even have something to contribute.'

'OK ... But not here. Let's meet somewhere else after I've finished for the day.'

We agreed that the simplest would be to meet at my office in Strandkaien at around six-thirty and I promised I would have some coffee ready for when she came.

She was there five minutes early, knocked to let me know she was there, then waited until I opened the door. My waiting room had been consigned to history, but the hotel had allowed me to keep the sign.

'I thought this entire building was a hotel,' she said with a surprised expression.

'Not all of it. I had a clause inserted in the contract, so I'm sitting here now like Robinson Crusoe on his island.'

Once in the office, she had a good look around, curious now rather than surprised. 'In fact, this is the first time I've been in a private investigator's office.'

'I can tell you it's far from the first time I've had a police officer visit me.'

'I suppose not.'

I pulled out a chair for her and poured some freshly brewed coffee into a clean cup, which I placed on her side of the desk. For myself I had my not-quite-so-clean cup, and sat down opposite her.

'Grandad should see us now,' she smiled.

'Yes, who would've believed it?'

With her usual efficiency she got down to brass tacks. 'What did you mean by your contribution?'

'My understanding was that you had an arrest warrant on you for Geir Gravdal the day you went to Sørneset. I know he'd gone to earth over the weekend, so I assume that was why you hadn't already arrested him.'

She sent me an expectant look. 'I see. Carry on.'

'Atle Helleve happened to mention to me, at the meeting with PST, that you had clear leads, and even you said, while we were talking that day, that you had forensic evidence.'

She arched her eyebrows ironically. 'I hear what you're saying about Helleve and me, but I'm more interested in hearing what you thought *you* could bring to the case.'

'OK. I spoke to Marita Svanøy last Friday. She told me that the day Jonas and Mona went missing, Geir Gravdal had accused Mona Martens of being a kind of undercover agent for her father and his colleagues. Gravdal had even alluded to emails that proved this. It had ended in a row. Jonas and Mona had left the area, and when the others went back to Bergen, Gravdal was left on his own. To make his own way home, they presumed. That's what Marita told me.'

She was listening attentively now. 'And then?'

'Well, we can imagine of course. What we *know* is that Mona and Jonas ended up in the sea off Markatangen. That is, the camper van did. With Mona inside, at any rate. We can probably assume Jonas was there too, but he managed to open the door and escape without being discovered by … hm, well, who? What do we think happened on the quay? My guess is you know a little more about that than me, as you claim you have forensic evidence. You've invested a great deal of work in tracking down the famous black car that Guri Leitet had seen passing her house. I assume you've located it now and it's with reference to that you have what you call forensic evidence?'

She looked at me with an expression I found hard to read. Was it patronising? Was she considering what I had just said, to assess the likelihood of it, or was she considering how much she was able to tell me?

As she didn't say anything, I carried on. 'Let's imagine the following scenario: you see, there's not only a political conflict here. There could also be a love triangle, where jealousy may well have been a trigger for Geir Gravdal's actions, both that day in September and this Monday.'

She still remained silent.

'I can visualise Jonas and Mona sitting in the camper van down on the quay. Then Geir Gravdal rolls up in his car. What happens next? Does he go out and confront them? Maybe. But he's already done that, in Sørneset. Perhaps he has a more drastic plan. Perhaps he drives right into the back of them and shunts them into the sea, thus killing one of them.' I paused before continuing. 'And if that's what happened I'm sure you'll find evidence of the collision – on both the vehicle that was recovered from the water and on Gravdal's, if you found it. Perhaps remnants of paintwork on one or both vehicles. Am I right or am I wrong?'

She stared at me. Again, it was hard to read her expression. We were at a sort of impasse. 'I can't say anything at all, Varg, because of the ongoing investigation. But let's say if you were a few decades younger, there'd be a job for you with us, if you got sick of freelancing.'

'From which I glean I'm not far off the conclusions you'd come to?'

She sent me another of her secretive smiles, then put down her coffee cup and thanked me.

'We'll be seeing each other again,' I said.

'I'm afraid so,' she said, sending me another smile as she left.

I was left to think through everything one more time. I tried to picture how it must have been for Mona and Jonas, the water closing over them, the vehicle sinking, being strapped in. Gasping for air, struggling to unbuckle the seat belt, Jonas getting free, but not Mona. Because he hadn't helped her? Or because he didn't have time before he had to get out himself? It was difficult to imagine the situation without finding yourself short of breath. But I felt fairly sure that was what had happened, more or less, with Geir Gravdal as the guilty party, who apparently had done nothing to rescue them from the vehicle and who had driven away without a backward look.

*

In the following weeks I followed the case in the media. The bombing occupied the public's attention. Cause and effect here were so obvious that it didn't take long for the prosecuting authorities to assemble a preliminary charge. It accorded well with what people had already assumed would be the outcome. The deaths of Mona Martens and Jonas Kleiva were still under investigation though, and the murder of Guri Leitet, which was part of the case, had never even reached the media's ears.

It was a week into November before I rang Signe again. She didn't want to meet me face to face, but she went as far as admitting that, yes, I had been right with regard to the forensic evidence they had, on both Jonas Kleiva's VW and Geir Gravdal's car – a black Volvo 740, 1992 model. Geir Gravdal had, following advice from his lawyer, admitted culpability for the collision on the quay at Markatangen, but had claimed he had acted in the heat of the moment and that when the vehicle went over the edge he had panicked and left the scene without making any attempt to save Jonas and Mona.

There were still some unanswered questions regarding Jonas's actions after the camper van went into the water up until the moment he was found dead, in all probability murdered, three weeks later. Geir Gravdal vehemently denied having anything to do with this, and the police were checking through his movements the weekend Jonas's corpse was found in the fjord. Signe made it clear that they were still fully focused on the case and were continuing their enquiries with all the staff they had at their disposal. Before ringing off, she said in what I perceived as very large capitals, that I should still give this case a wide berth and leave them to get to the bottom of it.

Two days later, sitting in my car on my way to Solvik, I philosophised on how to interpret the expression 'give a wide berth'. I suspected that we had two quite different interpretations.

47

I had arranged to meet Edvard Aga at the usual place: Solvik Store & Café. He was sitting in his customary seat at the window table and raised a hand in welcome when he saw me coming from my car and approaching the steps into the store.

When I entered, Stein Solvik stood up from the same table. *'Coffee and a roll, Veum?'*

'Yes, please.'

He disappeared into the back room as I nodded to Aga, who had remained seated. He already had a cup of coffee and there were crumbs from a roll on the plate in front of him. On the other side was Solvik's cup.

I went over, but stood waiting until Solvik was back.

'That was quite a spectacle out there in Sørneset,' Aga said.

'There were intense emotions at play, yes.'

'Were you there?'

'Yes, I was.'

Solvik appeared with a tray, on which were a cup of coffee and a roll sliced in two on a plate. *'I heard what you're talking about. I'm afraid it's left deep scars in the village. Folk are talking about nothing else, even now, three weeks later. Take a seat, Veum.'*

He pushed the used cup aside and placed the tray on the table in front of me. *'I'll just get a Thermos of coffee. Is it alright if I join you?'*

'By all means,' I said.

He went out again, returned with the coffee, filled Aga's cup, then his own, and put the Thermos in the middle of the table. He took a seat at the end, ready to jump up if any other customers came in.

'Like everyone, we've been following the news, on the radio, TV and in the papers,' Aga said. 'My reading is that it was the same man behind the terrorist attack in Sørneset and the murders of Jonas and Martens' daughter in Markatangen.'

'We-ell,' I said. 'That particular issue is still being investigated, from what I understand.'

'Oh, yes?'

'Hm,' Solvik commented with a gloomy glance at me. *'It's going to take even longer for the dust to settle in the village, then.'*

'Good chance, yes.'

Aga leaned forward. 'But you've got your finger on the pulse … The police obviously had good leads to follow, didn't they? There was hardly a car in the village that wasn't checked.'

'Including yours outside.'

'Yes, mine too. All clear, I was informed.'

'They found what they were after on another car. Geir Gravdal's. Or the terrorist, as he's called now. I suppose I can say that too, but that's all I know about the case. Gravdal admitted driving into the back of Jonas's VW and that was how they ended up in the sea.'

'So what do you think happened after the shunt then?' Solvik asked.

'There's absolutely no doubt that, whatever went on inside, Jonas got out of the camper. Gravdal maintains that he panicked and left the scene without doing anything to save either Jonas or Mona. So Jonas was free to scramble out and escape. Perhaps he tried to get Mona out, but failed. That's one question we'll never be able to answer, as they're both dead.'

The other two sent me sceptical looks. I allowed myself a bite from one half of the cheese-and-ham roll.

I looked at Aga. 'We've discussed this before and I informed the police about it. When you and I were up by Stølvatnet lake, we both had a sense that someone was watching us. The same someone we found traces of in the house. And we both thought it could've been Jonas, who, for some unknown reason, had decided to hide up there.'

Aga nodded. 'That's right.'

'But it was only when Jonas was found that we talked about it. Until that moment, we'd kept it to ourselves, hadn't we?'

'Yes, I don't exactly meet so many people...' He glanced at Solvik. 'I don't remember if I told you anything about it?'

I clearly remember you two talking about it one of the times Veum was here.

'Yes, of course. You're right.'

'Then Harald Eide, and I suspect Knut Sørnes, found Jonas,' I said. 'He had the same injuries to his head as Klaus Krog had two years earlier.'

'Really?' Aga said, looking me in the eye. 'Do you mean to say there's a link between the two deaths?'

'It's not impossible.' I took a mouthful of coffee. 'Poor Guri Leitet became a kind of main witness in the case. She'd noted down the number of the black car that had followed Jonas and Mona to Markatangen that September evening. What if she'd done something similar the evening Klaus Krog "died", to use the official terminology?'

'I see. But that was two years before and there was never any talk of other cars then.'

'No. Unfortunately the local police didn't take the incident seriously enough. They didn't carry out a proper investigation of the case. No one spoke to Guri Leitet at the time. Nevertheless, when the police were going through her papers this autumn, because of the suspicious death, it was conspicuous that one of her diaries with all her meticulous observations was missing – the one for 2002, when Krog was *murdered*, I venture to insist.'

'Do you mean you've solved the case, Veum?'

'I'm fairly sure I have, yes. There was another thing the police failed to do in 2002. But I did it when Betty asked me to investigate Krog's death, i.e., to read the unfinished manuscript of his book.'

'Did he leave a manuscript?'

'Yes, and what's more, towards the end of the manuscript, where he'd written a kind of summary of what he still had to do, there was a small list of the appointments he had the week he ... died.'

'Appointments? Mentioning the people concerned by name, I assume?'

I played a little fast and loose with the truth here, and nodded. Actually it was only the initials, but ... 'And I wasn't the only one to read it, either. Jonas did, too, when he stayed overnight in what had once been his bedroom, but which was by then taken over by Krog.'

'But I still don't understand. Where are you going with this?'

'As so often in such cases, we're probably talking about a sort of love triangle.'

'A love triangle? Between Betty, Klaus Krog and...?'

I held his gaze.

He gesticulated. 'Surely you don't mean ... me?'

'You'd known Betty from when you were young and she lived with your parents in Bergen. You came here because of her. In 1983 you were competing with Fredrik Martens for her favour – and lost. But you didn't give up, did you. Then another rival appeared. Klaus Krog.'

'This is senseless, Veum.'

I cast a quick glance at Stein Solvik. 'I can tell you both something Betty told me in confidence. I won't go into any detail, but she said Klaus Krog was the best thing that had ever happened to her. For the first time she had experienced true love. But as most of us know, there's a dark side to love, and its name is jealousy.'

'I've never ... Alright, I'll admit I was smitten by Betty from the very first moment I met her when she was a young girl in my parents' house in Kvernabekkvegen. I was unhappy when I heard she'd got married – and so young. And, yes, it was because of her that I first came here, and many, many more times later, and ultimately built my cabin here. It was like … just being in the vicinity of a dream, however unachievable, gave me some satisfaction in life, something to live for. Well…' He shrugged and opened his arms. 'I experienced disappointments. When she was widowed, I thought that … But then Kåre Kleiva showed up. And when he jumped ship, Klaus Krog jumped on board. I just had to confront the truth. For Betty I was never more than an acquaintance. Not even a first reserve. But I can tell you, Varg, I never felt any form of jealousy.'

I turned to Stein Solvik. 'You did, however.'

'*What do you mean, me?*' He burst out with what sounded like laughter. '*Jealous of the men who Betty…?*'

'From the moment I arrived here, you've been bad-mouthing her. You warned me against her, you said she ate men for breakfast. I haven't heard you say a good word about her. But you've known her longer than Edvard has. Right from your schooldays, as you're about the same age. And I'm quite sure you've suffered the same disappointments as Edvard – when she married Mons Marken, later Kåre Kleiva and finally got together with Klaus Krog. But she wasn't the loose-living girl you tried to present her as. She went into each relationship with enormous seriousness. The only slip-up, to my knowledge, was with Fredrik Martens, with whom she had her first child, Jonas. You knew what jealousy was, what it did to you, and finally you let it gain the upper hand – when you attacked Klaus Krog on the steep slope down from the summer pastures.'

'*What are you babbling on about?*'

'The circumstantial evidence is strong. There's a note in Krog's manuscript that is easily interpreted. He had an appointment with S.S., it says. There's even the date. Sunday, 22nd

September. The only day in the week the store's closed. The day Krog died. Or, to be accurate, was killed, by a rock to the head. But which the police never documented as anything but an accident. Two years later, when you suspected that Jonas was alive, you went into the mountains to check. Had he perhaps indicated, on an earlier occasion, that he had something to discuss with you? Perhaps it was precisely this that was keeping Jonas up on the mountain farm. Maybe he had a plan to have a confrontation – after reading what I've now read and having drawn the same conclusion. I suppose the meeting by the fjord was chance, but the outcome was the same. You found the person you were looking for and killed him, in the same way that you'd killed Klaus Krog two years before.'

The blood had drained from Solvik's face. *'And how do you think you're going to prove these fantasies?'*

Edvard Aga glanced from me to Solvik in disbelief and back again. He moved his lips mutely, as if asking the same question.

'As I said, there is strong circumstantial evidence. I have the note in the manuscript. And we have Guri Leitet. You delivered shopping to her every week. You knew she never locked the door. No one could've put a pillow over her face long enough for her to suffocate more easily than you. This method of killing leaves no traces, according to a pathologist I consulted. Especially when an older person is the victim. And why, of all the diaries, would the one for 2002 in particular be missing? Because the police went to such lengths to locate the black car, it reminded you that you had used your own car that day you were going to show Klaus Krog the remains of the old Solvik mountain pastures – as you had arranged. In which case that would probably be in Guri Leitet's diary too, should anyone make that link. And that was exactly what someone did do.'

'You did.'

'Yes, I did.'

'In which case, you're as guilty as me, as regards what happened to both Guri and ... to Jonas.'

'Of course, you're wrong there. You killed Jonas because he confronted you with what he'd read in the manuscript. You killed Guri Leitet to protect yourself. I've done no more than Betty commissioned me to do. To try and find out what happened to Klaus Krog in 2002. I'm fairly sure I have the answer now, whatever the consequences might be.'

There was silence in the room. We were three adult men. We had each lived our own lives and accumulated our own experiences. Because of what had become my profession, perhaps I had a few more than the other two. But that wasn't very significant now.

Aga broke the silence. 'Is this true, Stein? Is that how it was?' With amazement in his eyes, he stared at the man he had known for many years.

A distant, hardened glaze had taken over Stein Solvik's features. 'No, Edvard. It's all lies, the product of an overactive imagination.'

I pushed my chair away from the table and stood up. 'I've said my piece. A written version of all this is on its way by post to the Bergen police. I sent it before leaving town today, to be on the safe side. The decision is yours, Solvik. You can contact the police yourself and give yourself in. Or you can wait until they come knocking at your door and start asking questions. There's one more thing to do before I leave Solvik this time.'

Stein Solvik didn't say another word. He sat staring gloomily into space, as if transported to a different existence, to a country where the sun never shone and nothing could grow. A country so deserted that only lost souls could settle there.

Edvard Aga got up from his chair. 'And I'm going to jump in my boat and go back to my cabin. I've heard more than enough for one day.' As we made for the door together, he added: 'And the rest of my life.'

Outside, we went our different ways. I walked the short distance to Betty's house. She had seen me through the kitchen window and stood waiting in the doorway for me to arrive.